INVITATION

INVITATION

CYCLE ONE OF THE HARBINGERS SERIES

THE CALL BY BILL MYERS

THE HAUNTED BY FRANK PERETTI

THE SENTINELS BY ANGELA HUNT

THE GIRL BY ALTON GANSKY

a division of Baker Publishing Group
Minneapolis, Minnesota

Published by Bethany House Publishers
11400 Hampshire Avenue South
Bloomington, Minnesota 55438
www.bethanyhouse.com

Bethany House Publishers is a division of
Baker Publishing Group, Grand Rapids, Michigan

Printed in the United States of America

Library of Congress Cataloging-in-Publication Data is on file at the Library of Congress, Washington, DC.

ISBN 978-0-7642-1974-0

Cover design by Gearbox

17 18 19 20 21 22 23   7 6 5 4 3 2 1

CONTENTS

In this fast-paced world with all its demands, the four of us wanted to try something new. Instead of the longer novel format, we wanted to write something equally as engaging but that could be read in one or two sittings—on the plane, waiting to pick up the kids from soccer, or as an evening's read.

We also wanted to play. As friends and seasoned novelists, we thought it would be fun to create a game we could participate in together. The rules were simple:

RULE #1

Each of us would write as if we were one of the characters in the series:

Bill Myers would write as Brenda, the street-hustling tattoo artist who sees images of the future.

Frank Peretti would write as the professor, the atheist ex-priest ruled by logic.

Angela Hunt would write as Andi, the professor's brilliant but geeky assistant who sees inexplicable patterns.

Alton Gansky would write as Tank, the naïve, big-hearted jock with a surprising connection to a healing power.

RULE #2

Instead of the four of us writing one novella together (we're friends but not crazy), we would write it like a TV series. There would be an overarching storyline into which we'd plug our individual novellas, with each story written from our character's point of view.

Bill's first novella, *The Call*, sets the stage. It will be followed by Frank's *The Haunted*, Angela's *The Sentinels*, and Alton's *The Girl*. And if we keep having fun, we'll begin a second round and so on until other demands pull us away or, as in TV, we get cancelled.

There you have it. We hope you'll find these as entertaining in the reading as we did in the writing.

Bill, Frank, Angie, and Al

THE CALL

BILL MYERS

For Angie Hunt:
The Wendy to our Peter Pan

CHAPTER 1

There's four of us. Well, five if you count the kid. We don't know each other, we don't like each other, and we sure didn't ask for any of this. But here we are. "The probability of fate," Andi calls it.

I call it a pain in the butt.

Anyway, we each got our own version of what's been happening, so here's mine. . . .

It was Friday night. I was tired and business was slow. Time to shut down. I was already cleaning tips and grips when three white boys—football jocks from the community college—roll in. They'd played some big game earlier and it must have been a sweet victory by the way they waved around their Buds and staggered in, giggling. Well, two staggered in giggling—the one they carried between them was barely coherent.

"Hey there, Brenda." The buzz cut on the right had been a recent customer.

I glanced up from where I was cleaning my stuff. "Sorry, boys, all closed up."

He acted like he didn't hear. "We got ourselves an honest to goodness virgin."

The one in the middle, six-three, 275, raised his head and opened his watery eyes just long enough to greet me with a Texas drawl, "Ma'am," before nodding back off. But it wasn't the good-ol'-boy charm that got me. It was the face. The same one I'd been sketching for over a week.

Buzz Cut laughed. "Twenty years old and not a mark on him."

"Pure as driven snow," his buddy agreed.

I looked at the clock. Like I said, business was slow and I was getting tired of ducking the landlord. "You got money?"

All grins, Buzz Cut dug into his pocket and pulled out a wad of cash.

I swore under my breath and motioned them to the beat-up barber chair in the middle of the room. "Set him there."

They plopped him down.

I popped a sterilized pack and began prepping a tip. "What do you have in mind?"

"You know," Buzz Cut said. "Do your hocus-pocus thing."

"My what?"

"Where you tat out his future. Like you did me." He pulled up his sleeve to show a broken heart spurting blood from a bullet shooting through it. "I'm gonna be a heartbreaker, man." He grinned at his buddy. "A real lady killer. Ain't that right, Brenda?"

"If you say so."

"Chicks go for a man in uniform. Wherever they send me I'm gonna leave a long line of broken hearts."

I rolled up Cowboy's sleeve and started prepping the arm.

"So do the same for him," Buzz Cut said. "Tat out his future."

"You really do that?" his pal said.

I reached for a blade and began shaving the arm. "I just ink what I see."

"Well, shoot, do my future, too."

"You ain't got one."

"Huh?"

They both laugh, thinking it's sarcasm. I wish it was.

I sterilize and goop the arm, all the time staring at it.

"So how much?" Buzz Cut says.

"Free form?" It was a lie. Like I said, I'd been sketching stencils for a week. But they didn't have to know.

"Sure."

"Two fifty," I said. "Half now, half on completion."

"So that's . . ."

Thinking wasn't his specialty, so I gave him a hand. "One hundred fifty now, one hundred fifty when the job's done."

"Sweet."

He peeled off the bills, counting as he set them in my palm. "Fifty, one hundred, one hundred fifty."

He figured he was done, but like I said, it was a slow week and he was a slow thinker. I gave him a look and glanced at my hand, making it clear he was short.

"Oh, right." He peeled off another fifty.

"I gotta piss," his buddy said.

Buzz Cut nods. He motions to the empty bottle in his hand. "And it's time for a recharge."

His buddy leans over Cowboy and says, "Don't go nowhere, pal, we'll be right back."

Buzz Cut adds, "Get some sleep. It'll be over 'fore you know it."

Cowboy doesn't answer, so he shakes him. "Hey . . . hey!"

He opens his eyes.

"Get some sleep."

He nods and drops back off.

The boys turned and headed for the door. I stared at the arm, pretending to wait for an image to form. But as soon as they're gone, I crossed to the desk and pulled out the stencil I'd been working on—four grown-ups and a ten-year-old kid walking toward us. I didn't recognize the kid or two of the adults. But, like I said, I recognized Cowboy. And I recognized the woman beside him. Black. A few years older. Dreadlocks. A dead ringer for me.

The job took less than an hour. Another hour passed and still no one showed. It was late and I'd had it. I tossed down the magazine. I butted out my cigarette and crossed over to him. He was snoring like a chainsaw.

I shook him. "Hey."

He kept snoring. I shook harder. "Hey!"

He opened one eye, gave a polite "Howdy," and went back to sleep.

I shook him again. "Your friends? Where're your friends?"

Nothing.

Enough was enough. I lifted his arm and slipped under it. Getting him to his feet wasn't as easy.

"Come on, come on," I said. "A little help wouldn't hurt."

Somehow I got him to the door. I hit the lights with my elbow, staggered outside, and leaned him against the wall to lock up. I barely got out my keys before he started sliding.

"No, no, no—"

He hit the sidewalk with a thud. I finished locking up and knelt down to him. "Hey. Hey, Cowboy."

Nothing.

"Okay, fine." Prattville was safe enough. A small town in the middle of the desert. And the night was warm. He could just sit there 'til his buddies remembered where they left him.

I turned and headed toward my beater Toyota. Once I got there, I reached through the window to open the door. I glanced back at him. Big mistake. He sat there all alone and helpless-looking.

I swore and started back.

Two minutes later I'm loading him into the passenger seat.

He does his best to help, which was next to nothing. Once all the arms and legs were inside, I got behind the wheel. "Okay, Cowboy," I said, "where to?"

He mumbled something.

I shook my head and sighed.

Suddenly the car shook as something roared overhead. I stuck my head out the window just in time to see a private jet shoot by. It was three hundred feet above us, with smoke and flames coming from its engine.

I looked around, then dropped the car into gear and hit the gas.

CHAPTER 2

The jet took its sweet time to come down. We'd been on the road fifteen minutes and still hadn't found it. But we would. I saw the direction it was going and doubted it would be making any turns. I'd have called someone, but as usual my crap phone battery was dead.

"Where . . . are we?"

I turned to see Cowboy coming to. "Well, look who joined us. Hope you got cash. Door to door delivery is extra."

He frowned. "Sorry?"

"I'm driving you home."

He managed to turn his head and look out the window. "But . . . I don't live out here."

"We're taking the scenic route."

He sat up. "That's real kind of you, but—" He spotted the cellophane over the tat and pulled at it. "*Ow!*"

"Yeah, that's going to be a little tender," I said.

He looked at it. "Wow. Did you all do that? That's real nice. Who are them people?"

"No idea." I glanced at it. "That big guy's you, obviously. But those others . . ." I shrugged.

"What about—Ow!" He'd touched it again. "Her?"

"What about her?"

"She kinda looks like you."

"What do you mean, 'kinda'? That's a great likeness."

"Watch out!"

I turned back to the road just in time to see some old dude and a girl. I yanked the wheel to the right, swerving, barely missing them. Well, mostly missing them. I must've clipped the old guy, cause the next thing I know, he's out of sight.

I slammed on the brakes. The car barely stopped before I leapt out of it. He was on the ground twenty feet behind.

"Are you all right?" I shouted, racing to him, "You okay?"

"Professor?" The girl, a twenty-something redhead, was already at his side. I could only see her back. "Professor!"

He was sitting up when I got there. Even in the moonlight, I recognized the face. It set me back, but not much. When you sketch like me, you're never too surprised when the stuff shows up.

He was the third person in Cowboy's tattoo. His neatly trimmed beard and silver hair made him look like a senator, all polite and genteel . . . until he opened his mouth.

"Moron!" he shouted. "There's nothing but desert out here and you couldn't see us?"

"Sorry," I said.

"What type of idiot are you?"

"I didn't see—"

"Stupid women drivers."

"What?"

"You heard me."

Normally I'd be sympathetic, 'specially with not paying my insurance the last couple years. But he was a real piece of work. "Maybe if you didn't walk down the middle of the highway, you'd be easier to miss."

"A highway, is that what you call it?" He tried moving his leg and winced.

"Professor—"

"You people should try using some asphalt, or put a white line somewhere so we'd have a clue."

"Professor, you're hurt."

"I'm fine." He winced again.

The girl bent closer. Little Orphan Annie curls blocked her face.

"Were you with the plane?" I asked.

He didn't bother to answer. "How far are we from town?"

"Were you with the pla—?"

"Are you okay?" Cowboy interrupted as he joined us. "It looks like you're hurt."

The old man shot him a glare then turned back to the girl. "Are mental midgets the only indigenous life-form here?"

Cowboy smiled that dumb smile of his and kneeled down to join us.

The girl kept checking his leg. "We were flying to UCLA. That's where the professor will be delivering his next set of lectures. They're very informative and the reviews have been extremely positive." She looked up at me, shaking back those curls as she kept chattering. But I barely heard. I was looking directly into face number four.

"So our engine experienced some mechanical difficulties, at about"—she looked at her watch—"actually, exactly one hour and eight minutes ago. And the pilots, nice men both of them—an older gentlemen with a moustache and a younger one who forgot to button his fourth shirt button from the top—decided to set the plane down back there"—she motioned over her shoulder—"approximately one point two miles."

"Incompetent boneheads." The old man tested his leg again and winced.

"They okay?" I asked. "The pilots?"

"Until I sue them for attempted manslaughter."

"Professor, they saved our lives."

"Which they'll live to regret."

"No one injured?"

"Everyone's fine," the girl said. "They're flying in a mechanic first thing in the morning, and they called a taxi for us."

"But you didn't wait."

The professor answered. "I've developed serious trust issues with them in the matter of transpor—Ahh!" He turned to Cowboy, who'd put a hand on his leg. "What are you doing?"

"Sorry," the big guy said.

The professor turned to me. "So do you have hospitals out here? Or do you just leave people on the side of the road until they expire?" He spun back to Cowboy, who was touching him again. "What are you . . . where's that heat coming from?"

"Sorry."

He looked to the girl. "Andi, get on the phone and call 9-1-1. Tell them I expect a vehicle to be sent immediately and—" He stopped and shouted at Cowboy again. "What's that heat? What are you doing?"

Cowboy gave no answer, and the old man pulled his leg away.

"That's strange," he said.

"Professor?"

He moved it. "What on earth?" He reached down, touched the leg, then moved it some more. "How very odd."

"What's wrong?"

He didn't answer but kept testing his leg. Finally, he rolled over onto his hands and knees.

"Professor, be careful, you're hurt."

"Nonsense." With some effort he managed to stand.

The girl took his arm. "Please, Professor, we don't know what's—"

"I'm fine." He shrugged her off. "Let go. I said I'm fine. I must have pulled something." He began walking. "See, I'm fine now."

I glanced at Cowboy, who avoided my gaze.

"So, how far to the nearest town?" the old man demanded.

"Nine, ten miles," I said.

"Good. Then you will take us to your finest hotel—provided, of course, you are able to stay on the road without hitting anyone or anything else."

I turned for the car. "Let's go, Cowboy."

"Don't worry," the old man said. "We'll pay."

"I'm not a taxi service."

"Twenty-five dollars."

I turned. "You think you can just buy me like some—"

"Fifty."

"Seventy-five."

"Don't be absurd."

I continued toward the car.

"Surely you don't intend to leave us out here."

"Enjoy the walk."

"All right, all right," he said. "Seventy-five."

"Per person."

"That's robbery!"

"Take it or leave it."

He stood, anything but happy.

I shrugged, knowing I had him. "That's how us mental midgets do business."

CHAPTER 3

Cowboy, because of his size, sat up front with me. The professor, because of his mouth, sat in the back with Andi.

But that didn't stop Cowboy's down-home charm. "So, how come you're a professor and all, but you ain't teaching at a college?"

Andi, who had the enthusiasm of a fourteen-year-old and energy to back it up, answered, "He's on a national lecture tour. Lots of universities. Come next spring we've even been invited to the White House."

Cowboy grinned. "You don't say."

"And before that we're going to the Middle East and Europe. Maybe even the Vatican."

"That sounds real nice. And what, exactly, do you all lecture on?"

The professor didn't answer, which didn't stop Cowboy. "S'cuse me, Professor, what did you say your lectures are about?"

More silence.

"Professor?"

Finally the old man said, "What's your name, son?"

"Bjorn Christensen. They call me Tank for short."

"Well, Tank-for-short, during this lovely tour of your desolate countryside, do you suppose for one minute we could enjoy some silence?"

I shot the man a look in the mirror.

Miss Congeniality answered. "The professor lectures on the toxicity of believing in God in a postmodern culture."

Cowboy stayed quiet, which I got to admit was a bit of a relief. But it didn't last long.

"I'm sorry. I don't mean to be rude or nothin', but why do you want to go around telling people there ain't a God?"

"I don't tell them there isn't a God. I tell them they're intellectually stunted if they believe in one."

Cowboy frowned. "But I believe in God."

"Yes, I'm sure you do."

I glanced back in the mirror. "So you're an atheist," I said.

"I'm a realist."

"You tour the world to mess up people's faith?"

"I tour the world as penance for the lives I've ruined."

"He was a priest," Andi explained. "A Jesuit."

"That was a long, long time ago," he said.

"But—" Cowboy turned back to him. "I'm confused."

"I'm sure you are."

"If you're a priest, how come you don't believe—"

"Stop the car!" Andi shouted. "Quick, stop the car!"

If it was the professor who yelled, I wouldn't have bothered. But the girl I almost liked, in spite of her perkiness.

"What's up?" I said as we slowed.

"There!" She pointed off to the right. "Over there."

A hundred yards away, you could see pillars of rock shining in the moonlight. Like giant stalagmites. Some rose a hundred feet high. Around them were a bunch of buildings, a fancy school I had some history with.

"Those are the Trona Pinnacles," Cowboy said. "Kinda famous around here."

"There's nine of them, right?" Andi asked.

"That's what you see from the road," I said, "but there's plenty more"

"And this is September sixth." She turned to the old man. "Nine, six, Professor."

"Please, I am in no mood for your—"

"And what time did our plane leave?"

"Andi . . ."

"We were supposed to leave at eight o'clock."

He sighed. "But because of mechanical difficulties we were delayed an hour."

"Actually one hour and six minutes."

"Andrea—"

"Putting our departure time at—"

"Ms. Goldstein—"

"9:06."

He looked at me in the mirror. "She has a thing for numbers."

"Not just numbers," she said. "Patterns. Everything's a pattern. The Fibonacci Numerical Series and the Golden Ratio, DNA, Scale Rotational Crystal Growth. Please stop the car."

The professor sighed. "Better do as she says."

I pulled to a stop in the school's driveway, under its sign.

"What are those buildings?" Andi asked.

"Some hotshot prep school for geniuses."

She squinted at the sign. "The Institute for Advanced Psychic Studies."

"Like I said, it's a—"

"That's six words!" she cried.

"Andi—"

"And the date! Look at the date!"

Locals who never got over the Institute buying up the place used the sign for target practice. But you could still read the date it was built. At least part of it.

"—996!" Andi practically shouted.

"Excuse me?" I heard another voice, from outside. I glanced at my side mirror and saw some skinny teen walking toward us.

"Wonderful," the professor sighed. "More local color."

The kid came up to my open window. "Where have you been?" He had an accent like from India or something.

"I know you?" I asked.

"I am Sridhar. Sridhar Rajput."

He stood a moment, then reached out to shake my hand. I didn't feel inclined to take it. "What can I do for you, Sridhar Rajput?"

"It has been three hours." His voice cracked. Sounded like nerves. "I have been waiting nearly three hours for you to come and address my concerns."

"Waiting?"

"My dreams, they indicated you would be here at 11:00 p.m. and now it is nearly 2:00 a.m."

CHAPTER 4

As we headed down the Institute's drive, the kid dumped a truckload of info on us. Most of it I already knew, and I'll tell you about it in a minute. Of course, the professor, in his usual charming manner, made it clear he didn't buy any of it.

"So why are you coming with us?" I said. "If you think the place is a crock, you should have stayed in the car."

"I have no inclination to sit alone in some godforsaken desert waiting to be mugged or run over again."

Of course it was a lie. He was as curious as the rest of us.

The Institute had always been a mystery. Our private Area 51. It started back when some geologists tried digging a well into the earth's mantle. They got nine miles down when the drill started to wobble, then flew out of control. They said they'd hit a giant cavern and couldn't go on. Maybe they did, maybe they didn't. Whatever the reason, there was plenty of talk about smelling sulfur and hearing voices. Some claimed they heard animals howling. Others said people.

The point is, they shut down the place until another organization came along and bought it. They built the fancy boarding school. Once in a while we see a teacher or student from it, but for the most part they stick to themselves. They don't bother us and we don't bother them. No one gives them a thought, except for the rumors—everything from a vacation spot for extraterrestrials to an assembly plant of spare body parts for superheroes.

Truth is, like the sign says, it's a place where they study psychic stuff. They fly kids in from all over the world who are supposed to be gifted. I don't care how you cut it, for me that makes the place interesting. That's why when some kid appears in the middle of the night begging us to follow him and check something out . . . well, here I am.

We were twenty yards from the main gate and guardhouse when I said, "You guys had to take lots of tests to get in?"

"Yes, we have had many examinations. Physical, psychological, intellectual. They even studied our DNA."

I nodded. "To make sure you were worth the investment."

"That is correct. But you must not feel bad. You came extremely close."

"Say what?"

"You think I would not know? I did my homework, Brenda Barnick."

I gave him a look. The Institute was the reason I dropped out of school and moved here in the first place. With the pictures and stuff I see, I figured I might get in. No such luck. But that was a long time ago.

"And you." The kid turned to Cowboy.

"Me?"

"Did you ever wonder why a small community college would offer a football scholarship to a student three states away?"

Cowboy shrugged. "Some folks think I'm kinda good."

"They wanted him nearby?" I asked. "They paid the college to bring him here?"

"So they could monitor him, correct."

"We got a pretty good season so far," Cowboy said.

Andi spoke up. "When you use the term *they*, who, exactly, do you mean?"

"Dr. Trenton, our director, calls them *the Gate*. Though I believe even he is not entirely sure who they are. We are merely their training camp. One of several. They are very secretive and"—he lowered his voice—"that is one of my many concerns."

"Right," she said. "You mentioned concerns."

"Which is why you have come."

We traded looks with each other.

"Please," he said. "I am not complaining. It is a great privilege to attend here. My parents could not be more proud. And the placement they offer after graduation, you cannot imagine. Nevertheless . . . well, you shall see. My dreams said you would come to help me decide, and I trust my dreams."

"Of course," the professor said dryly, "that explains everything."

"When did you first come here?" Cowboy asked.

"Our gifts surface during adolescence. Precognitive skills, psychokinesis, astral projection, telepathy—"

"And, in your case, dreaming," Andi said.

"Yes. Originally it was lucid dreaming. But with my concentrated training it has grown much greater. And after the induction service tomorrow, it will become so great I shall be able to serve the nations."

"Nations?" Andi said.

"One of last year's students graduated in my same area of expertise. She now lives in Brussels and assists the European Banking Federation."

"The Illuminati all filled up?" the professor asked.

Andi ignored him. "And you? Where will you go after graduation?"

He looked down. "That is why you are here. The ceremony will be tomorrow and—"

"Tomorrow?"

"—and I am not entirely sure of its safety. The Institute can be quite strict and demanding."

"Which is why they allow you to wander off campus anytime you wish," the professor said.

"Not exactly." The kid lowered his head and pushed back the hair on the back of his neck. There, at the base of his skull, was a piece of metal the size of a dime. It glowed and pulsed a faint blue.

"Is that some sort of tracking device?" the professor said.

The kid nodded.

"They know you're here?" Andi asked.

He smiled. "Yes and no. Come." He motioned us to the guard shack. Once we got there, Sridhar opened the door and we stepped inside. The place looked like something out of a sci-fi film—rows of flashing lights, TV monitors, and other high-tech junk. Some Arnold Schwarzenegger-wannabe was asleep in front of the control board. The TV screen directly in front of him was playing a cheap porn flick. But he was sound asleep—head tilted back on the chair, headphones over his ears, snoring away.

"Security at its finest," the professor said.

"Actually, I provided a little help." The kid reached into his pocket and pulled out a bottle of some over-the-counter sleeping aid.

"You slipped him a sleeping pill?" I said.

"Actually, three. At his request."

"Guys," Cowboy said. "I really don't think we should be here."

I glanced over and saw him staring at the floor. "Why not?"

Without looking, he gestured to the porn flick.

"Does that embarrass you?" Andi asked.

"No, ma'am. But if it's all the same with you"—he started

toward the door—"I'll just step outside 'til you're all done here." Before we could answer, he headed back out into the night.

Andi turned to the kid. "I'm still confused. Why would the guard ask you to put him to sleep?"

Sridhar pointed to a set of eight monitors to the right. Each had six photos of kids with a few statistics printed under them. I stepped closer to look. The photo of Sridhar was flashing red.

"That indicates I have stepped off the grounds," he said.

"And?"

"Not only can I manipulate my own dreams, but I've learned to manipulate others'. Mr. Hanson—the guard—has agreed to let me leave the grounds if I provide him with enough . . . incentive."

"Sleeping pills and a porn flick?" I said.

"I have directed his dreams to experience everything he hears in the movie."

"As if he's living it?"

"Precisely. In his dream, he is immersed in the movie as if he is there, as if it is really happening to him."

"That's sick," Andi said.

I shrugged. "Sounds like a win-win to me. You get what you want and so does the Incredible Hulk here."

"Except—" the kid hesitated. "He is never satisfied. Each time he insists upon more explicit material. It is becoming increasingly difficult to meet such demands."

"Everyone has his weakness," the professor said, moving to study the switches on the board.

The kid sighed. "Which we are carefully taught to exploit." He hit a button on the panel. The iron gate in front began to open. "Come, we haven't much time."

"Before?"

"Dr. Trenton discovers you are here."

"How will he know?" I nodded to the sleeping guard.

"The Travelers will awaken him."

"Travelers?"

He didn't answer, just motioned for us to follow. We stepped outside and joined Cowboy, who was humming, hands in his pockets, and gazing up at the stars. We headed toward the opening gate.

"That's it for your security?" the professor said.

"Pardon me?"

"A fence, some security cameras, and a sleeping pervert? Out here in the middle of the desert I would have expected more."

"As I said, we are merely a training facility. However, we do have one further line of defense."

The gate finished opening and we stepped through.

CHAPTER 5

The grounds were like I remembered. A couple of three-story buildings to our left, two more to our right, and a smaller round one straight ahead. The stone pillars rose between them. Some were as wide as thirty feet. Others ten. Some twenty feet tall. Others over a hundred.

It all felt very familiar and very strange. Stranger still was the kid stopping to put on a pair of John Lennon granny glasses.

He saw us looking at him and explained. "They reveal the location of the security field that is repositioned every week."

"Security field?" Cowboy asked.

"It is an energy field that scans the brain waves of any intruder. It reads their greatest fears, then runs them through a central computer that amplifies them. They are then broadcast back into the brain many times stronger."

"Of course," the professor said. "One of those."

"What I wish to show you is in the auditorium just ahead. But you must stay behind me and follow my route. You must not leave the path I follow." He turned to the right and walked almost parallel to the fence.

Me and Andi traded looks, then followed. So did Cowboy.

Not our resident cynic.

Andi was the first to notice. "Professor?"

"You're going to this building less than fifty feet in front of us, correct?"

"That is correct."

"So why the circular route?"

"As I said, you must follow the prescribed path or you will—"

The professor snorted and started walking straight ahead.

"Professor, no!" Sridhar called. "You must not do that!"

"Watch me."

"Professor—"

Nothing happened, at first. Two, three, four steps. Nothing. Then the old man slowed and looked down.

"Professor?"

He turned to us. "What's going on?"

"Professor—"

"My mind . . . it's—"

"Professor, you must step out of there. Step out of the field and follow—"

"It's—" His face filled with concern. "I can't . . . I'm . . . my thoughts, I can't—" He grabbed his head. "What's happening?"

Sridhar stepped around us and doubled back, careful to stay on the path.

"I don't . . . I—"

"Professor!"

He looked up, his eyes wide. "Help me . . . I can't—" He bent down, still holding his head. "I'm . . . I can't remember."

"It is an illusion." The kid stepped as close to him as he dared. "It's what you fear most."

"My memories, they're . . . Sartre. Jean-Paul Sartre. He stated that . . . in 1890, he stated . . . No, that wasn't Sartre. He wasn't born until . . . ahh, I can't . . . when did Sartre live?"

Andi called to Sridhar. "Do something! Help him!"

The kid shook his head. "No one can go in there. He must—"

"Kierkegaard, Søren Kierke—what did he, who?" He looked up at Sridhar. "Help me."

"You cannot fight it, Professor. You cannot fight fear. You can only replace it."

"I don't understand!"

Andi started toward him. I grabbed her arm and shook my head.

Sridhar spotted us. "Stay there. You must stay on the path."

"Pi." The professor looked around in panic. "Three point one four one—" He stopped. "Three point one—three—I can't, I can't remember pi!"

"Professor, listen to me." The kid tried to sound calm, but wasn't doing so good. "We cannot fight our fears. We can only replace them."

"I don't—"

"Think of something good. You must think of something pleasant to replace your fears, something you really enjoy."

"I enjoy my intelligence."

Sridhar shook his head. "No. A place. An activity."

"I don't—Books, I like to learn. I like—"

"No. A person. Is there a person you are fond of? Just one person."

"Better try another approach," Andi said.

"I . . . She was a long time ago."

"Who? When?"

"Mindy . . . Mindy Buchanan. Junior high."

"Think of Mindy Buchanan. What did she look like?"

He closed his eyes, frowning.

"Think of her clothes. Her hair."

He kept thinking.

"Good . . . that's good."

The professor opened his eyes and looked at Sridhar in surprise.

"That's right," the kid said. "Keep thinking about Mindy. Think about Mindy and start moving toward me."

The old man nodded and took a step. Then another.

"Her voice," the kid said. "Remember what her voice sounded like."

The professor slowed, then stopped. He was three or four feet from Sridhar but couldn't move.

"What's wrong?"

"She called me . . . stupid." The man scowled. "She said I wasn't smart enough."

"No, no. Think of the good."

"She said I'd never amount to—" He cringed.

"No, Professor."

He grabbed his head. "I . . . can't remember."

"Professor!"

"What did . . . I . . . can't."

There was no way he could go on. He was so close, but there was no way he—

Suddenly, without warning, the kid leaped off the path. He stepped into the field and grabbed the professor by the arm.

"What are you doing?" the professor shouted. "What are you—"

The kid tried dragging him out. When that didn't work, he ran behind the professor and pushed, slamming the man hard into his back. They both fell out of the field and onto the ground, the kid on top of him.

"What are you doing?" the professor yelled.

"I was—"

"Get off me, you ignoramus! Clumsy oaf. Get off! Get off!"

The kid scrambled away. The professor got to his feet, then brushed off his slacks and adjusted his sport coat, grumbling all the way.

He'd obviously made a full recovery.

CHAPTER 6

The auditorium had two, maybe three hundred seats. At one end there was a stage with a lectern. Behind the lectern sat six high-back chairs with armrests. Behind them were a couple of risers. And in front of the stage was another platform, more like a cube. Five by five by five. Bronze. In the center was a sealed pipe that stuck out another six or so inches.

I turned to Sridhar. "Is that—"

"Yes, that is the well."

"And those chairs?" Andi asked. "Up on the stage?"

"That is where we will sit for tomorrow's graduation. Mine is the sixth and final one to the right."

"Six?" Andi said. "Did you hear that, Professor? There are six graduates."

The professor ignored her. He'd spotted a large control board at the back of the auditorium and was heading up the steps to check it out.

Earlier, when we followed Sridhar and the spiraling path into the building, Cowboy wouldn't come in. He just stood at the side door in the hallway that surrounded the auditorium.

"What's wrong?" I asked.

"The place gives me the willies."

"Like the guard shack?"

"No. Yes. Different. Yeah, but kinda the same."

I shook my head, then turned to the kid. "What's the deal with the well?"

"It is sealed for now," he said. "But during tomorrow's induction, it shall be opened."

"And why is that?" Andi said.

"It is best that I show you." He turned to the center of the auditorium and called, "Computer. Please play last year's ceremony."

The air above the middle of the room sparkled, then filled with light. Suddenly we were looking at a 3-D hologram of the auditorium filled with people. This time, up on the stage, there were eight kids.

"That is last year's class," Sridhar said.

The students looked comfortable enough, all prim and proper in their white gowns. You barely noticed their wrists strapped to the armrests or their ankles strapped to the legs of the chairs. On the risers behind them stood a dozen younger kids. Up at the lectern, some pompous, slick dude in a three-piece suit was giving a speech:

" . . . leaving selfish ambition behind to enter a new fraternity, an order that will guide us from the old paradigms of self-centeredness and destruction into a new era of peace, wisdom, and freedom."

The audience clapped.

"Computer," Sridhar called, "go to the induction."

The image flickered. Now the students on the risers were singing. One of those medieval chant things, only higher and creepier. As they sang, two older dudes dressed in red robes came up to the cubicle. They carried a long silver pole that they slipped into the ring on the pipe's lid. Then, as one stood at each end of the pole, they lifted the lid.

"Come," the slick speaker called. "Travelers of the future, come fill these newest vessels with your ceaseless knowledge."

The singing grew louder and creepier. Wisps of green smoke started rising from the pipe. It grew thicker until it became a green cloud that glowed and pulsed with the music. It rose until it was ten feet above the cube.

"Guys!" Cowboy yelled over the music. "I don't like this!"

I glanced over my shoulder. He had inched his way into the auditorium a few feet.

The cloud drifted over to the stage. As it did, it divided in half. Then those halves split again, so there were four. They split again, so there were eight. Eight little clouds pulsing in perfect unison to the music.

"Guys?"

The clouds drifted until each one floated over a graduate. The students watched, not quite as relaxed as before.

"The time has arrived!" Slick shouted over the singing. "All of your hard work and diligence shall be rewarded. Now is the time to reap your reward. Now is the time for induction."

The singing amped up until it almost sounded like screaming. The students kept staring up at their clouds.

"And so, let it begin!"

The clouds began to churn. The music got louder. Finally, one of the kids opened her mouth. Wide. And she kept it open.

"Come!" Slick called. "Now is the time!"

Another opened his mouth. And then another. And another. They looked like baby chicks waiting to be fed. The clouds kept pulsing and churning until the last kid opened his.

Then Slick shouted, "Receive your destiny!"

In a flash, the clouds shot into their mouths. At first the kids resisted. They rocked back and forth, pulling against the straps holding their hands and ankles. If they screamed, you couldn't hear it over the music.

It lasted only a few seconds. Pretty soon they stopped fighting and relaxed. One by one, they closed their mouths and lowered their heads. They looked calmly out over the audience.

And the crowd broke into cheers and applause.

"Hologram, off," Sridhar said.

The image disappeared and we stood in the silence, trying to digest it all.

Finally Cowboy spoke. "It's the devil."

I turned to him.

"Those are demons straight from the pit of hell," he said.

"Demons?" Sridhar sounded surprised. "Dr. Trenton says they are time travelers. They have returned in time through a portal in the earth's crust to warn us and save our planet."

I turned back to Cowboy. "So you don't think Sridhar should be a part of this?"

"I don't think we should even be inside this room."

"Andi—" the professor shouted down from the console. "Can you come up here a moment?"

"It's creepy," I said to Cowboy. "I'll give you that. And those kids on stage weren't exactly thrilled."

"Until their training took over," Sridhar said. "After the initial shock they were fine. Better than fine."

"And you've talked to them?" I said. "Afterward?"

"Yes. Many are my good friends and now they work closely with world leaders. Everything is well and good."

"Except for them being possessed," Cowboy said.

"Guys?" Andi called from the console. "Check it out." She hit a few switches and motioned to the stage.

The same smoke we'd seen in the hologram was rising from the pipe. Only this time the pipe was covered.

"That's not possible," the kid said. "The well won't be unsealed until tomorrow."

"Looks like it has different plans." I moved in for a closer look.

"Miss Brenda—" Cowboy warned.

By the time I got to the cube, I saw something wasn't right. It took a moment to work up my courage, but I finally stretched my hand into the smoke. Only there *was* no smoke. My hand lit up green and I could see smoke on it, but there was no smoke. I wiggled my fingers. I waved. Nothing. It was just a projection.

The professor called down from the console. "Behold, your demons."

I pulled back my hand and turned to him. "Another hologram?"

Andi flipped a couple of switches on the console. The smoke rose and pulsed just like before. It divided. First into two clouds, then four, then the last one divided again, making six. They drifted until one floated over each of the chairs.

"It's a light show," I said. "Just special effects."

"But—" the kid moved beside me. "What about the graduates?"

"What about them?" the professor said.

"Surely you saw their reaction when the travelers first entered them."

"I saw eight susceptible teenagers programmed for months, perhaps years, to believe whatever they saw and heard."

"But . . . our training, our classes—"

"Take a good look, son. It's all smoke and mirrors."

"Not entirely."

I spun around to see Slick himself standing in the center of the stage.

CHAPTER 7

Dr. Trenton." Sridhar took a step toward the stage. "I am so sorry. Let me explain. I was—"

Slick held up his hand and the kid stopped. Then the man turned to me. "Ms. Barnick, it's so good to see you again."

It took me back, but I held my ground. "We never met. I don't know you."

"You may not know me, but I certainly know you." He shoved his hands into his pockets, all relaxed. "So tell me, how's life as a tattoo artist?"

I nodded toward the clouds. "How's your life as a con artist?"

He smiled, all superior-like. "Yes." He called to the back of the auditorium, "Andrea? Would you be so kind as to shut that down, please? It can be so distracting."

"How do you know my name?" Andi called.

"The controls are to your left. But apparently you've already discovered them."

"Yes, I have, and they're very impressive." She punched a few buttons and the clouds disappeared. "But how did—"

"Thank you. And Dr. James McKinney, tell me, what do you think?"

The professor was unfazed. "Time travelers? Is that the best you could come up with?"

"You don't believe in time travel."

The professor motioned to the stage. "Apparently, neither do you."

"Oh, that." Slick chuckled. "It's an audiovisual aid. Merely something for weaker minds to put their faith in."

"So it's all fake?" Andi asked.

"No, dear. It's an icon. As real as the Kaaba in Mecca, the crosses in churches—"

"Or the face of the Virgin Mary in a burrito," the professor said.

Slick gave that smile again, this time for the professor. "Whether you care to admit it or not, those beliefs, however misinterpreted by the masses, have a trace of truth."

"I prefer my truth less delusional."

"And what truth would that be, Professor? Existentialism? Postmodernism? What's your flavor-of-the-month today?"

"It's certainly not *Star Trek* reruns or wherever you're getting your inspiration."

"That's right, you're a good eighteenth-century scientist, aren't you? A classical materialist who believes only in what he can see."

"I'm a realist. If it can't be measured, it doesn't exist."

"So you have no belief in the multiple dimensions surrounding us."

"No more than the Easter Bunny or Santa Claus."

"Even though theoretical mathematicians have clearly proven them as fact."

"*Theoretical* and *fact* do not belong in the same sentence."

"Like the theory of evolution?"

"Please," the professor scorned.

"Or dark matter."

"That's an entirely different issue."

"No, that's 72 percent of reality. And every physicist worth his salt knows it. It can't be touched, it can't be measured, but they know it's here. The same goes for dark energy making up an additional 24 percent. So congratulations, Professor, you believe in 6 percent of reality."

"Who are you, really? What's this place about?"

"It's a doorway to our future. As is every student here." He gestured to Sridhar. "Each one carefully trained to bring us back from the brink of extinction and usher in a new age of peace and prosperity for all."

"Break out the incense and love beads."

"Oh, you are a tough one, aren't you." Slick paused, then added, "I believe in—"

At that same moment, the professor said, "I believe in—"

Both men stopped. The professor frowned.

Slick smiled. Then he said, "What are you?" just as the professor said, "What are you?"

Again they stopped. The professor frowned harder.

Slick smiled bigger. Then he said, "What's this?" just as the professor said, "What's this?"

They kept going. "Another one—"

"Another one—"

"Of—"

"Of—"

"Your—"

"Your—"

"Tricks?"

"Tricks?"

The professor was anything but thrilled.

Slick just grinned. "Now, how did I know you were going to say that?"

"Actually, that's a very good question," Andi said. She left the console and started down the steps, moving toward the stage. "How *did* you know?"

"I didn't. But the time traveler I'm hosting did. In fact, if I allowed him, he could recite our entire conversation before it began."

He paused, then added, "That's ridic—" just as the professor said, "That's ridic—" and stopped.

"Yes." There was that smile again.

Andi joined me at the cube in front of the stage. "So there's absolutely nothing coming out of this tube?" she asked. "It's all special effects?"

"Yes and no. The time travelers will be gathered all about this stage tomorrow. The special effects are merely a way of priming the pump, of helping the audience visualize what is actually occurring. The same goes for the graduates. It provides a point of reference, so when the indwelling occurs, they are not startled or alarmed."

He turned to the kid. "And Sridhar, I'm afraid this must remain our little secret. As you can imagine, I am not pleased to find you and your friends skulking about, and uncovering such information, especially before our big day. And it may make your own induction tomorrow less pleasant. Nevertheless, it is imperative you not share this with the other graduates."

"Yes, sir."

"The music, these effects, all are designed to create an environment more conducive to receiving your travelers. Without focusing upon them, your natural defenses will resist—a painful penalty for your disobedience. However, there is no need for your fellow graduates to also suffer. Wouldn't you agree?"

"Yes, sir."

He turned back to us. "With or without the assistance of these special effects, the travelers *will* enter the graduates where they will continue to expand each host's giftedness in order to help and enlighten the world."

"Demons," Cowboy called from the doorway. "They're demons sent by the devil himself."

Slick looked at him sadly. "Yes . . . little wonder you weren't admitted into the program." He turned to the rest of us and clapped his hands. "Well, as much fun as this has been, I'm afraid you'll have to come back some other time. Tomorrow's activities await and it will be a very busy day." He turned to Sridhar. "As for you, my young friend, it's off to bed with you. Try and put that curious mind of yours to rest. Tomorrow will prove to be one of the most important days of your life."

The kid looked at him a moment, then lowered his gaze.

"What if he doesn't want to go?" Andi asked.

"Excuse me?"

"The boy has had second thoughts," the professor added.

"I'm sorry, that's not possible."

"Possible or not, it seems to be—"

Slick made a sharp motion with his hand. The kid grabbed the back of his neck and cried out. "Ahh!"

"Is that correct, Sridhar?" Slick asked.

The boy was in too much pain to answer.

"What are you doing?" Andi demanded.

He calmly repeated, "Sridhar? Is that correct?"

"I—" the kid gasped.

"What's going on?" Andi cried. "What are you doing?

"An electronic leash," the professor said.

Slick smiled. "Very good."

The professor continued. "Not only does it serve as a tracking device, but apparently as a method of control as well."

"Only for the less compliant," Slick said. "Time to call it a night, son." He waved his hand and the kid cried out again, this time doubling over in pain.

"Stop it!" Andi shouted. "You're hurting him!"

"Let him go!" Cowboy's voice joined with Andi's. "Stop it!"

Sridhar kept gasping. "Please . . . please—"

"Stop it!"

All right. Enough was enough. They could yell all they wanted, but there's only one way to stop a bully. I took off up the steps and went across the stage, heading straight for him. He had me by twenty, thirty pounds. I had him by surviving the streets.

I heard Cowboy shouting behind me, but I didn't need his help. I lunged at Slick and shot straight through him like he was thin air. The reason was simple. He *was* thin air. Another projection. I spun around and tried again. Same thing. Only now he was laughing.

"Please, Dr. Trenton," the kid begged. "I shall go. Please!"

Slick's projection turned to him.

The kid stood panting. Sweating.

"Go" was all Slick said.

The kid nodded and staggered toward the opposite exit.

"Sridhar!" Andi shouted.

"Big day tomorrow, son," Slick called after him. "Need to get that beauty sleep."

"Wait!" Cowboy shouted. "Hold on, now." He raced toward the boy, but was too late. The kid never looked back as he stepped through the door and let it slam behind him.

"Sridhar!" Cowboy got to the door. Pushed it. Slammed into it. Pushed again. It didn't budge.

Andi spun back to Slick's image. "You can't hold him against his will."

"Actually, he looked more than willing, wouldn't you say? And as for you—" He glanced at his watch. "I have deactivated the security field for the next two minutes. That should give you all ample time to leave the auditorium, cross the yard, and exit through the gate."

"And if we don't?" the professor said.

"Then I shall have you arrested for trespassing and breaking and entering."

"We were invited," Andi argued.

Slick looked to where Sridhar had exited. "That may be difficult to prove." He glanced back at his watch. "One minute forty-four seconds."

We stood a moment. No one knew what to do.

"Better hurry," Slick said. "As the professor can attest, the effects of the field can be quite unpleasant. One minute thirty-two. I believe you have played out all of your cards for this evening, wouldn't you agree?"

The professor was the first to turn. He hesitated, then started for the exit.

"Professor?"

"I'm not going through that field again," he said. "Trust me, none of you want to."

"An excellent choice, sir."

Without warning, Cowboy bolted for the stage.

"No!" I shouted. "He's just a projection." I waved my hand through Slick as a reminder and Cowboy slowed to a stop.

"Seventy-six seconds," Slick said. "Dear me, it will be close."

I looked after the professor, then glanced at the others. Finally I turned to leave.

"Miss Brenda, what are you doing?"

"Nothing," I said. "There's nothing any of us can do. At least not tonight."

"Very good," Slick called after me. "Run, run, run away; come back to fight some other day."

What I wouldn't give for him to be real. Just long enough to land one punch. But he wasn't real and there was nothing we could do.

Those were the facts. The same facts that led Andi to eventually turn and follow me. And finally, Cowboy.

We stepped outside and barely made it across the field in time. A groggy guard had opened the gate and we walked through. It closed with a mournful creak, followed by a dull thud.

We headed back to my car. Nobody said a word. Nobody wanted to. We were all alone with just our thoughts and the dark, violet band stretching across the horizon.

CHAPTER 8

I wanna make it clear, I'm no pushover. Just because some kid I don't know gets into something over his head doesn't make it my business. It happens all the time. Hookers, gang members, drug runners . . . if they can get out, fine. If not, it's called survival of the fittest.

Despite Cowboy's whining and Miss Do-Gooder's pleadings, I'd had enough. And for the first time I could remember, me and the professor agreed. Of course we'd called the cops, and of course they said they'd look into it, which of course they wouldn't. Not with all the money the Institute had to throw around.

I dropped Cowboy off at his place around six. Took the professor and Andi to our best (and only) motel around six forty-five. I was dead-dog tired but hung in the parking lot just long enough to hear the professor rant and rave about the accommodations. After all the drama, I figured I was entitled to a little entertainment. Of course, we'd all exchanged phone numbers (my mistake) and agreed to contact each other if someone had an idea, but I wasn't holding my breath.

I got to bed but didn't sleep good. Way too many dreams.

First it was the usual suspects—making rent, shop troubles, Mom, a guest appearance by Jimmy Jack, who knocked me up at fifteen, and little Monique. Sweet, baby Monique (who I secretly named and held for five minutes before the Brady Bunch couple showed up and swept her away). A day doesn't go by that I don't hate myself for that decision, worry about where she is and how she's being treated. She'll be eleven next month. Same age as the boy I tatted on Cowboy's arm.

The boy who never showed.

But the dream that wrecked me was about Sridhar. He was in one of those cattle chutes they drive sheep through on their way to slaughter. In my version it led to the Institute's auditorium where we all sat watching. Slick was up on stage in his three-piece suit holding shears. When Sridhar got to him, he shaved off the kid's clothes like wool. And the kid? He just stood there looking at me like I'm supposed to do something.

Once Slick finished and the kid was butt naked, two security guards showed up. They tied his feet and hands and hung him up on a conveyer belt with hooks. It carried him off stage through curtains spattered with blood. I knew what was coming next and forced myself awake . . . both times.

There might have been a third if Cowboy hadn't called.

"Did you get it?" he asked.

"Get what? What time is—"

"The dream. The one me, Andi, and the professor got."

"What are you talking about?"

"Where Sridhar is getting butchered?"

Ten minutes later I was in the car driving to pick them up. Besides the dream, a picture kept forming in my head. More like a pattern. I kept pushing it away but it kept coming back. A sign it might be legit. I rummaged through the glove compartment of McD wrappers and parking tickets 'til I found a pen and an envelope from a delinquent water bill.

I sketched as I drove. Pretty simple, really. Just a circle with three spiral arms shooting from it.

I picked Cowboy up first. He gave me that good-ol'-boy smile. "Mornin', Miss Brenda. How you been?"

Andi greeted me with her usual enthusiasm. "What a fantastic morning. It's great to see you again!"

The professor didn't bother.

We wound up at the local St. Arbucks getting a much needed caffeine fix. Andi chattered the whole time, making me think she'd had a few shots beforehand.

"Since the beginning of time, dreams have been taken seriously by every known people group. The ancient Babylonians put great stock in them. Besides the Persians and the Greeks, there were the Romans. Of course, we can't forget the Jews, who even included them in their holy scriptures. Not to mention the Muslims, Christians, and every Eastern belief and culture. In fact, did you know—and you'll find this incredibly interesting—an indigenous tribe of New Guinea once based their entire government upon the dreams of—"

"Your point?" I said as we grabbed our drinks and settled in at a back corner.

"My point is, this is definitely not a coincidence. The odds of three people having an identical dream with identical details is nearly impossible."

"Nearly?"

"Approximately one to ten to the one hundred fifty-seventh power."

I gave her a look.

"Approximately," she said.

The professor, who'd been quiet as a tomb, dug a pack of powdered creamer from his pocket. He answered my look. "Lactose intolerant."

"So it was Sridhar, right?" Cowboy said. "The little guy put the dream into my brain."

"A wonder he found room," the professor said.

Andi ignored him. "Before his training, Sridhar started off as a lucid dreamer—"

"Which is an entirely different crock of—"

"Which is something the United States government invested millions of dollars developing during the Cold War. They called it Remote Viewing, and it was somewhat successful."

"The government paid millions of dollars for people to dream?" Cowboy asked.

"I rest my case."

The professor tore open the creamer and dumped it into his coffee. He'd just picked up a stirrer when Andi cried, "Wait! Look!"

We followed her gaze to the professor's cup.

"Did you see that?" she said. "Did you see the way it swirled?"

The professor sighed wearily. "Really?"

"No, I'm serious. No substance swirls into a liquid like that. It was a perfect circle, a perfect ring with three symmetrically placed arms spinning out of it. It lasted only a second, but surely you saw it?"

She turned to Cowboy, who shrugged.

Then to the professor.

He gave the cup an extra stir.

She looked at me. My face must have given something away. "You saw it, didn't you?"

I pulled out the water bill envelope and shoved it across the table at her.

"There!" She pointed at my sketch. "See! See!"

"See what?" Cowboy asked.

"A nine. Don't you see it? That's the number nine. It doesn't get any clearer than that."

Once she mentioned it, it was kinda clear. A nine, spinning out of the circle.

"And this spiral up here at the top right. See the way it makes a perfect six? And this one at the top left?"

"Another six," Cowboy said.

She tapped the paper. "Nine, six. It was September sixth when we got there last night."

"It still is," Cowboy said. He was catching her enthusiasm. "What about that other six, the one on the left?"

"It could be anything. The minute our plane took off, the number of words in the Institute's name, or—"

"The sixth chair of the sixth graduate in today's ceremony," I said.

Andi and Cowboy looked at me.

"It's a joke," I said. "I wasn't—"

But Andi's eyes were wide. "The sixth day of the ninth month with the sixth participant. It's Sridhar! It's got to be!"

Cowboy frowned. "So, besides the dreams—"

"Someone or something is telling us to help!"

The professor closed his eyes in exaggerated patience.

"That's why we're here!" she practically shouted. "The plane crash, the nine pinnacles, the same numbers over and over again. They're telling us to rescue Sridhar and to rescue him today!"

I shook my head. "You may not have noticed, but we already tried that."

Andi reached into her handbag and dug around. "So we have to try again."

"That's right," Cowboy said eagerly. "Practice makes perfect."

She pulled out a pencil and notepad. "We have to devise a plan. Between the four of us there must be some way to save him. Professor? Come on now, we need your help." She drew a rough sketch of the Institute.

The professor looked at me and sighed. Between Cowboy's bighearted naïveté and Andi's over-the-top enthusiasm, we were outnumbered.

I'll save you the boring details. It was late, but after too many cups of coffee and way too many pastries for breakfast, and then lunch, we had no fewer than six plans for breaking into the Institute during the ceremony. Because of Cowboy's involvement, most looked like football plays with *x*'s and *o*'s, but at least we had them. One might have actually worked if it weren't for Andi's text message.

"No way," she said, looking at her phone.

"What?" Cowboy asked.

"It's from the Institute." She looked up. "We're on the list."

"List? What list?"

She read it out loud. "'Please stop by Security and pick up your on-campus pass. A fun day to be had by all. Dr. B. J. Trenton.'"

The professor swore under his breath.

I joined him.

CHAPTER 9

We're standing at the back wall of the auditorium watching the show. Slick, the real one, had been onstage forty-five minutes, rambling on about how privileged the kids were and how they'd be making the world a better place. The good news was they'd shut down the security field, so once we got our passes we just strolled on with the rest of the doting parents and whoevers. The bad news was we had to listen to his drivel.

" . . . leaving selfish ambition behind to enter a new fraternity, an order that will guide us from old paradigms of self-destruction into a new age of knowledge, peace, and prosperity. Graduates, are you ready?"

The six students behind him nodded. Like the others we'd seen the night before, they were strapped into their chairs looking excited and nervous. Except Sridhar. Even where I stood you could tell he was pretty drugged up.

"Then let us begin the induction!"

The choir on the back risers began to sing the same creepy music. Like before, two hooded guys came forward with a long pole. They slipped it into the ring on the pipe's lid and lifted it off. And, like before, glowing green smoke seemed to billow out.

"Arise!" Slick called. "Travelers of the future, come fill these newest members who have prepared so long for this moment with your great and wondrous knowledge."

I glance over to the control board a dozen feet away. Some guy in a shaved head was sipping a Jamba Juice and running the show. By the looks of things, everything was going according to plan. Everything but us. We still didn't have one. Even if we did, the two burly guards on either end of the stage could be a problem.

Sridhar and the others watched as the music grew louder and the smoke turned into a cloud that divided into two, then four, with the last two dividing to make six.

"We gotta do something," Cowboy whispered. "Maybe we could ask them to make an announce—"

"Shh," Andi said. "Listen."

He paused a second. "All I hear is singing."

"Exactly."

"What's that got to do with—"

"Shh. Don't you hear that? The rhythm? The pattern?"

"It's just music."

"And a rather loose description of the term," the professor added.

"No, listen." She took a breath and blew it out. "Hear it?"

We didn't.

She did it again—breathed in and out. She motioned to the stage and did it a third time. "See? See how Sridhar and the other five are aligning their breathing with the music?"

"To help them relax," I said. "Like the guy told us last night."

"But those bass notes, hear their rhythm? The way they throb? Underneath?" She tapped her fingers into her palm. "Bum-bum, bum-bum, bum-bum . . ."

"It's like a heartbeat," Cowboy said.

"Precisely. And it's lined up to match the light pulsing inside those clouds."

I looked on as Sridhar and the other kids closed their eyes and tipped their heads back. "So it *is* to help them relax," I said.

The professor shook his head. "No. It's to manipulate their limbic systems."

"English?" I said.

"It's creating a trance-like state. Lowering their resistance, making them susceptible to hypnotic suggestion."

"Or to whatever wants to enter them," Andi added.

I turned back to the stage. The clouds were moving into position over each of the students. "So what do we do?"

"If we're to help Sridhar, we better act now," Andi said, "or it'll be too late."

I gestured to Shaved Head at the control panel. "We could take over the board." I turned to Cowboy. "You could take him out, right?"

He shook his head. "I wouldn't want to hurt him."

"You take out guys every week on the football field."

"Not on purpose. If I do, I always try to patch 'em up when I'm done."

I just looked at him.

"There's another way," Andi said. "If I go backstage and confuse the singers' rhythm, if I can shift it so it's actually conflicting with the flashing clouds—"

The professor scoffed. "You think you can create enough dissonance to break their hypnotic state?"

"And disrupt the ceremony? Maybe."

He dropped his head and shook it in disbelief.

"And then what?" I said.

"I don't know. If there's enough confusion, maybe Tank could sneak in from backstage. Maybe he could free Sridhar and get him out of there."

"And maybe pigs can fly," the professor said.

I looked down at the stage. The clouds were over the students' heads and pulsing brighter. The kids were beginning to open their mouths.

"We have to do something," Andi said. "Does anyone have a better idea?"

We didn't.

"All right, then. Tank, you come with me." He nodded and they headed for the back door to the hallway circling the arena.

I looked at the professor. He leaned against the wall, as noncommittal as ever. I turned back to the control board and Shaved Head. Andi's plan was iffy at best. It wouldn't hurt to have a backup.

I headed for the board.

There was a four-foot wall around it. The closer I got, the more Shaved Head looked big and impressive. But I had a few impressive attributes of my own.

Once I got there, I tugged down on my V-neck, making sure my attributes were visible.

"Psst!" I whispered. "Hey!"

He glanced up from the board.

I smiled and leaned forward, making sure I had his full attention. He crossed to me.

"Can I watch?" I whispered.

He frowned.

I motioned him closer and whispered into his ear. "I really think it's hot the way you run all this stuff." He looked at me. I nodded and mouthed, *Really hot*. He broke into a smile that had most of his teeth.

I reached for the little gate separating us. "Can I watch?"

He hesitated.

I smiled, tugged at my shirt again. He opened the gate.

Happy to show off his manly prowess, he returned to work. Happy to find an external hard drive, I slammed it into the back of his head. He slid to the floor. No one noticed—except the professor, who almost looked impressed.

I turned to the board with all its switches and blinking lights. Where to begin?

Up on stage, Andi had slipped beside the last choir member and was singing her little heart out. You couldn't hear her, but you could see the choir staring. Slick too. No one was happy.

The professor arrived and pushed open the gate to join me.

I nodded to the stage. "How's she doing?"

He listened and shook his head. "Not enough."

I motioned to the board. "Plan B?"

He nodded. "Shut her down."

"Any idea how?"

He didn't have a clue. Well, except for Shaved Head's Jamba Juice. The one he picked up (Tropical Fruit, I believe) and poured over the board.

It was like the Fourth of July—lights and sparks everywhere. And not just the board. The whole auditorium went dark. When the emergency lights came on, one of the security guards spotted us and took off up the steps.

"Now what?" the professor said.

My solution wasn't as original as his but probably just as effective.

"Run!"

CHAPTER 10

I went for one back door. The professor took the other. By the time I circled around and got to the stage, things had definitely changed. For starters, the clouds were shorting out. The images kept repeating themselves, floating from the pipe to the students, from the pipe to the students. The choir had quit singing and the audience was anything but happy.

"A hoax?" someone yelled. "This is all a hoax?"

Another shouted, "We've been watching a light show?"

Of course, Slick did his best to fix things. "Please, we're currently having some technical difficulties." And all the teachers, about a dozen in the front row, were on their feet trying to quiet everyone.

Cowboy had unstrapped Sridhar and was holding off the other guard. "Please. I don't want to hurt you," he kept saying. "We'll just be takin' this boy and be on our way."

I moved to the kid and helped him to his feet.

"What happened?" he mumbled. "What's going on?"

Slick spotted us. "Stop them!"

"You two best be going, Miss Brenda," Cowboy said.

I looked into the auditorium and saw the other guard coming for us.

"What about—"

"I'll be there in a jiffy. Me and the fellas just need a little talk."

I looked over to see Andi waving from the side exit. "Over here!"

The kid and I started toward her. The lights flickered again. The crowd had grown even more restless and was getting to their feet.

"My child wasted two years of her life here?"

"A fraud. This is all a fraud!"

"You'll be hearing from my lawyers."

"I *am* a lawyer!"

Slick and the teachers definitely had their hands full. Still, he managed to shout at us, "I've engaged the security field, so you're going nowhere!"

We joined Andi and stepped into the hallway as Slick repeated, "I said you're going no—"

The door slammed shut behind us.

We crossed the hallway and opened the exit door. The yard was in front of us. The gate forty feet away.

"Now what?" I said.

"We followed a spiral," Andi said.

"What?"

"Last night, we circled the building. We followed a spiral path to this location."

"A path we can't see without those special glasses." I turned to the kid. "Unless you got them now."

He shook his head.

"Wait a minute!" Andi said. "That pattern you drew of the numbers? The one identical to the creamer in the professor's coffee. Do you have it?"

I pulled the envelope from my pocket and handed it to her.

"Yes!" she cried.

"What?"

"The route."

"That's no route. It's numbers and dates. You said so yourself."

"And it's the route."

"It can't be both."

"Maybe not in three dimensions. But if Trenton is correct about multiple dimensions, then of course it is."

"Of course?"

"Multiple dimensions function at multiple levels. Therefore, they should have multiple meanings. They *must* have multiple meanings." She pointed where the arc of the number met the circle. "If this is our current location, we must follow this exact route back to the gate."

It made no sense to me. So what else was new?

The door opened. Lots of noise came from inside as Cowboy stepped out.

"The guards?" I asked. "They cool?"

"They'll be a little cranky when they wake up, but yes ma'am, everything's good."

"And the professor?" Andi said.

"Right behind me."

"Let's go, then." Andi held out the diagram as we headed into the yard. We'd gone about twenty feet when the professor showed up at the door.

"Wait for me!" he yelled.

"The path!" Andi shouted. "Avoid the field by following our path."

The old guy froze. Guess he didn't want an encore of last night's performance.

I saw where we'd been. "Keep going," I said. "I'll go back and get him."

"Stay on the path," Andi repeated.

I nodded. When I arrived, the professor was his usual sunny self. "I hope she knows where she's going."

The lights in the building beside us flickered.

"What did you do?" I said.

"There was some extra Jamba Juice."

"And?"

"I found the main circuit room."

We headed after the others. We got about halfway when the door flew open and both security guards piled out.

"Let's move." I grabbed the professor's arm and pulled him along faster.

"Be careful," he groused. "Stay on the path! Careful!"

The guards gained on us. The fact they didn't drag around a whiny windbag made it easier. That, and their John Lennon glasses.

Andi, Cowboy, and the kid reached the gate. We were just feet behind them when I suddenly thought of baby Monique. Only now she wasn't a baby. She was the same age she'd be today. They had her locked in some dark room. A closet. And she was sobbing. Her face streaked with tears. All alone.

It was only a thought, but so real I had to gasp, "Monique . . ."

Over her tears I heard another voice. Old and white: "You'll stay in there until you wash *all* those dishes."

"Momma?" she cried. But not for them. For me. "Momma!"

I could barely catch my breath. "Monique, is that—"

"No!" The professor yelled. I looked up to see him grab his head. "Not again! Somebody help me!"

"They changed the security field!" Andi shouted.

"Momma . . ." More images flickered. Sharper. Clearer. Monique stood barefoot in a cold, wet cellar. She was shivering. Hard. Her arms raised. To me! "Momma? Momma, help me!"

"Oh, baby—"

"Grab my hand, Professor!" Andi shouted. "Grab my—"

"I can't remember!" he cried. "I don't—"

"Grab my hand!"

"Miss Brenda!" Cowboy yelled.

I blinked. Saw Cowboy reaching for me. He was six feet away. The professor was beside me, doubled over.

"Miss Brenda!"

I fought off Monique's image long enough to grab the professor by the waist.

"Help me!" he cried. "Help—"

It took all my strength, but I flung him past me. He stumbled out of the field and into Andi's arms.

"Momma!"

I spun back to Monique.

"Momma, it hurts. Momma, they're hurting me! Momma—"

"Miss Brenda!"

I tried focusing on Cowboy's voice, pushing her out of my mind. But I couldn't. How could I, when what I feared most was happening right in front of me?

CHAPTER 11

"Father, please . . . please, forgive me!" Monique huddled in the corner of a fancy bedroom. Stuffed animals. Canopy bed. Everything pink and frilly. "I'm sorry, please . . ."

A human tub of lard stood over her, belt in hand.

"It was an accident, I—"

Slap. He hit her hard across the face. I felt the sting on my own. I grabbed my cheek and staggered forward. "Monique!"

"I'll teach you to respect my property."

Slap!

"Miss Brenda!" Cowboy's voice was far away. "Think of somethin' good!"

Now Monique was looking out a window. Rain streaked it. Her face was wet with tears. Outside, the Brady Bunch loaded their brats into a van, preparing to drive away.

"Momma . . ." She choked out the word. "Momma, where are you?"

I stood at the door, tears in my own eyes. "Right here, baby. I'm right here."

"Fight it, girl!" The professor's voice called. "It's an illusion—fight it!"

He was right. I concentrated with all I had to push her out of my head.

The image flickered.

I tried harder.

She disappeared.

I turned around and saw Andi, eight feet away, reaching for me. "Hurry!"

I started forward, two, three steps before I heard, "Momma . . ."

She sounded so real. So lost. I knew I shouldn't, but I had to.

"Miss Brenda!"

I turned and there she was. So alone. So frightened.

"Oh, baby." I started forward. "Momma's right here."

"Brenda!"

I was nearly there. Stretching out my arms. Suddenly her face darkened, twisted into rage. "Stay back!"

"Baby—"

"I hate you!"

I slowed. "Sweetheart, I—"

"I hate you! I'll always hate you!"

I stopped.

She kept shouting. "You gave me away! To strangers, you gave me away!"

"No, I—"

"Like garbage! You threw me away!"

"Miss Brenda?"

I closed my eyes. Trying to force her out of my mind.

"And now I have to suffer. My whole life I'm suffering."

But the harder I tried, the stronger she became.

"It's your fault. It's all your fault!"

I heard Sridhar's voice, faint. "You cannot remove it. You must replace it!"

"Think of somethin' good, Miss Brenda. Replace it with somethin' good."

"You've ruined me. You've ruined everything!"

"Somethin' good."

"I hate you!" The words punched me in the gut. "I hate everything about you!"

"Think of somethin' good!"

I thought of her delivery, back in the hospital. Not the pain, but afterward.

"A girl, Ms. Barnick. " The doctor smiled down at me. "A beautiful baby girl."

I remembered her tiny weight when they put her on my belly. Her warmth. The crying, the squirming. She was a part of me, but more. Another human. Completely me, completely different.

"You gave me away . . ." Her voice began to fade.

I thought of her eyes. Those puffy slits squinting against the light. People say newborns can't focus, but she saw me. She opened them and looked right at me. And we connected. Mother and child. My heart swelled.

"Miss Brenda!"

I turned to see Cowboy and the others motioning to me.

"Hurry!"

I took a step toward them, still seeing my baby, still hearing her cry. Another step. The crying stopped for an instant and she smiled. At me. Another step. I was smiling, too, my heart bursting . . . as I took the final step and fell into Cowboy's arms.

"You okay?" he asked.

The memory faded. I nodded and he helped me to my feet.

Suddenly Sridhar screamed. I turned around to see the kid grabbing the back of his neck and doubling over.

"Did you honestly think you could leave that easily?"

I turned and saw Slick standing in the middle of the field,

glasses on, definitely not happy. He pressed a small remote in his hand. The kid dropped to his knees, shrieking in pain.

"And without even saying good-bye?"

"Stop it!" Andi yelled. "You're killing him. You're killing him!"

"He should be so lucky."

CHAPTER 12

"Please—" The kid gasped.

Slick showed no mercy. "You're the first, did you know that? The only graduate to ever refuse induction."

Lights from another building flickered, then went out.

"You think we wouldn't make an example of you?"

"I'll . . . come back. I'll—"

"It's a little late for that." He cranked up whatever gizmo he had in his hand. The kid cried out, curling into a ball, trying to breathe.

"Stop it!" Andi yelled.

"He's just a boy!" Cowboy shouted.

Slick ignored them. "You have no idea who you're dealing with, do you?"

"Release him," the professor called. "Release the boy and we will go."

Slick broke out laughing. "Go? Oh, you'll go, all right. But trust me, you won't be leaving. Not this war."

"War?" Andi shouted. "What war?"

"Do you think you four were brought together by accident?

Are you really so naïve as to think there are not greater forces at work here?"

"What are—"

"Please . . ." the kid whimpered, gasping.

"You'll not succeed. They're too powerful. You may have won the battle but the war has barely be—"

He was cut off by a muffled explosion at one end of the auditorium and a small puff of smoke rising. At the same time, the kid groaned and seemed to relax. Apparently the pain had stopped.

Slick wasn't so lucky. "Ahh!" He doubled over. "No!"

We traded looks.

"The security field?" Andi asked.

The professor frowned. "It must be shorting out."

"No! No . . ."

Cowboy shook his head. "I don't think—"

"I've done everything you've asked!" Slick cried. "I've—" He began to stagger. "No!" He threw up his arms, slapping away at something no one could see. "No!"

"Those are some ugly fears," I said.

He fell to his knees and began choking, gagging.

"Them ain't fears, Miss Brenda."

"Stop this!" A different voice sounded. It came from Slick, but it was deep, guttural. "Stop this at once!"

Slick's normal voice came back, pleading. "No . . . don't—"

"Stop!" The other voice started cussing. Worse than me on a bad day.

Slick's hands shot to his face. He began scratching at it, clawing until it was covered in blood. He spun back to us, his eyes wild. "Help me! Help—"

"Shut up!" the deeper voice yelled. "You are a failure!"

"No! No, I did every—" He screamed and threw himself on the ground, where he began to writhe.

"That's enough!" Cowboy shouted. We turned to him. Before any of us could stop him, he stepped back into the field.

"Tank!" Andi called.

"Ain't nobody deserves that," he said, and kept walking forward.

"Cowboy!"

He kept right on going. You could tell he was hurting. His back was to us, but you could tell something real bad was running through his head. He stumbled, almost lost his balance.

"Tank!"

But he kept pushing forward. The air over the yard crackled like electricity. For the briefest second it filled with sparks.

Cowboy staggered, but kept right on walking.

It happened again, crackling louder and longer. Sparks, like glitter, filled the air.

I turned to Andi, but she didn't have a clue.

"He's overloading it!" the professor yelled.

"He's what?"

"Whatever he's thinking, he's overloading the system."

"That's not possible."

"Tell *him* that."

I turned back to Cowboy. He kept walking. The crackling got louder. The sparks brighter. Finally he reached Slick.

By now the man was screaming uncontrollably, convulsing and rolling on the ground. Cowboy knelt down to him. He took him by the shoulders and said something so soft no one but Slick heard. The man showed his appreciation by spitting in the big boy's face. Cowboy barely noticed. He just kept on holding Slick and talking.

And Slick kept on struggling. But it did no good. He gradually got weaker and weaker until he finally wore himself out. When he quit struggling, Cowboy let him go. But the man wasn't done. He threw up his fists and began beating on Cowboy's chest and shoulders, tried punching his face, all the time screaming and swearing. Cowboy was unfazed. He just grabbed Slick again, held him, and kept talking.

Slick's eyes bulged in frustration, but he couldn't move. His face grew red. The veins in his neck bulged. It looked like he was going to explode. Then he threw back his head and let go a chilling scream. A howl like an animal's. It went on until he ran out of air.

He finally collapsed into Cowboy's arms. This time it was real.

The air over the yard stopped crackling and sparking.

"Tank?" Andi shouted. "Tank, are you all right?"

The big guy turned to us.

We all waited.

He broke into that good-ol'-boy grin of his. Then he scooped Slick up into his arms and rose to his feet.

EPILOGUE

The 130-mile drive to Bakersfield was as long as it was boring. I didn't mind. Not this time. It was the first peace I'd had since our visit to the Twilight Zone. A couple weeks had passed since our fun and games at the Institute.

Of course, Cowboy had carried Slick to their infirmary. And of course they threw us out, with promises we'd be hearing from their attorneys. Not that I blamed them. Between the professor's electrical work and Cowboy's voodoo, we'd pretty much destroyed the place. At least their credibility.

I wish I could give you a "happily ever after," but it didn't roll that way. The evening we finished, Andi and Professor Sunshine took a taxi to the airport. He had lectures at UCLA the following day—which left no time for long good-byes, which I'd try to get over.

Cowboy wasn't so easy to get rid of. But I'll get to him in a minute.

It was the kid, Sridhar, that haunted me. I let him stay on my sofa the first couple of nights—back when he was calling his folks in Sri Lanka for money to fly home. But they never connected. They'd either moved or changed their number. The kid didn't buy it for a minute. Something else was up. To keep him safe, we made plans to ship him to my mom's over in Arizona. It never happened.

He disappeared. Just like that. One morning his blankets were folded, the pillows stacked, and he was gone. My first thought was the Institute. I called the police. They said I had to file a missing persons report.

"Can you at least drive out there and check?" I said.

"You think he's at the Institute?" a bored voice asked.

"That's what I said."

"So if you know where he is, how can he be missing?"

I hung up and drove out there myself.

I wasn't sure what I'd do. It didn't matter. When I got there, the place was deserted. Completely. In seventy-two hours everyone had packed up and disappeared. The gate was open, the auditorium gutted, the classrooms and dormitories empty. A ghost town. Talk about eerie. That night, for the first time in a long time, I locked my doors.

A few mornings later Cowboy swung by the shop. He wanted me to touch up his tat where it had scabbed.

As he sat in the chair he said, "He didn't leave a note or nothin'?"

I shook my head and began inking.

He kept sitting there thinking, or whatever he does when he isn't talking. Finally he said, "You ever wonder what that headmaster guy meant when he said we weren't brought together by accident?"

I did, but kept my mouth shut.

Cowboy didn't. Or couldn't. He looked down at my work. "I miss 'em already, don't you?"

"Not exactly."

He motioned to the boy that I'd tatted with the four of us. "You ever wonder about this little guy?"

"I just ink what I see." I finished up and began smearing on the Aquaphor. "I got a question for you."

"Shoot."

"How come that security field never bothered you?"

"What do you mean?"

"I mean it put me and the professor through hell. It barely touched you."

"Oh, yeah it did. Something fierce."

"'Til you replaced what you were afraid of with something better."

"That's right."

"Which was?"

He didn't answer.

I taped on the cellophane. "What'd you replace your fear with, Cowboy?"

He broke into that goofy grin. "If I told you, you'd just say I'm preaching."

"What'd you replace it with?"

"God. I kept thinking how much He loves—Ow! That's tender."

I didn't bother to apologize. "Somebody still owes me one fifty for this."

"I'll take care of it."

"Plus another twenty for interest."

"Yes, ma'am."

"Alright, we're done here." I peeled off my gloves.

He climbed out of the chair. That's when he spotted the envelope with the numbers or the symbol or whatever it was that I'd sketched and left on the counter.

"Wow," he said, moving closer.

"Wow, what?"

"Did you ever notice that if you turn this around it's not a six, a nine, and a six? If you keep turning, it's a six, a six, and another six."

"And thanks for stopping by." I ushered him toward the door.

"I'll drop off the check tomorrow."

"Mail's fine."

That had been two weeks ago.

I parked the car six blocks from the Bakersfield airport. It was gonna make me a little late, but it was worth it, not paying for parking. I cleared security and headed for my gate. Some tattoo business I'd never heard of up in Washington State had e-mailed me. They said they'd seen my work and wanted to discuss building a franchise. It was obviously a mistake, but not mine. So when they wired me a couple hundred and e-mailed me the ticket, I figured let them worry about it. A little vacation wouldn't hurt.

At least that's what I thought, 'til I heard the voices at the gate.

"This treatment is unacceptable. You should have been aware of the weather long before we departed, long before you dumped us in this godforsaken . . . where are we again?"

"Bakersfield, Professor."

"Bakersfield."

The professor was fighting with the attendant behind the counter, Andi beside him.

"Sir, please try to understand. First class is entirely booked. There is no possible way to—"

"Look at this ticket!" the professor said. "Do you see it? What does it say?"

"First class, but—"

"We had first class out of Los Angeles and we expect first class out of, out of . . ."

"Bakersfield, Professor."

I got in the boarding line and turned my head so they wouldn't see me. Too late.

"Oh, look, there's Brenda!"

I pretended not to hear. But Andi was as persistent as she was cheery. "Brenda. Brenda!"

When it was clear everybody heard her but me, I turned and acted surprised. "Hey."

"Are you on this flight, too?"

I nodded. "What are the odds?"

"A good question. I'll let you know."

"I bet you will."

"Pardon me?"

I shook my head.

"We'll see you on board, okay?"

"Right."

Once I got on the plane I moved down the aisle, checking my seat number. The good news was I was way in the back. With luck, the professor would get his way and wind up in first class. The bad news was—

"Miss Brenda! Miss Brenda!"

I looked up. There was Cowboy in the last row, all grins.

"What are you doing here?" I said.

"It's incredible. The University of Washington, they want me to fly up there and talk to them."

"Talk to them?" I continued down the aisle toward him.

"For a scholarship! They want to talk to me about a scholarship."

I glanced at my ticket, fear growing.

"Think of it. I might become an honest to goodness Husky! Go dawgs! Isn't that fantastic? Isn't God good?"

"Well, He's something."

"What seat do you have?"

"Thirty-eight D."

"Are you kidding me? I have 38 E!"

I searched for another empty seat. Any would do. But I was late and the plane was packed.

"Did you see the professor and Andi? They're on the same flight, too. Isn't that amazing?"

I stuffed my backpack into the overhead. With no place to go, I dropped into the seat beside him.

"This is so cool. I mean, really, really cool."

I sighed and buckled in. Like so many times before, Slick's voice echoed in my head. *Are you so naïve as to think there are not greater forces at work?*

Cowboy continued his chatter. "I mean really, when you stop to think about it, how lucky can we get?"

I leaned back and closed my eyes, knowing whatever was happening, whatever was going on . . . it had nothing to do with luck.

THE HAUNTED

FRANK PERETTI

CHAPTER 1

Clyde Morris

Clyde Morris looked entirely the part of a wraith: neck tendons tuned like a harp, white hair wild, fogging corneas following unseen demons about the old dining room. "My life, my years, all over. Done! Can't reach them from here, can't change them, no more chances!"

His frumpish wife, Nadine, could make no sense of his ravings, his clenching and unclenching hands, his rising, pacing, sitting again, his seeing horrible things. She reached across the table to touch him but drew her hand back—it felt chilled as with frost.

He leaned, nearly lunged over the table, his face close to hers. "It knows me! It knows all about me!"

From down the hall came the shriek of door hinges. Clyde's eyes rolled toward the sound, his veiny face contorted. A wind rustled the curtains, fluttered a newspaper, swung the chandelier so it jangled.

Clyde stood and the wind hit him broadside, pushing him toward the hall.

"Clyde!"

He reached across the space between them but the wind, roaring, carried him down the hall along with cushions, newspapers, the tablecloth.

A doorway in the hall, glowing furnace red, pulled him. He craned forward to fight it, stumbled, grappled, and slid backward toward it.

The doorway sucked him in like a dust particle. A high-pitched scream faded into infinite distance until cut off when the door slammed shut.

The wind stopped. The newspaper pages settled to the floor. A doily fluttered down like a snowflake. The chandelier jangled through two diminishing swings, then stopped and hung still.

Now the only sound was the wailing of the widow, flung to the floor in the old Victorian house.

CHAPTER 2

The Phenomenon

When A.J. Van Epps first called to relate what had happened—or allegedly happened—to crusty old Clyde Morris, I fidgeted, perused lecture notes, indulged him. Why would a learned academic and researcher like Van Epps trouble himself—and now me—with a campfire tale too easily debunked to warrant the effort? The largely one-sided conversation took a feeble turn toward interesting only when I discerned in Van Epps' voice a tone of dread so unlike him, and it was after that hook was set that he sprang his proposal: Would I come and assist in the investigation? Would I help him regain his objectivity? Would I lend my knowledge and experience?

Oh yes, exactly what my frayed nerves needed. Being in a near plane crash and hauled into a misadventure in a so-called "Institute for Advanced Psychic Studies," not to mention having my personal and deepest fears vivisected by one and the same, was a sleepy, monotonous ordeal. I needed the change.

Besides . . .

We were old friends and associates. I would be lecturing at Evergreen State College in the Puget Sound area in the next few days. Of course I could afford a side trip to help him look into the matter. I agreed to come—and kicked myself the moment I ended the call.

McKinney here. Dr. James McKinney, sixty, professor of philosophy and comparative religions, emeritus, at large, published, and so on and so forth. Generally, a scholar of religious claims and systems, but specifically, a skeptic, and it is to that last title I devote the most attention. This, I trust, lends explanation for why I and Andrea Goldstein, my young assistant, drove our rental car through the meandering and sloping village of Port Avalon and located the quaint Victorian residence of Dr. A.J. Van Epps.

Van Epps, thinner and grayer than I remembered, took our coats, then expended no more than a minute or two on greetings and how-are-yous before he led us to his kitchen table and brought up a photograph on his computer: A two-story Victorian home, dull purple, richly detailed, turreted, with a covered porch and sleepy front windows.

"My interest, of course, is to ascertain how it works, what empowers it, what measure or means of controlled stimuli will produce predictable results."

Andi and I studied the photo. I saw a house; it was Andi's way to see more, always more, which was one reason I took her along.

"Seven panels in the door," she said. "Each window has seven panes. There are seven front steps."

Not that I appreciated her timing. "Save it for later," I advised, then asked Van Epps, "So this is a house here in town?"

Van Epps inserted an artful pause before answering, "Sometimes."

This whole affair was ludicrous enough. "A.J., I'm not known for my patience."

"Check out the landmarks: This tree with the large knot; this fire hydrant; this seam in the street." He arrow-keyed to a second photograph, what one would call a vacant lot: some brush, some trees, nothing else . . . save for the same knotted tree, fire hydrant, and seam in the street in front. "I took this soon after the first. The house was there, and then it wasn't."

I didn't stifle an irritated sigh. "If I may—just to cover the obvious—these photos are digital."

He sighed back. "I didn't alter them. No Photoshop."

"And you've presented them in the order you took them?"

"Yes."

"So I'm to take you seriously?"

He leaned back and held my gaze with his own. "I've found something, James, something atypical. As you'll observe, Port Avalon is one of those . . . *alternative* kinds of town that attracts all brands of superstition, so the locals have their legends about the House, how it's a harbinger of death, how it knows you, follows you . . ." With an unbecoming cryptic note, he added, "Takes you."

I rubbed my eyes, mostly to buy time. I was at a loss.

"I came to Port Avalon with the specific objective of encountering this House in order to study it, know it. I saw it for myself a month ago, even before the incident with Clyde Morris, and yes, there is *something* about it that would trigger such legends, so I have to ask, what is it really? And can we control it—maybe harness whatever powers it?"

"Harness? What are you talking about?"

He fidgeted, composing an answer. "Some friends and I are interested in occult power—not as occult power, you understand, but as . . . power. Power that could be useful."

"Friends?"

"Investors, shall we say."

I knew he wouldn't go any further into it. Maybe another time. "A.J., if you want me to bring balance to this—"

"Absolutely! I can see the handwriting on the wall, this is no plaything."

"Then I'll be skeptical. Digital photographs? Legends? To waste my time is to insult me. Show me evidence beyond this."

"There's Nadine, Clyde Morris's widow. You should hear her account. She was there, in the House, when it took him."

I rose deliberately. "Then we'll go there now." I turned to get my coat.

The closet door was locked.

"Other door," Van Epps said.

I found the closet, grabbed and put on my coat. Andi threw hers on.

"There's more," said Van Epps, clicking on another file.

It was my role to get him on track and I persisted. I recognized his favorite jacket in the front closet: fine leather, and a distinctive smell. I grabbed it and held it out to him.

With his eyes turned away from his computer, he swiveled it to show us another photo, that of a ghostly old man with glassy eyes and hunched shoulders glaring at the camera. The lighting was rather dim, the photo taken outdoors at dusk or later. "Clyde Morris."

I would have none of the chill I felt and shook it off. Andi showed the same chill plainly. "He could have been dead already." I was being sarcastic.

"He was," said Van Epps. "He died a week before I took this."

CHAPTER 3

Encounters

Nadine Morris took one look at Van Epps' photo of the House and looked away, tears once again filling her reddened eyes. She nodded yes, and Van Epps gave me a look.

"And where was it?" he asked her.

We were sitting in her small, long-dated living room. She pointed through her front window at the woods across the street. "It was right there, like it was waiting, like it was watching me."

Andi immediately pointed out the knotty tree, fire hydrant, and concrete seam.

I had to look around Andi's explosive red hair—like a sea urchin with a perm—but I expected as much.

Nadine continued, "And then it was here. It wasn't our house anymore, it was *that* house, and I was sitting in it and . . ." She trembled. "There was Clyde, sitting in the dining room." She broke into a whimper. "But he was only a spirit. His time had come."

"He'd passed away a week before—" Van Epps began.

I cut him off. "I want to hear it from her."

"At Daisy Meadows," she said. "The assisted living facility. He died in his sleep. But the House wouldn't let him rest. It chased his spirit around town until that night when it caught him . . . and sucked him into hell."

Ravings. I ventured a challenge. "How do you know he was sucked into hell?"

"He was a difficult man, wasn't he?" Van Epps asked.

Nadine stiffened. "He didn't mean to hurt me. It was the drink, you know."

"Objectivity! Scientific method!" My voice was raised. It gets that way when people don't think. "You are a researcher, a debunker! What's come over you?"

Van Epps sat hunched and self-protective at his kitchen table while I paced about the room. "I thought it could pertain."

"Whether Clyde Morris was deserving of hell? What bearing could that possibly have on an explainable phenomenon?"

He had to work up an answer. "I was exploring the phenomenon through her point of view."

"You were leading the witness!"

Van Epps and I had had our heated discussions before. I took it in stride when he lashed out, "I came eye to eye with a posthumous manifestation of Clyde Morris! I photographed it! I felt the intensity of it! There *is* a human element here and we have to consider it."

"From an objective base, which you no longer have."

He halted, then raised a hand in surrender. "No. No, I don't. That's why I need you here." He drew a breath, recovering a measure of professionalism. "The House exerts a strong effect on the human psyche, and I could be a case in point. When it first appeared, I truly felt it was looking into me as if it knew me. As if—note this—it knew my sins. And that look I got from Clyde Morris . . ."

I sat next to him. "Religious guilt?"

He smiled, nodded. "I'm sure you can relate."

"Of course." Van Epps knew of my ill-fated days in the priesthood, and he'd shared a little of his Sunday school background. "I've found a good dose of reason and logic can make it go away . . . usually."

"And the power of suggestion can bring it back. In this town there's plenty of that."

I rose. "Which, if I'm to be clinical, I need to apprise. Andi, get online. Find out if there's any precedent for what we're seeing here, any other cases of a house appearing and disappearing and . . . holding people morally accountable." I looked at Van Epps. "Fair assessment?"

He nodded, chagrined.

"Want to come along?"

"No. I'll write up what we have so far. That should clear my system of . . . whatever this is."

"Good enough."

Port Avalon was a small town nestled on the forested hillsides above the Puget Sound. I drove less than four minutes to reach the town center, and could surmise from the boats, docks, and harbor the town's origins as a fishing village.

That, I guessed, had to be before the sixties and the influx ever afterward of the mystical set who favored seclusion, nature, and the nearness of the sea. Such mundane businesses as an Ace Hardware, a pharmacy, and a floral shop held precious ground amid a disproportionate measure of Eastern, animist, and mystical enterprises: tarot readers, fortune-tellers, psychic healers, shamans, meditation centers, and pagan temples. Here the objects of worship were goddesses, ascended masters, Mother Earth, any growing thing.

I walked about, "fishing" for data and beginning to understand Van Epps' conundrum. Port Avalon was saturated with the human need for explanation, for an answer to the question *Why*, for a basis of knowing good and evil or even the existence of such things. I had long ago established to my comfort that such cosmic questions developed only from our need for survival and holding our societies together, but as this town demonstrated, those who could accept morality as a matter of utility and not "truth" were few, and the pervasive norms of this place could easily aggravate the old "pang of conscience." Poor Van Epps. This place was getting to him.

And getting to me as well, I thought, halting on the sidewalk. Across the street I saw what an unprepared mind could take to be a cosmic coincidence.

There, engaged in conversation with the gypsy-costumed proprietor of Earthsong's Psychic Readings, was the brusque and urbanesque tattoo artist, Brenda . . .

I'd forgotten her last name and that was fine with me, but her dreadlocks and slinking posture were unmistakable.

A plague on this town! In that moment I nearly believed some game master somewhere was moving us about like chess pieces. It was more than enough that she'd been on the same plane Andi and I took to Seattle, and not only she, but the wide-eyed giant we called Tank, and all by happenstance. Yes, I argued with myself—and the town—happenstance, even if Tank should show up in Port Avalon as well.

Perish the thought. The last time Andi, the tattooist, the giant, and I were lumped together, it was to invade that ridiculous Institute—trespassing, vandalizing, and resorting to pointless acts of heroism. Heroism! Now there was another conundrum: If in this random and purposeless universe there was no basis for right and wrong, how could there be any point to heroism?

I deliberately gave my head a shake to cast off all this tizzy. I thought I would turn away.

If anyone ever attributes my decision to fate, luck, God, or any other capricious power, I will fervently deny it. I was, after all, "fishing," and if the fish might be across the street . . .

I crossed, though it pained me.

"Well—" was as far as my greeting went before Earthsong got whammy-eyed.

"Ohhh!" she said with serpent-handed histrionics. "You are looking for someone!" She reeked of incense and her bracelets jangled. It was strictly carnival. "Would you like to know more?"

Brenda—I recalled her last name was Barnick—seemed pleasantly surprised at the sight of me. "Oh, this is the guy! I was—"

"Yes," I said. "I'd like to know more, anything you have to say."

Brenda made a face that telegraphed *are you putting me on?*

I'd been struck in that moment by another coincidence. I had a fish on the line, tugging. I wanted to land it.

CHAPTER 4

Earthsong

I felt in violation of my own precepts, sitting in Earthsong's mystical, candlelit parlor, listening raptly as she went through a well-rehearsed spiel. Yes, the crystal ball was there in the center of the table; the incense was burning and tainting everything, including ourselves; a carved, ruby-eyed raven perched above our heads lending mood and . . . vibration? Brenda shot me many a sideways glance through the proceedings, but I suggested by my own behavior the role she should play: gullible, enraptured. She fell into it quite well.

"I see . . . a child!" said Earthsong, waving her fingers over the crystal ball. "Young . . . innocent . . . blond hair. Strangely silent." She then sneered. "Ha! He is thought to have a gift, but next to me, he is nothing! He knows nothing of the real powers! It was a waste to consult him! A waste!"

I was not experienced in discerning drug-affected behavior,

but I had to suspect she was high on something. I would definitely consult the streetwise Brenda afterward.

The fortune-teller continued. "He was a prisoner but broke his bonds and is free! And now . . ." She made eye contact for effect. "You seek him!"

"And where is he?" Brenda asked.

Role playing? At least it spurred the conversation.

"This is the cry of the powers! Where is he? Where is he?" Earthsong consulted her crystal ball. "Ask the House. The House will know. The House . . ."

From there she went into a fit, something she must have learned by watching the channelers on television in the eighties. We got nothing more from her except the amount of her fee: Twenty dollars.

Brenda and I made our way up the sidewalk, chained to each other by curiosity.

"What does she mean, ask the House?" Brenda mused.

"What the devil are you doing here?" I demanded, turning to her.

"What are *you* doing here?"

I explained Van Epps' invitation, meaning I had to detail the bizarre reasons as well—and explain what I could of the House.

She returned my favor, explaining, "Got an invitation, plane ticket and everything, from a tattoo agent in Seattle, something about starting a franchise. Called himself a tattoo *broker*! That should have been a clue right there. It was a rip-off. They get me the work and take a percentage, but the fine print says I can only work through them and they own my designs. So screw 'em, but thanks for the free ride."

"But what are you doing *here*?"

"Don't get your boxers in a wad. I saw a poster in the agent's

lobby, said you were lecturing at Evergreen State. I said, 'Hey, what're you guys doing plugging a don't-believe-in-nothing guy like this?' The agent tears the poster off the wall and throws it in the fireplace."

I could see her watching it in her mind's eye.

"I saw you burning, curling up, going to ashes. I called Evergreen—what's that face for? Yeah, I called 'em, and they said you were coming up here to see a friend."

"You came here because somebody burned a poster of me?"

"Listen, I'd need more than that to trouble myself over you." She dug in her shoulder bag and brought out a sketchpad. "I saw *this* right after that."

She showed me her drawing of a snaky logo with scaly lettering: Psychic Readings, Fortunes Told. We both looked back to verify the same logo above Earthsong's front door.

"You saw this on the bulletin board?"

She sniffed her impatience and pointed to her head. "In here, man. I see things in here and I draw them. That's why I stopped there to talk to the lady. I said, 'Hey, I'm trying to find somebody,' and right then, there you were. Now you do what you want with it, but that's what happened."

"So that's how she got the idea we were looking for someone . . ." I mused. "Except I wasn't. Not you, not the little blond kid." I chuckled. "She couldn't have been further off."

"So why'd you spend the twenty bucks?"

We'd come to my car. I nodded to the passenger door. "Let's have a chat."

Inside, I cautioned her to secrecy and continued. "It seems my friend Van Epps has a close relationship with that lady. The moment I reached her front door I caught the odor of her incense—it's a smell that permeates Van Epps' leather jacket. He's been to her place on a regular basis."

"Did you see the needle tracks on her arms?"

"I was going to ask you—"

"She was high. Heroin. I've seen it."

"High and careless. Being a charlatan, she guessed wrong and told us somebody else's fortune. But the information is likely true: Somebody's looking for a child—"

"I've seen the kid."

"—and I have to wonder what Van Epps knows about it."

"Are we talking or just you?"

"Sorry?"

"I've seen that kid."

I had to clarify. "Where?"

She indicated her head again.

"I suppose you have a drawing?"

"Not on me."

"Hmph."

"It's on Cowboy's arm. A little blond kid, standing there with the rest of us."

We were going over a cliff. I applied some brakes.

"Let's categorize what we have. You claim to be here following information gained through some kind of psychic means—"

"No I don't!" she argued.

"Whatever, all right? Just for now?"

"I don't do trances and I don't trip out . . . and I don't have a freaky carved raven!"

"Granted. But let's put all that here in this category"—I indicated a small corral with my hands, then indicated another beside the first—"and another category here, for data gathered the old-fashioned way, through observation."

She was either bored or miffed, looking elsewhere.

I proceeded anyway. "In the second category, Earthsong is tied to Van Epps, and that being the case, he may know something about this child, something he's chosen not to talk about."

She looked at me again. "She's jealous of the kid, you know that."

I nodded. "He supposedly has a gift she went out of her way to discredit."

"So he's a threat, so he's real."

"I agree."

"So what about the rest of it? The kid in prison and breaking out and somebody wondering where he is . . ."

"And the House knowing . . ." We now had a bag of pieces that didn't connect. "I'll have a word with Van Epps about it, if only to get his reaction." Then, wanting data first and accepting explanation later, I added, "In the meantime, let me know if you see any more pictures."

She gave me a look.

"No, please do."

CHAPTER 5

Gustav Svensson

Van Epps disappointed me—not for lack of information I could at least infer, but for lack of honesty with me, his old compatriot in skepticism.

He asked me about my walk through the town. I recounted my impressions and introduced Brenda. He asked if we'd noticed the overburden of mystics and charlatans, and of course we had.

"Places like . . . Earthsong's Psychic Readings," he said with a sardonic wag of his head. "So typical."

How notable that he brought up the fortune-teller without my mentioning her. I pursued it. "We gave her a try, as a matter of fact. She put on quite a show."

He sneered, he scoffed, he chided me for wasting my time and money.

"She spoke of a missing child," I said with a mockery to match his. "Obviously, a 'reading' that had nothing to do with us."

He laughed along with me but drummed his fingers nervously and would not dwell on the subject.

From there, things went into a limbo that became more and more constricting. We went to several homes around the neighborhood and town, but the reactions we got were as Van Epps predicted from his own experience: No one talked about the House.

After that, a day passed, then another, and we became like survivors in a lifeboat, stuck in close proximity with nowhere else to go. Van Epps and I fell into quarrels over old information when we weren't exhausting each other in protracted academic discussions. His house was sizable enough for his guests but not sizable enough to prevent friction between myself and the two women.

Andi, lacking something to do, began jabbering about patterns: The dimensions of the cupboard doors were golden rectangles, the teakettle played a continuous tone progressing through ten degrees of the scale and ending on an accidental, the pattern of the living room carpet repeated every forty-eight inches, which was the same number of flowers in the pattern multiplied by four, so there had to be more twelves or multiples of twelve somewhere. There was no turning her off.

Brenda, always edgy, wandered, explored, got to know some people, but the idleness weighed upon her and she simply could not find something to like. She didn't like the town, she didn't like the house, she didn't care for Van Epps and, of course, she could not accommodate herself to me—a mutual feeling I had no incentive to correct.

And all along, Van Epps kept pressing us: "It'll show up again. Count on it. You'll see."

Then came October 6. The day held no significance for me, but for Andi, it was the number six, the number the Institute seemed so fond of, which was divisible into twelve, which constituted the pattern she was waiting for. "It's the sixth! I think we're going to get something today!"

I got out of the house—alone. That was the point.

I walked the same loop around the neighborhood, past the same trees, hedges, yards, and yapping dogs I'd memorized by now, vexed by the monotony, the sameness, the cyclical repetition . . .

Until I noticed a different sensation. Beneath my vexation, a sense of gloom moved in like a mood swing on a cloudy day . . . feelings associated with the memory of a woman I could not have . . . shadows of regret . . . anger . . . the day I tore off my clerical collar.

Blast! I had long ago buried all such issues. It had to be the town, the idleness, and now my being exiled as it were, a solitary soul on an empty sidewalk in a strange town. I dashed the memories from my mind—

And felt a sense of foreboding as if being followed. Watched.

I looked about. No one behind me—

The moment my eyes came forward, I saw only twenty feet away . . . Him? It? I will use the term *specter* to convey the appearance of the man and, I admit, the chill, the danger I felt. He was motionless, like a post. His eyes, pasted over like those of a dead animal, were locked on me. How he could make such an instant appearance and from where, I could not tell.

He was dressed like an aged mariner: old slicker, drooping hat, work boots. His complexion was cold and gray, and he was dripping wet, standing in a puddle of water though it was a rainless day.

He took a step toward me, and then another, the grim expression steady as a mask. Intuitively, I considered my size and strength and so resolved to stand my ground. The boots squished and left wet footprints on the street. The slicker dripped as if being rained upon.

Now he seemed he would move by me, so I stepped aside. He passed by, his pasty eyes probing me, and it had to have been Van Epps' prior description that made me feel he was looking into me, knew me, knew my sins.

The specter's back was to me now. I fumbled for my cell phone to snap a photo. Even as I composed the picture, he stopped and looked back. *Click*. A photo I might fear from that day on.

What? The man gave his head a little jerk as if to say, *Come this way*.

I followed him at a distance even as I swiped and tapped my phone to raise Andi's number. When she answered, I found myself whispering. "Come quickly, all of you."

Oh, the frustration!

"Come where?" she said. "Where are you?"

Somewhere in Port Avalon, blast it! "I don't know the street name. I'm near the big white house with the black mutt."

"Well, where's that?"

I came to a street sign. "Mossyrock." The man kept walking around a corner, up a hill. "Make that 48th."

"Forty-eight!" she exclaimed.

I hated how she could make me curse, especially to her. "Do not start, Andi! Just get down here!"

She indicated that Van Epps knew where I was. I tapped Off and holstered the phone.

The specter rounded a wooded corner and went out of sight. I ran to catch sight of him again.

There he was, relentlessly walking, squishing, dripping.

And just beyond him, at the end of the street where, I'm sure, nothing but woods had been, was a house. Two-story Victorian, dull purple, richly detailed, turreted, with a covered porch and sleepy front windows.

CHAPTER 6

The House

The "posthumous manifestation" of whoever this was seemed in no hurry. Rather, he stepped and squished up the seven steps to the front porch of the House, turned, looked at me, then waited until the others arrived.

Andi and Brenda spilled out of Van Epps' car. "Who is it?" "What is it?" Then they stood next to me and gawked.

"Looks like an old fisherman," Andi observed.

Brenda chose to respond by invoking the sanctity of excrement.

I was relieved that they saw it too.

Van Epps remained in his car, hiding, it seemed, behind the steering wheel even as the apparition stared at him with much the same expression as Clyde Morris had in that photo. A pattern there, but now I could relate.

The specter scanned us as if taking attendance. The front door opened by itself. He went inside, and the door closed with a creak and a clunk.

Only then did Van Epps scramble from his car with a video camera and tripod. "See? I told you! There it is, right in front of you!"

"Looks real enough," said Andi. "Different landmarks, though. No knotty tree or fire hydrant. Not this time."

Emotions were running high, mine included. I dared not be fooled. I studied the House, cautious to sort reality from illusion, scanning the lines of the walls, gables, roof. The windows drew my gaze, and I found myself looking the House in the eyes, if such a thing were possible. Van Epps' observation was not unfounded, though subjective, as mine was at that moment: I couldn't shake the impression that the House was staring me down, just like the old fisherman. I couldn't ask the ladies what they might be feeling lest I suggest the idea to them. I tried moving from side to side. Still, the gaze of the windows followed me. *I know all about you*, said the House. *I know all about you.*

By now, word had filtered through the town. People showed up in little clusters, keeping their distance, gawking, taking pictures with their cell phones.

It was Gustav, someone said. Gustav Svensson. They tossed the name around, repeated it, passed it from one to another.

I listened. I counted and recorded faces, trying not to stare too long at a man and woman stationed behind the others. I may have seen them before, but impressions were questionable at the moment.

Brenda and Andi were looking to me for the next move. I looked at Van Epps. He was behind a tree with the camera.

"Shall we have a closer look?" I asked.

"Yes, by all means," he answered. "Go ahead. I'll keep recording."

"Recording what?"

"It might move again! It might—we need a record."

I looked at the ladies. "Shall we?"

Brenda, clearly unsettled, swore again. I couldn't have said it better.

It was getting dark, which seemed to be a cue for the crowd. They began to back away, then disperse in ones and twos.

A glow appeared in an upstairs window and there were gasps from those remaining—and from Andi.

"Hey," said Brenda. "Somebody's home."

"Yeah," said Andi, "the dead guy."

"Ghosts don't need lights."

Van Epps called from behind the tree. "We need data. You should go inside and check around. I'll keep the camera going in case something happens."

Reading Van Epps' voice and body, I agreed. "Yes. I think you should stay out here."

The walkway was real, as were the front steps, as was the porch. Brenda thumped on a porch post and gave a little shrug. Andi was counting things: the lap siding, the light fixtures, the—

"Hey," she said, "there's no house number!"

She could even get excited about the lack of numbers.

Since the House was real enough, I thought I should try a real knock on the door. No answer. I knocked two more times, but still no answer. I tried the door. Locked. Brenda had to try the door for herself. Still locked.

The daylight was fading to a steely gray. I led the way around the House while we could still see the details: concrete foundation embedded in the ground; small yard with grass a bit shaggy; planting beds, but flowers withering this time of year; moss growing on the roof; some paint peeling.

We continued to circle, breathing easier. For a phantasm, the House was so normal as to be disappointing—

Until we caught a glimpse of something or someone moving around the corner toward the front of the House, and Andi, her nerves wound tight, screamed. I found a windfallen branch on the lawn and picked it up for a weapon—which had to look silly, more like I wanted to build a campfire than assail an enemy. Nevertheless, the ladies followed close behind as I, their masculine protector, wielded my tree branch. We inched our way around the front corner. . . .

"Well, howdy!"

We wilted with relief.

"Whatcha guys doin'? Buildin' a fire?"

I dropped the branch. It would have been nice if Tank, our gentle giant, *were* an illusion, but of course that was not to be. He was carrying a duffel bag over his shoulder, a traveler just arrived. Brenda and Andi embraced him, their high-pitched greetings as pleasant to me as worn brakes: "*How'd you get here?*"

So this was their new masculine protector, I supposed.

"Hitched a ride. A techie was coming right by here on his way to Port Townsend."

"So how'd it go?" Andi asked.

Tank was gushing with the news. "Gonna be a dawg! Full scholarship, baby!"

Ah yes. His football scholarship to the University of Washington. A wonderful, happy subject to take up time and distract all of us from the enigma now demanding our attention.

Brenda frowned. "I don't know much about college football, Cowboy, but how is it that you're eligible to play in the middle of a season?"

Tank shook his head good-naturedly. "They just tell me to play football, and I do."

"So why are you here?" I cut in. "Don't tell me. You had a vision, or God spoke from a cloud, or . . ."

Tank's eyes went mystical. "I . . . received a message!"

Of course. I rolled my eyes.

"Andi called me." He stood there grinning at his own cleverness. The three shared a laugh—at my expense.

I directed an icy employer's look at Andi, who justified herself. "Calling him was logical, objective, totally pragmatic! Case in point right here."

She looked at Tank and nodded toward the front door. "It's locked."

"So?" he asked. After his neurotransmitters connected, he wagged his head. "Eh, I dunno. That's somebody's house, you know?"

Van Epps called from behind the tree, "Just open the door!"

Tank looked for where the voice had come from. "What's he doin' back there?"

"He thinks the place is haunted," Brenda whispered.

Tank's face went blank. "Really?"

"Perhaps you might justify your presence here," I prodded.

Tank acquiesced and went up the front steps with the rest of us in tow. I was about to advise the ladies to give the big fellow some room for safety's sake—

He simply turned the knob and the door creaked open. He gave us a puzzled look. I looked at Brenda and she shrugged back.

"Hello?" Tank called.

Of course, he hadn't been here earlier. He hadn't seen the apparition or heard all the background. He walked right in as if his mother lived there. Still nursing our trepidations, we followed.

CHAPTER 7

Explorations

We couldn't find a light switch anywhere, and the daylight coming through the windows was quickly fading. Andi got out her cell phone and used the flashlight feature to produce a sharp beam she could play about.

So what were we expecting? A decaying netherworld draped in cobwebs? A flurry of frightened bats and ghostly glows against the walls? Trapdoors, secret passages, mysterious wailings in the dark? As our eyes adjusted to the dim light and Andi helped with her cell phone, we found ourselves in a residence clean and furnished as if the housekeepers had just left and the owners were due home any minute. We could admire the entryway with its hall tree and grandfather clock; the ascending staircase with finely turned balusters and railing; the living room, furnished in Victorian style, and beyond that, the formal dining room with high-backed upholstered chairs, eight place settings, and jeweled chandelier. The place was benign, dignified, even welcoming.

So what the deuce caused this trembling in my hands, this animal sense of being cornered? Power of suggestion? The eerie sight of our ghostly guide? Perhaps the darkness and the unknown.

I handed Andi my cell phone. She activated the flashlight while I watched and found out how to do it—learning new technology from her was becoming a routine with me. Brenda and Tank got the same idea, and soon we were moving about like techno-fireflies, pinpoints of light casting stark shadows. I held my phone in both hands to steady the shaking, angry at the dread I couldn't quash.

A door clicked and swung open in the hallway. I heard a toilet flush. "Toilet works," Andi reported.

Well. Something normal. I was grateful.

The next door she checked refused to open, apparently locked, but I stopped her from asking Tank to try it. Maybe it was the House's effect on me, but I felt such a barrier should be honored. We were being invasive as it was.

The floor of the entryway was slippery. I lowered my light to find a trail of drippings and wet boot prints leading toward the stairs. Perhaps only to remain the cold and objective investigator, I reached down, wetted my fingertip in the drippings, and put the sample to my tongue.

Seawater.

Brenda called from the kitchen. We gathered there like bees to a hive, lights hovering, snooping.

On the kitchen table were a jar of jam, one of peanut butter, a loaf of bread, and an uneaten quarter of a sandwich left on a plate.

Tank's voice made us all jump. "Hello? Anybody here? Hey, we're your friends, we won't hurt you."

Something bumped somewhere in the House. I looked in each face and got a shrug, a wag—*It wasn't me.*

Brenda shook her dreadlocked head and laughed—at herself and us. "Somebody's living here and we are gonna get busted."

"But it wasn't here before!" said Andi.

"You sure about that?"

I interposed, "May we at least resolve the question of the old fisherman? We all saw him, did we not?"

"Did we *not*?" said Tank. "Yeah, I didn't."

"We do have his boot prints and water dripped on the floor—seawater, by the way—leading up the stairs."

Oh, the pall of doom that fell over Brenda's and Andi's faces! As for Tank, for some reason he just wasn't getting it.

It was my idea, so I led. Tank followed me. The ladies followed, but several steps behind. We agreed not to sneak, but to walk benignly up those stairs, calling hello as we went. Our lights went where our eyes went, meaning everywhere, and frantically.

There was no light switch at the top of the stairs, and the hallway was an unlit tunnel save for our cell phones. The boot tracks, now dark, wet imprints in the carpet, led to a doorway. I knocked. I called. There was no answer. I tried the door and it opened.

There was only a dark bedroom on the other side. There was no light switch, and we found soon enough there was no occupant.

"But isn't this where the light was on?" Brenda wondered.

Andi searched the ceiling with her light. There was no lighting fixture, no lamp in the room. "Well . . . it was a light, but that doesn't mean it was an electric light. . . ."

"Don't, don't do that."

Shining my cell phone and feeling with my hand, I carefully traced the boot prints to a wet spot in the center of the room. There, they ended.

"Okay," said Brenda. "Now how about we get out of here?"

I wanted to agree, but Van Epps would be waiting behind his tree wanting data and trusting me to be the unaffected gatherer. "We haven't learned anything."

Andi tapped off her light. "Save your batteries."

Our phones winked out, and despite my efforts, I felt the dark closing in on me and fear twisting my viscera like a seizure. Blast it! I could turn my phone light back on, but they would ask why; I could explain, but that would plant a suggestion that would skew our observations. It could also make me look like a coward.

"So what now?" Andi asked. Her voice was weak. Perhaps she was feeling the same visceral reaction.

I loathed the answer even as I spoke it. "If we leave for the night, the House may relocate. There are no lights and our phones can only provide so much. We need to go through this place in the light of day." I felt I was delivering a line from an old horror movie: "We'll have to spend the night."

CHAPTER

During the Night

If I'd been given to flights of imagination, I would have imagined the House expecting our visit. Though it was early October, the House was pleasantly warm; though there were no lights, there was running water and the toilets worked; the bedrooms were fully furnished, the beds made up with fresh linens.

"We are gonna get busted," Brenda moaned.

We laid out a plan, beginning with two escape routes should anything strange occur. There were four upstairs bedrooms; each of us would take a room and stand watch for a two-hour slot during the night while the rest slept—assuming any of us could sleep. We would remain clothed in case we had to make a sudden exit. If anything strange should occur, we were all within shouting distance.

"Any questions?" I asked. There were none.

I advised Van Epps of our plan. While I remained to moni-

for the camera, he drove home and returned with a chair, an extra coat, and a thermos of coffee. I left him at his station and returned to the House, the front door admitting me without resistance.

We all said good-night.

If I may personify, the House had a plan as well. We never saw the morning from inside those confining rooms or that dark hallway. The House saw to it.

My two hours came first. Needless to say, I wasn't sleepy. I found a seafaring novel on the nightstand and sat in a comfortable chair to sample it by the light of my cell phone. Less than one chapter in, I found Andi was right regarding cell phones as flashlights—the typical phone cannot last long as a typical flashlight. After one final look around the room, I tapped out the light to save the phone's battery.

As I feared, the darkness closed in on me again. My insides tightened like a dishrag being wrung out. I felt like bait awaiting a predator.

Blast this House! Blast this fear, this consuming, irrational phobia! What was the dark but the absence of light, and nothing more? What lurked in that darkness other than a bed, a nightstand, a picture on the wall? Nothing!

I tapped my phone—my hands were shaking so badly it took several tries. At last, the tiny light came on, proving, of course, there was nothing there but a bedroom with its furnishings. I tapped the light off.

Immediately, I knew, I just *knew* that darkness was a living, malevolent thing.

Then the phobia brought delusion. The House could have spoken audibly, the impression was so real. *I know all about you*, said the House. *I know all about you.*

Shades of my church experience: the ever-present thumb of God upon the back of me, the insect! I fought to regain mastery. No, I thought, and then I muttered, "*No*, there is nothing here. This is a figment of my imagination."

Oh? the House seemed to answer.

"You are a lifeless structure of stone and wood," I said, mostly to convince myself. "You have no mind, no plan, and you don't know me!"

I know all about you. I know all about you.

I would not engage this lifeless thing in moral arguments; I would not justify myself to a pernicious phobia! I tapped my cell phone for precious light and locked my eyes on the painting over the bed: sailboats heeling on white-crested waves. Just look at the sailboats, I told myself. Happy. Alive. Tangible. Something real. A tether to sanity.

The light began to dim to a yellow glow, weaker, weaker. I strained to see the painting—

Before my eyes, like black mold growing in time lapse, tiny specks percolated through the wall, widened into patches that widened into areas, surrounded then covered the picture, thickening, ever thickening—toward me.

I suppose it was logic, pragmatism, and yes, my own vanity that kept me in the chair, none of which deterred the phenomenon. It boiled out of the wall, an inky eruption. In the faint orange light from my phone I searched for the picture on the wall—it was inundated, gone. The bed disappeared next, then the nightstand. The *presence* obscured the top of the door, then the top half, filling the room, expanding downward. The closet was nowhere to be seen. As if with a diabolical mind, it saved my little corner for last, swallowing up the space on my right, on my left . . . above me.

The light from my phone went dead.

CHAPTER 9

Four Messages

I had no thoughts, no theories, nothing left but instinct. I dropped to the floor because it was the only place to go. I rolled, groping about for bearings, trying to find the door.

I felt a weight on my left shoulder, and then a painful compression as if something had taken hold of me. It was not by my choice that I ended up flat on my back, sightless in the dark, fighting, grappling, contacting nothing, while something directly above bore down with a weight that expelled the air from my chest. My very next breath . . . would not come.

I pounded the floor, kicked, screamed without sound. As consciousness, as life itself, broke away in pieces with the passing seconds, I was lost to panic.

I cannot say, for I do not recall, that I prayed. I cannot say what transaction, if any, may have occurred in the blackening remnants of my consciousness. I can only guess that for whatever reason, the House was satisfied, its message delivered. The weight lifted. Air rushed into my lungs. My reawakened limbs got me to the door, out of that room, and into the hall.

The moon had risen, casting precious light through a window at the end of the hall. I thought only of breathing as I labored to my feet, leaning against the wall to support myself. My mind returned with the question of calling for the others—

The very next door burst open and Andi, a dripping, spewing silhouette, tumbled into the hall, rebounded from the opposite wall, and collided with me, coughing, flailing as if drowning. I wrapped my arms around her to bear her up. She spewed water from her mouth and nose, splattering me, the wall, the floor, and I recognized the briny scent, even caught the taste once again, of seawater. She gagged, coughed, gasped for air.

"Easy now," I said, not wanting an explanation, only wanting to calm her, to save her. "Breathe, girl, just breathe."

She calmed, quit flailing as I held her, and with admirable intention drew several wheezing breaths.

"That's it, that's it."

She was dripping wet as if plucked from the sea. Shivering. Her nose was running. Blood from a head wound streaked her face.

She was my employee, but in that moment she could have been my daughter. I bolted into the room that had nearly smothered me. Defiant, not caring what the House might do, I tore the comforter from the bed and returned, throwing it over Andi's shoulders. She wrapped it around herself, calming, breathing steadily.

"All right?" I asked.

She nodded, willing each breath. "I was in the ocean . . . the whole room was filled with water . . ."

By now I was oxygenated and thinking again. "We'd better check on the others."

We knocked on Brenda's door but didn't wait for the answer

we didn't get. We found her flopped on the bed as if lifeless. We shook her, called her name, with no response. I felt the artery in her neck. She was alive but barely breathing. "Let's get her up."

Taking her arms over our shoulders, we bore her from the room. She was limp, nodding off, muttering as if drugged.

"Come on, walk," Andi coached her. "Walk!"

A few feet into the hall, Brenda jerked as if startled. Her legs went to work, bearing her up as her eyes opened and rolled about. "Whaz 'appenin'?" We propped her against the wall. "Whaddaya guys doin'?"

Andi checked her arms. "Look!"

Both arms bore the needle tracks of an addict. The vein in the crook of her left arm bore a needle mark that was recent, red, and swollen.

For an instant I wanted to confront her, rebuke her for such wanton, self-serving, irresponsible—

But then I noticed that Andi's hair, silhouetted in the patch of light at the end of the hall, was wild again. "Excuse me." I reached and felt it. It was dry.

She felt it, then felt her clothing under the comforter, which prompted her to look once again at Brenda's arms.

The needle tracks were fading.

And so was Brenda's stupor. Her eyes focused. She stroked her arms. "Where'd the guy go?"

"What guy?" asked Andi, her eyes inches from Brenda's.

Brenda recovered further and shook her head. "I was dreaming. Some guy shooting me up . . ." A wave of emotion. She covered her face.

I checked for the wound on Andi's head. It was gone, along with the blood that had streaked her face.

And it was in that moment that I saw beyond her frizzy hair, stark in the moonlight at the end of the hall . . .

A child.

I froze. Brenda and Andi followed my gaze and were as stupefied as I was.

He was a lad of ten years or so, dressed in jeans, untucked shirt, and tennis shoes. His backlit hair glowed like an aura around his head. Despite all our clamor, he didn't seem frightened, but fascinated, studying each of us.

"Please tell me you see that," I whispered. I caught Andi's, then Brenda's eyes. Yes, their faces told me, they saw it too. We looked again—

In that instant of inattention, the lad had vanished. Nothing remained at the end of the hall but an empty patch of moonlight.

And then came the laughter. As if we had become the brunt of a cruel joke, from somewhere came a riotous, mocking laughter, the very stuff of ghost stories and horror movies. We all jumped, quivered. The ladies cowered against the wall, arms protective. I found myself in the center of the hallway, vulnerable on every side and spinning to look for . . . what? Surely not a ghost.

But where was that laughter coming from?

We looked about, narrowed it down . . .

The last door, at the end of the hall. Tank's room.

This was not appropriate, not in keeping with anything we'd experienced. He'd scared years off our lives. What the devil could that big oaf be laughing about at a time like this?

We hurried—I stormed—down the hall to the bedroom door. I rapped on the door so hard I hurt my knuckles.

He was still laughing, whooping, hollering.

I flung the door open and there he stood, enraptured, grinning, wagging his head in wonder as he looked all around the room at—

We saw nothing but a dark bedroom.

"This is so incredible!" he whooped. "Wow! Can you believe this?"

"Believe what?" I asked.

He wagged his head in spellbound wonder. "It is just so beautiful, so perfect!"

His joy made Brenda feel no better. "He's on acid or something."

"Look at that sky!" said Tank. "It just keeps going and going . . . and . . . you hear that music?"

Of course, we didn't.

"Man, can they sing!" Then he sank to his knees in . . . well, a religious moment. "I can see Him! I can see Him standing right there!"

"We need to get him out of here," said Brenda.

"We all need to get out of here," said Andi.

I'd had all the scientific inquiry I could bear for one night. "I heartily agree."

"You can't see this?" Tank was desperate for us to share his experience.

No. We couldn't see it.

"It's heaven! It's gotta be!"

Of course there would be no tearing Tank away from his visions by physical force. We had to talk him back to earth, tell him we were concerned about safety, tired . . .

Scared to the point of a complete emptying of our bowels, Brenda said—I'm paraphrasing.

Tank was elated, satisfied, bolstered in every inch of his being, and that was a lot of inches. He came with us, talking about the flowers, the smells, the music, the joy of the place, the love he saw in "His" face. We got him through the front door and across the street to the woods.

Even in the dark, Van Epps could tell we were out of kilter. "What happened? What did you see?"

"Data we should only discuss by daylight and under calmer circumstances," I insisted.

"I didn't see anything from out here," he said. "I'm afraid I've wasted drive space on—" He went blank, eyes peering across the street.

We turned.

The House was gone.

CHAPTER 10

A Heated Debriefing

We gathered in the supposed safety of Van Epps' home for the few remaining hours before daylight. We needed sleep, but of course we couldn't get it.

When morning came, our eyes were burning and our nerves were raw. We were in no condition to butt heads over findings and procedures. Tank, wiser than I'd given him credit for, went for a morning jog to depressurize. The rest of us entered into battle, our pointing fingers our swords and coffee cups our shields.

"It's gone," said Van Epps. "And so is the opportunity! The House was yours and you let it get away."

Brenda's crazed eyes and dreadlocks made her a veritable Medusa. "Now listen here, you—" She described him from a library of expletives. "You weren't there! You didn't see it, you didn't feel it, you didn't almost get killed!"

"So where's the data? How do we control this thing? Tell me!"

"Whatcha got on your video besides three hours of static?" She turned to me and Andi. "Guy can't even run a camera!"

Van Epps came back at me, finger waving. "I did not desert my post!"

Fearing Brenda might round the kitchen table to scratch his eyes out, I intervened. "The data can only be understood by calm and objective minds in the light of day—"

"Oh, shut up!" She was just as angry with me. "Don't give me that super scientist crap! You were about to piss in your pants."

"Yes! Yes, I admit being terrified, but that's my point. On a human level—"

She mimicked me, " . . . on a *human* level . . ."

Disrespect always sets me off. "On a human level we can't trust our impressions because they are skewed by emotion."

Andi—my employee!—jumped in. "But emotions are part of it—they're part of the message. We were supposed to be scared!"

"We are not dealing with a message. We're dealing with an explainable phenomenon, with observations, data, that's all."

"The House was trying to get our attention!"

"Well, see, now you've assigned it some kind of personality."

Brenda's long fingernail pointed like a weapon. "She didn't assign nothin'! She's right, that thing's talking and, baby, I'm hearing it and you'd better listen too if you want to save your sorry ass!"

Van Epps had a mini-fit in his corner of the room. "So this is the team you brought?"

How dare he? "I didn't bring them!"

He shot a glance at Andi.

I pointed to Brenda. "Well, I didn't bring *her*!"

Brenda slammed down her coffee cup. "That's it, man! I'm outta here!" She addressed Andi on her way to the hall. "This guy ain't human and that's why he's missing the whole point!" She glared at me. "You got as much sense as a refrigerator!"

She was looking for the closet to get her coat. The door she tried was locked. She struck it with her fist.

"Other door," I said.

Andi perked up and went into the hall.

"You're not leaving as well?" I asked.

She ignored me, preoccupied by that locked door.

My cell phone—our phones were the only thing among us recharged—played Beethoven's Fifth. "Yeah?"

"Hey, howdy!"

I was so emphatically, even dangerously *not* in the mood. "What is it?"

He told me but I had to ask him to repeat it. He did.

My world changed.

Brenda was coming out of the hall, headed for the front door. I waved at her to stop. She flipped me off. "It's Tank!" I tried again. "Please. Please wait."

Invoking Tank's name worked. She rolled her eyes at the ceiling, but she stopped. Andi was all eyes and ears.

I got a quick report from Tank, found out where he was, and ended the call.

We had to come back from the brink. Hand raised and voice quiet, I said, "All right. We have more data. Now. Calmly, in the daylight, let's agree, please, that we will hear all sides on this." I made eye contact with Brenda. "And that includes me. I will listen to you."

Brenda sniffed in disgust and looked away, but she stayed where she was.

"Andi . . . a word."

I led Andi into the living room, cautioned her to silence, and spoke into her ear. "Have you found any precedents for this, any case of a House . . . carrying messages, as you put it?"

She seemed to be confessing. "No, but—"

"I have some research I need you to do . . ."

Andi went into the kitchen and asked Van Epps for his camera. Van Epps was about to protest, as I expected, but I deftly changed to a more pressing subject. "The House is back. It's right down the street."

That worked. As if everything up to this point, especially our quarrels, was forgotten, we all poured into the street.

I hardly had to direct everyone's attention. I merely looked down the hill and so did they, and we saw the two-story Victorian sitting there as if it had been part of the neighborhood for years.

I expected Van Epps would fly into a seething, four-letter rage, and so he did. So much for logical and practical. This was not the man I once knew, and that seemed to carry a message as much as anything else we were dealing with.

"If you can grant us another chance," I told him, "we'd like to go down there and complete what we couldn't complete last night."

He eased just enough to scold me: "Well, make sure you do!" He waved us on and stormed back into his house. For a moment I saw him pulling back the front blinds to watch.

"Andi, please get that information and join us when you have it." I could see a protest forming and averted it. "It's vital."

She went inside to fire up her computer.

"So where's Tank?" Brenda asked.

"He's in the House, even as we speak."

CHAPTER 11

Daniel

It was a short walk, during which Brenda and I said not a word to each other. I felt it would be a long time before we did.

Remarkable. The House appeared just as it had the night before: same yard, walkway, planting beds, everything.

Except this time, Tank was standing in the front door, smiling and waving.

I looked at Brenda and she afforded me a cold, wordless return. Even so, by her tentative gait up the walkway I could tell she felt the same familiar fear I did. We did not like this place.

As for Tank . . . his comfort, his joy with the House was so incongruous as to suggest a meaning of its own.

"Hey, y'all, come on in! I got someone I wantcha to meet!"

Tank turned and went in as if we would follow him.

"Well," I said, "it scared us, but it didn't kill us."

"First time for everything," she responded.

She'd said something to me. Bolstered, I ventured inside.

She followed, giving a closet door a side glance as we passed through the hallway into the kitchen.

Tank had taken a seat at the breakfast table, and there beside him, having a bowl of cereal, was the child. He was dressed in the same untucked shirt and jeans, and now that he was sitting with one foot boyishly askew, I noticed he was missing a sock.

"Everybody, this is Daniel."

The boy looked up at us, munching on his breakfast, expression neutral. I smiled, stumbling over myself to be nonthreatening.

Brenda seemed to have her own issues where a child was concerned. Her cold exterior gave way to an abrupt and inexplicable sorrow that she fought back. At length, she took some deep breaths, then stooped to the boy's level with a smile I'd never seen before. "Daniel, it's great to meet you, baby."

Tank gestured toward an empty chair next to Daniel. "And this is . . . well, I called him Harvey but Daniel didn't like that. So we don't know his name."

Daniel looked up at an invisible someone sitting in that chair, a sizable person, judging from his eye line. I looked at the empty chair, at a loss. Nothing was ever going to be normal again, was it?

Tank must have read my face. He laughed, and it was a kind laugh; I took it that way. "Oh, you're all right. I don't see him either. But Daniel does."

Daniel exchanged a smile with the friend who wasn't there.

Brenda asked, "Well . . . is Daniel . . . ?"

Tank reached over and tousled the boy's hair. "Oh yeah. He's real."

Brenda pointed at Tank's tattoo, the one featuring our motley four and this small boy.

Tank shook his head in wonder. "Ain't that wild?" Then he stood. "Hey buddy, we're gonna go into the next room and talk a bit. You just finish up your breakfast, okay?"

The boy gave Tank a smile of complete trust.

Brenda and I went with Tank into the living room, and I noticed how much better I felt. Brenda seemed much more at ease as well. It could have been Tank's carefree and comfortable manner, plus the fact that the living room—indeed, the whole House—was lovely in the daylight, not threatening or mysterious. In any case, I was thinking clearly, and that was indispensable.

We stood in a tight triangle in the finely furnished room.

"Is this the boy you saw last night?" Tank asked.

"He's the one," said Brenda as I nodded.

"I was out jogging, you know, and here he comes running out from between those houses just down the hill, and he's looking scared like somebody's chasing him, and I hollered, 'Hey, bud, you okay?' He acted like he knew who I was because he just came running to me with his arms out, and I picked him up and he put his arms around me and just hung on.

"But—" Tank paused for effect and then wagged his finger to make a point. "I saw two people right on Daniel's tail, and you know what? They were there last night, standing there with the other folks watching the House and watching us."

"A man and a woman?" I asked. "She had short black hair, and he was young, six feet tall, close-cropped hair?"

"Wearing black. Last night and today. They must like black."

"Go on."

"I asked 'em, 'Hey, you want something?' but they just got out of there, didn't say a word." Tank made sure to meet our eyes. "I think they were up to no good. Daniel was scared of 'em, but now they had to deal with me so they took off. Good thing."

"Did Daniel know who they were?"

Tank shrugged. "He didn't say anything . . . but he doesn't usually." He hushed his voice and leaned in. "But here's something for you: I was gonna bring him back to Van Epps' place, and he wasn't about to go there, either. Looks like he knows that place and he's really scared of it."

"But this place doesn't scare him at all?" Brenda wondered.

"Hey, I tell you what, I was just trying to figure out what to do with him when, bammo, man, here's the House, right here. He dragged me through the front door like he wanted to hide in here, so here we are."

I suggested, "So he's the one who likes peanut butter and jam sandwiches?"

"There's food in the House, stuff that's easy to fix. I guess he's been living here, or hiding here."

"So . . . who is he? Where'd he come from?"

Tank could only shrug. "Guess we could ask him."

We went back into the kitchen. Brenda had the heart, the gentleness to try the direct approach. "Hey, sweetie, we're kind of wondering, just what are you doing here? Do you know why you're here?"

Daniel looked at his invisible friend as if for an answer. Then he directed a long, studying gaze at me and said, "Not yet."

Perhaps it was an answer to Brenda's question. Strangely, I felt it was a message to me.

CHAPTER 12

One Final Message

Hello?" came a call from the street.

It was Andi, planted timidly on the pavement. I beckoned from the front door. "Come on in, the coast is clear."

She kept eyeing the House, every step cautious as she came up the front steps and through the doorway. Meeting Daniel helped dispel her fears, though it left her as puzzled as the rest of us.

"What did you find out?" I asked as we four clustered in the living room.

Andi kept her voice low for the child's sake. "I got a report from the assisted living facility. Clyde Morris must have been quite a crumb; they didn't have anything good to say about him. But it's kind of pitiful: They say he died from suffocation. Apparently he rolled over into his pillow and couldn't right himself."

"And Gustav Svensson?"

Andi nodded. "He was a real person, an old fisherman who

lived on his boat in the harbor. People say he was a nasty old coot, but he died four days ago." She took a breath, maybe to be sure she still could. "He drowned. But he had a blow to his head. Folks figure he slipped, hit his head, and fell off his boat."

We all met each other's eyes as the pieces came together.

"So," said Brenda, "Mister objective, scientific, poo-poo-the-supernatural-stuff, what do you say now?"

I knew she wanted to corner me. That wasn't about to happen. "Whatever this is . . . it is what it is."

"Oh, that's good, that's real good."

"This is a scientific inquiry. Consequently, even though the means by which we acquire the data is open to question, the data itself could be true. Whatever this is, and however it works, we can't rule out what the House seems . . . to be telling us."

Tank nodded toward the kitchen and young Daniel. "And still is. By the way, his last name is Petrovski. It's written on his shirt collar, and there was a phone number under his name." He handed me a torn corner of paper napkin with the number scrawled on it. I handed it to Andi.

"I'm on it," she said.

"Okay," said Brenda. "So, believing what the House is saying . . . who died from a drug overdose?"

"Or still might?" I said. "And the files in Van Epps' camera?"

"Three folders, one hour each, nothing but static."

Brenda reiterated, "Guy can't run a camera."

"And there is still . . ." I looked toward the door in the hallway that was locked the night before and, I guessed, still was. "One final message, wouldn't you say?"

Andi and Brenda exchanged a look. They were sisters on this one.

Andi led the way to the door. "Have you seen this before, seen it elsewhere?"

Clearly, we all had.

"Looks just like the same stupid closet door that wasn't the closet door back in Van Epps' place," said Brenda.

I nodded. We were together on this. "You and I both mistook that door for the closet, and both times, it was locked."

"But here it is," said Andi, "a direct copy, and locked just like the other one."

"Hold on," said Tank. He spoke quietly again. "Daniel won't use this hallway. He always goes the long way around, through the dining room, to get to the kitchen."

"We have our next step," I suggested. I was just about to wonder how we might accomplish it when, to our surprise, a lawn mower started up in the front yard.

"What the devil—" I started to say, but was interrupted by the clatter of a chair in the kitchen.

Tank looked, then hurried. "Hey, bud! What's wrong?"

I caught only a glimpse of Daniel before he disappeared, terrified, inside a cupboard and closed the door after him. Tank looked at us, then toward the front door, nonplussed.

Neither I, nor Brenda, nor Andi, had felt comfortable closing the front door behind us, so it remained open, providing a framed view of the front yard. The mower's operator passed across that view, eyes locked ahead of him, a death grip on the mower's handlebar, pushing the mower for all he was worth.

It was A.J. Van Epps.

CHAPTER

13

The Prison

Data? Van Epps had become an unnerving source of data by his very behavior. He would not stop mowing the lawn even as I chased alongside him, trying to engage him over the roar of the mower.

"Behavioral Analysis!" he shouted to me, turning about and heading back across the lawn again. "We apply an input, such as doing the House a favor, such as mowing the lawn, and see if it triggers a response we can analyze, a change in behavior."

"A change in what behavior?"

He wouldn't answer me. I hurried beside him, almost tripping over the walkway, until I was tired of the game, the indirectness. "What are you afraid of?"

He stopped, but left the mower running, I suppose, to ensure our privacy.

"You can't see it? That thing's a predator, a—a vindicator! It has something against me, against all of us."

I refrained from saying *You're mad!* but I certainly thought it, and I suppose he read it in my face.

"Think what you will, but we—you and I—have become part of the experiment. It intends to take us like the others, and that means practical solutions, direct action."

He continued mowing, leaving me behind. I ran once again to catch up with him and called over the mower. "Do you have any gardening tools? We could help. We could weed the beds, edge the lawn."

That seemed to mollify him, at least for a moment. "In my garage. Help yourself. Please."

I signaled Brenda and Andi to come with me. We agreed with Tank that he should remain with the boy.

In Van Epps' garage we found the tools we needed: a large hammer and a crow bar. Within minutes the obstinate door in Van Epps' hallway splintered away from its lock and creaked open.

It was the doorway to the basement. Steep wooden stairs descended into a musty chamber of web-laced concrete, a netherworld of stacks, shelves, and piles of things unneeded and unused.

Directly opposite the base of the stairs was another door, yawning open, hanging crookedly from its hinges. It had been barred shut, but the two-by-four bar had been broken like a toothpick; the door had been locked, but the lock now lay in bent and broken pieces on the concrete, leaving a hole in the door like a shark bite. Strangest of all, the door had been broken *out*, not in, as if a formidable beast had been captive but was now at large.

We found a small room within. There was a bed with its covers askew, and a portable RV toilet. Some toys lay on the floor, some children's books and a box of crayons on the bed.

Andi found a single sock, clearly the mate to the one the boy was wearing.

We regarded once again the door that had sealed this room, the concrete walls with no window, the cold, the silence, the prison cell size, and a silence fell over us.

"Friend of yours?" Brenda said at last.

Only to my horror and dismay. It took effort to find my voice. "I . . . cannot defend him."

"Defend him? What for? This is all . . ." She mimicked my voice, my manner. "Entirely pragmatic! A logical step! A practical means to an end!"

"Enough—"

"We'll lock the kid up like a lab rat, purely for the sake of gathering useful data because after all, what are right and wrong but mere social abstractions?"

"You're not being fair—"

"Fair? What do you know about fair?" She waved her hand over the whole mess before us. "I'll tell you *fair*. If I was the House I'd be after him too, and I hope the House gets him!"

She had me on the ropes, but Andi, like the proverbial bell, saved me. "Excuse me? Have you seen this?"

She was referring to strange symbols the boy had scrawled on the wall of the room with a black crayon. It could have been a code, a language, I couldn't tell. I looked to Andi, but she seemed perplexed.

Until I remembered a phrase Van Epps had used: *the handwriting on the wall* . . .

That triggered something in Andi. She gasped, looked at the strange squiggles again, then grabbed a crayon from the bed and began to copy them on the same wall, but in mirror reverse, from left to right. "Oh no . . ." she said. "Wow. Unreal. It's in script, and he wrote it left to right. . . ."

"Keep going, baby," said Brenda.

Andi finished copying, then pointed at the symbols as she read: "May-nay, may-nay, Tay-kel, oo-far-seen."

I now recognized it. "Hebrew."

Andi nodded. "Every Jewish girl learns her Hebrew. This is a quote from—" Then she laughed and wagged her head in wonder. "From the book of Dani'el!"

Brenda was impatient. "So what does it say?"

"Mene," I began. "To count. Tekel: To weigh. Pharsin: to divide."

"The prophet Dani'el's warning to the wicked king Belshazzar," said Andi, her voice hushed with wonder.

"Written by the hand of God on the wall of the king's palace." To Brenda's questioning look I responded, "I was a priest."

Andi explained it. "God was telling Belshazzar, 'Your days are numbered and they've come to an end; You've been weighed in the balance and found wanting; your kingdom is divided among your enemies.'"

"So the boy Daniel has a gift," I mused.

"And one tough dude for a friend," said Brenda, eyeing the broken door and then pointing to a high basement window still hanging open.

"Harvey?" Andi asked.

Brenda shuddered. "Man, *I* ain't calling him Harvey."

"So as Earthsong told us, he escaped." I recounted the "reading" of the fortune-teller. "A child thought to have a gift . . . he was consulted . . . he was a prisoner, but he broke his bonds and is free and people are looking for him."

Andi eyed the writing on the wall. "God spoke in different ways in the Bible. You know the stories: the burning bush, the donkey that talked to Balaam, Gideon's fleece . . . the handwriting on the wall. I couldn't find a precedent for a 'house holding people accountable,' but maybe the House is another way for God to speak."

"In which case, I'd say Daniel delivered. He spoke for the House, only Van Epps didn't like what he had to say."

"And Daniel isn't the first prophet to be locked up by somebody who didn't like his message," said Andi.

"And Earthsong . . ." Brenda ventured.

I was having the same thoughts. "She knew all about it—and she was careless enough to tell us."

Brenda muttered—maybe a curse—as her hand went to her head.

"What?"

"You okay?" Andi asked.

"You wanted me to tell you if I got any more pictures. . . ." Brenda's eyes closed as if viewing something in her mind. "I see . . . blood on the floor."

"Where?" said Andi, looking around.

"In my head!"

"The fortune-teller," I said, my guts twisting.

Their eyes asked for an explanation.

"Your comments, Brenda, about Van Epps being unable to run a camera. We can say for sure he was minding that camera long enough to record three hours of static."

"But—" said Andi, eyes widening.

"Exactly," I said. "We were in the House for five."

CHAPTER 14

The Third Death

I assigned Andi to a safe and neutral position behind a tree on a small bluff overlooking the House and, just up the street, Van Epps' home. She was not to approach either one—which was fine with her—but to let us know if anything developed. In the meantime, she could follow up on the phone number Tank found on Daniel's shirt collar.

Brenda and I returned by back roads to Earthsong's Psychic Readings to find a CLOSED sign hanging in the window. We knocked, we called out, we got no response. Brenda drew upon her street wisdom, gained admittance through a side window, and let me in through the front door.

Upstairs, a sound system was playing psychedelic rock from the sixties. We ventured up the stairs to the living quarters, a dimly lit, cultural throwback with tie-dyed tapestries, black-light posters of Morrison, Hendrix, and Joplin, walls randomly splattered in pop-art colors.

We found Earthsong on her bed, two fresh needle marks in her arm, the syringe on the nightstand. She had nodded off and fallen into a deeper and deeper sleep until she was dead.

"Don't touch anything," I cautioned.

"So here's death number three," said Brenda.

"Murder number three, I'm afraid." I used a pen from my pocket to press the sound system's *off* button and immediately confirmed the stirrings I thought I'd heard downstairs.

I went to the top of the stairs and called out, "Lady and Gentleman, she's dead and we are witnesses; we have the child in our custody, and Van Epps will be convicted of murder. Now you can kill us and draw all the more attention, or you can abandon Van Epps right here, right now, and slink back under your secretive rock to fight another day."

Brenda, beside me, was clearly surprised to hear footfalls move through the building. We caught only the back of the man and woman going out the front door.

"Our error, leaving that door unlocked," I said. "They've been following us from the beginning. We've seen them before: scum from that Institute, damage controllers, trying to find Daniel and letting Van Epps know our every move—beginning with our visit to this very place. Earthsong thought you and I were them. That's why she showed off so much—and said things she shouldn't have."

"And Van Epps killed her?"

I felt condemned by my own concession. "As you reminded me, it was the pragmatic, logical, practical thing to do. It stands to reason that perhaps she was his mistress, which explains how she knew about Daniel, his gift, how Van Epps held him prisoner, and how he escaped. And being Van Epps' mistress, of course she'd be jealous when Van Epps brought in Daniel to consult instead of her. So she was jealous of Daniel and high on heroin, which made her blabby—a liability. If she mouthed off so freely to you and me, who else might she talk to?

"You noticed there were two needle marks? The first dose was administered by Earthsong to satisfy her addiction; the second fatal dose was administered by her lover, who knew where she kept her heroin—who no doubt supplied it in the first place, maybe in exchange for sexual favors. He was only minding his camera outside the House for three of the five hours we were inside. The other two afforded him the opportunity to come here, eliminate the risk of discovery, and return to meet us outside the House, his jacket freshly imbued with more of Earthsong's incense, by the way.

"As for Clyde Morris and Gustav Svensson, if we believe the pattern set by the House—which logic, not belief, compels me to do—it follows that the same person who engineered Earthsong's death is also responsible for the other two." I reached for my cell phone. "I would say it's time to call the police."

In my hand, my cell phone played Beethoven's Fifth. The screen told me it was Andi. "Yes?"

She was so frantic I could barely understand her.

"Van Epps! He's trying to burn the House down, and Tank and Daniel are still inside!"

CHAPTER 15

A House Afire

At perilous speed we drove back to where the House . . . used to be. At that location we found a field overtaken by blackberries.

Up the street, directly across from Van Epps' home, the House stood rock solid even as smoke poured from the windows and flames licked about the porch. The can of gasoline for the mower lay on its side in the front yard, emptied. Van Epps was just coming from his garage with another can and some empty beer bottles.

Andi ran to us as we screeched to a halt and burst from the car. "Tank and Daniel are inside!"

Before I could get to him, Van Epps hurled a gasoline-filled bottle through the front window. An explosion of new flames followed, roiling and engulfing the living room, the walls, the furniture.

I ran and stood between him and the House. "Are you out of your mind? Stop this!"

As if I were not even there, he raged against the burning building. "Come after me, will you? How do *you* like burning? I'll send you back where you came from, you filthy—"

He grabbed another bottle and would have filled it, but I blocked the action and the bottle shattered on the street. "A.J., come to your senses! Look at what you've become!"

For the first time he looked at me. "Become? *Become?* This *is* me, James! I am what I've always been, and this"—he indicated his arsenal of gasoline and bottles—"this is survival!"

The ladies were screaming for Tank and Daniel. The House was becoming an inferno, the flames roaring up the sides, black smoke venting out the eaves.

A chair crashed through an upstairs window, followed by a huge, smoking body. Tank! He plunged, rolled down the porch roof, took hold of a trellis as he pitched over the edge, and grabbed the autumn-deadened branches of a vine to break his fall. He landed and collapsed on the lawn, rolling in the grass to extinguish flames that I hoped had not ignited on him. The ladies and I were there instantly, checking him over.

He was blackened by smoke and soot, bleeding from scrapes and cuts, wracked with coughing, fighting for air. Yet still he managed to cry, "Daniel! Daniel!"

Flames were shooting out the window he'd just come through. Daniel. Oh, child! No one could still be alive in there.

Andi shrieked, "Daniel!"

I followed her horrified gaze across the street.

Daniel! There he was, crossing the street, hand in hand with he-whom-we-were-not-to-call-Harvey . . . heading for Van Epps' front door.

"He made it, he made it!" Brenda shouted to Tank.

Daniel met our eyes, our horror, with a look of such peace, I felt all reason leave me. *Child, what are you doing?*

Van Epps caught sight of Daniel even as the boy went in his

front door. Van Epps abandoned his pyromania and dashed toward his house, bounded up his stairs, burst through the doorway.

No! Oh dear God, no!

Tank was fallen, barely turned from the brink of death. The ladies were tending to him and hadn't the strength . . .

And for reasons only the heart, not the mind, can know, I ran for that door.

CHAPTER 16

The Monster

I bounded up the stairs two at a time. In one blurred moment I crossed the porch and burst through the front door—

And into a cage with a monster.

Van Epps held Daniel in a desperate grip, and a knife to Daniel's throat. "Stop right there, James!"

I stopped. I raised my hands. "A.J. This is—you must admit—highly irregular."

"But *you* must admit, entirely pragmatic!" His crazed eyes locked on the burning House; the glow of the fire played on his face. "A life for a life. I'm sure the House understands the concept!"

"It would only be another murder!"

"Murder?" He actually laughed. "Am I talking to James McKinney? Since when did murder become more than a social concept? Since when did you decide to be a hero?"

I was struck dumb. What could I say? Where could I go from here?

Van Epps was enjoying the upper hand. "Morris was a drunken, wife-beating wretch and deserved to die anyway. All I did was control the time of death."

To my own indictment, I understood his reasoning. "Controlling the conditions for observing the phenomena."

"And it worked: it produced a posthumous sighting and photographs of Clyde Morris; the House appeared again; we got the account from Morris's widow."

"So what about Gustav Svensson?"

"A blight on the face of the town! Constantly soiling the tourists' experience with his foul temperament. Hated! So we needed observable, repeatable results. I took the necessary steps—and we got them."

I erred in taking a step forward. His knife went anew to Daniel's throat. "Easy! Easy!"

I took a step back.

The knife stayed right where it was. "So don't you see, James? Repeatable results mean predictability, and predictability means eventual control. Had we understood the House, we could have controlled it. We could have harnessed it."

"*And* turned it aside?"

His glare was condemning. "Exactly."

I grimaced. A monster being reasonable. Another monster would have accepted his argument. I, at least, saw the logic in it. I felt sick.

"I suppose," I ventured, "Earthsong was only a complication?"

"She . . . and the kid." He waved the knife under Daniel's nose.

"He only delivered the message, A.J. Locking him up didn't change anything and killing him certainly won't."

"His life for mine, James. Behavioral control of that thing over there . . . until it burns to the ground."

"Not at such a cost! Never."

As if to confirm my words, there came a rumbling in the floor, in the walls, and then a shaking so severe the furniture danced. We fell. Daniel wriggled free. The noise shook my insides. Dishes, lamps, books showered down, and I felt I was riding the floor, fists clenching wads of carpet, as it heaved and bucked and the room spun about. Where was Daniel?

I saw the knife, fallen from Van Epps' hand and jittering upon the floor. I knew he would go for it, so I did. We collided in the center of the room, neither of us procuring the knife, both of us reduced to a savage brawl: rolling, kicking, striking—I even bit his hand. The degradation was appalling and my skills as a grappler nonexistent, but there we were, rabid animals in a huge tumbler, trying to kill each other.

Somehow Van Epps got hold of me from behind, and as he compressed my throat and I fought for my life, an infinitesimal part of my awareness took note of four facts: the room had changed, my friends were shouting and pounding on the front door, Daniel stood safely in a corner, watching, and . . . Daniel was also watching someone else, his eyes expectant.

Suddenly, Van Epps let out an *oof*, released me, and I tottered forward, turning in time to see him slam against the wall. That I would have such strength surprised me.

The advantage, however, was now his. He had the knife again and charged like a raging bull. I may have ducked when he thrust the knife. I only remember tumbling onto the couch while he went flying over it and then let out a cry.

I leaped from the couch, eyes everywhere, not seeing him—

A groan came from the archway between the living and dining rooms. The couch blocked my view, but as I rounded it I found my adversary fallen, a pool of crimson spreading beneath him, the knife up to the hilt between his ribs.

Only then, as I gasped for breath, did I realize the tumult and quaking had ceased. Only then did I recognize the dining room with its eight place settings and high-backed chairs. I was standing in the House. Except for the disarray Van Epps and I had caused, no harm was done, and not the slightest scent of smoke remained.

As if by the House's will, the front lock released, the door burst open, and in spilled Tank, Andi, and Brenda. Tank was scorched and tattered, but ready to . . . well, I suppose I beat him to it.

Aghast, they took in the scene, from Daniel safe in the corner to the upset furniture to the body of Van Epps, unquestionably dead. Brenda stared in recognition at the pool of blood on the floor, then at me.

"Duly noted," I replied.

"You're bleeding!" Andi cried.

Oh. A cut on my hand. Nothing deep or serious, but sufficiently dramatic. Even so, something else warranted my attention: an awareness, an urgency. "Get Daniel out of here."

"But—"

"Tank, if you would, please."

Tank hurried over and scooped Daniel up.

I could not say how I knew, and there wasn't time to sort it out. "It isn't over. Get out. Now."

Oh, the cacophony of voices, the static!

"What?"

"What are you talking about?"

"How do you know?"

"I just *do*, for God's sake . . . pardon the term!" The House shook, a familiar sensation. "Go!"

I shoved and herded them, surprised at my strength, ashamed

of my manners, and got them through the door. The latch fell into place and I caught my breath.

The quiet brought no comfort; a lull before a storm. Once again, I was afraid.

I felt a chill behind me and turned.

There stood Van Epps, ghostly white, eyes pasty, blood streaking his clothes, the knife in his hand.

CHAPTER 17

A Hero

The knife came down. I dodged it. Van Epps lunged for me; I leaped, tumbled over the back of the couch, got to my feet, and ran across the room—where he met me, plunging the knife again. I dodged again, and must have struck him with an elbow—he took a blow, jerking sideways, off balance. I put out my foot to kick him but missed; he fell anyway. When he came at me again I had a lamp in my hands, but didn't have to swing it. Inches from me, his body and face flattened as if he'd struck a thick pane of glass between us. He fell back and nearly tripped over something.

It was his own body, dead on the floor, the knife protruding.

From his guttural gasp and the way he wilted, I had a fair idea the fight was over. He teetered there, gawking, horror stretching his veiny face, a ghostly copy of himself, complete with a bloodstained knife. He dropped the knife—it dissolved before touching the floor—looked at me, looked at himself . . . then around the room.

His silence spoke though he could not. No arguments remained, no rationales. I could see he knew.

The House had him.

And as quick as that thought, three guests appeared, seated at the dining table: Clyde Morris, hunched and worn, resigned to his fate; Gustav Svensson, bitterness tightening his face, eyes glaring; Earthsong, her beauty fading even as she sat there, her eyes showing the wounds of betrayal.

I could not, I dared not move or speak. I could only hope, foolishly, that they could not see me, that I wasn't really standing in the same room, the same House, with the man now facing his accusers.

Van Epps and I had long assured and supported each other in our opinions. We had mocked those who believed in a God and any day of reckoning. In anger, in bitterness, I had killed God long ago and ever after wished Him dead. Though all appearances suggested it was Van Epps on trial, was I not partly responsible for his being there?

Clyde Morris seemed interested only in Van Epps as he produced a pillow—Van Epps' instrument of murder—and laid it on the table.

Gustav Svensson followed, producing a bloodstained rock.

Earthsong, saddened, produced the syringe used to kill her and set it beside the pillow and the rock.

Van Epps didn't speak. What was there to say?

A door in the hall answered, its hinges creaking, and immediately a wind moved through the House, swaying and jangling the chandelier, rustling the curtains. Van Epps' eyes rolled toward the hallway as if he knew what the sound was. The three accusers simply turned their heads; they already knew what it was.

True to the widow Morris's account, a powerful body of air hit me in the back and sent me reeling in the direction of the hall. Van Epps, caught in the same rush of air, stumbled and staggered ahead of me, arms fighting off flying newspapers, serviettes, doilies, a tablecloth, any and all things the wind could carry. I grasped a dining room chair but it only came with me. I could hear Van Epps screaming over the gale.

Just ahead of me, the three accusers, Morris, Svensson, and Earthsong, walked into the hallway even as their images dissolved into particles like sand before the wind. The doorway—yes, the House's precise copy of Van Epps' basement door—stood gaping, the glow of a furnace pulsating upon the opposite wall. Like specks of dust drawn into a vacuum, what was left of the three shot through.

Van Epps dropped to the floor, grabbed for the carpet, a server, a hutch, to no avail as the wind carried him—and me—toward that door. I could feel the heat.

It was not a thought, for there wasn't time. It was a knowledge: I'd been on trial with Van Epps. Hope as I might, argue as I might, the House was good with its promise: it knew all about me.

Van Epps blurred through the door with a shriek. The rectangular frame of fire filled my vision, I flew helplessly, headlong—

My body slammed against an unseen barrier stretched across the door, and I hung there, a gale force pulling my arms, legs, and hair into the throat of a flaming, roaring tunnel. Far ahead of me, Van Epps, a rag doll in silhouette, tumbled, kicked, screamed, shrank into oblivion.

How might I escape? How? I looked away from the fiery maw that would swallow me, desperate to know my situation. What held me here? How might I work my way to safety?

Only in that tiny and panicked measure of time did I realize my body had come up against another—I felt the shape of a powerful chest against mine and, on further groping for escape, I discerned what could have been huge arms. I looked up.

I saw the glow of the fire on the lintel of the door, the wall, and the ceiling above, but somehow, in the light of the flames and the shadows cast, I saw the outline of a face: the shape of a jaw, a brow, the crown of a head. Although I could not see the eyes plainly, I could feel them watching me. I looked where I knew them to be, and . . .

I could not plead. No words would come.

The huge arm to my left reached out; the door swung shut with a clamorous *bang!*

And I came to my senses on the floor, my body in a heap against the basement door in the home of the late A.J. Van Epps. His body still lay where it fell, a dim and crumpled shadow against the sweep of red and blue lights that came through the front windows.

CHAPTER 18

Reflection

The fire crew grumbled a little, trying to understand why they'd been called to a fire when now, search as they might, there was none to be found. There wasn't even a burning House to be found, only an old field with a long defunct chicken coop. I think some of them knew, but they weren't going to say anything.

The police had plenty to do, stretching their yellow ribbon around Van Epps' home and beginning the long process of piecing together his death, his basement prison, the prisoner, and three murders. According to their instructions, I waited with my friends on the front steps, shakily sipping from a cup of water. Along with our debriefing each other, we discussed lodging; getting everything explained was going to take a while.

Faithful Andi reported, "The phone number on Daniel's shirt got me the Norquist Center for Behavioral Health—it's a home for the insane. They've been looking for Daniel. Daniel's uncle and aunt came to take him for a few days but never brought him back, and as it turns out, they weren't his real uncle and aunt."

I nodded, theorizing. "Our charming couple from that Institute, no doubt. Van Epps had friends he wouldn't talk about—friends wanting 'power.'"

Brenda draped a blanket over my shoulders. "I'll bet they were tracking little Daniel the same as they were tracking me and Tank for our 'special gifts.'"

"And brought him here to help them . . . what? Make contact with the House? Well, what he provided was not to Van Epps' liking."

"Hey," said Tank, "it was God talking. You want to hear from God, you better be ready for the truth."

God. So many issues there. Such a long history. Such a long, long journey back should I even desire to make it. I didn't care to rebut Tank's faith, not today. I only asked him, for the record, "Did you really see heaven?"

Tank grinned. "Jesus was there. It couldn't have been anything else." Then with a sober, thoughtful air he added, "The House only tells the truth. For some it's good news; for others . . ."

Brenda put an arm around Daniel and drew him close. "I'll tell you something. Daniel's not insane. He's like anybody else folks don't understand."

I reached and touched the boy's cheek. "I'm glad you're all right, son." Then I added with a wink, "That's quite a protector you have."

Daniel replied, "Yes, sir," and smiled up at his invisible friend.

"So what do you suppose, Daniel? You heard the House's message. You wrote it on the wall. Did the House take Dr. Van Epps because he killed those people and almost killed you?"

"No, sir."

We waited for more.

"The House took him because he was the kind of person who would."

I could still see myself hanging in that doorway. There, but for the grace of God . . .

"It could have been me," I whispered.

I saw the same look I'd seen in Daniel's eyes the last time he said it: "Not yet."

THE SENTINELS

ANGELA HUNT

CHAPTER 1

I was sitting on the edge of my grandparents' deck, bare legs swinging in the sun, when Abby trotted out of the house and sat beside me. "Abs!" I slipped my arm around her back and gave her a hug; she returned my affection by licking my cheek. "Stop that, silly. You know I'm ticklish."

As if she understood, Abby straightened and joined me in staring at the sea oats and the white sandy beaches of the Gulf of Mexico. We had sat in this same spot hundreds of times in our growing-up years . . . me, the geeky high-schooler, and Abby, the ungainly Labrador pup. Somehow we had both outgrown our awkwardness.

I ran my hand over the back of her head, then scratched between her ears. My heart welled with nostalgia as tears stung my eyes. "I've missed you, Abs," I whispered. "All that time away at college . . . I wish you could have been with me. Maybe I wouldn't have been so homesick if you were there."

She whimpered in commiseration, then gave me another kiss.

My throat tightened at the thought of eventually losing her. Big dogs tend to have shorter lifespans, and all the books said

Labs lived an average of twelve to fourteen years. Which meant I'd only have my girl for another five or so years. . . . I had to get home more often.

Abby pricked up her ears, pulled away from me, then jogged down the deck steps.

"Abs! You know you're not supposed to go down to the beach."

When it suited her, Abby had selective hearing. She dove into the bed of sea oats. I couldn't see her in the thick undergrowth, but the tasseled heads of the stalks bent and trembled as she passed by.

"You're going to get sand spurs in your coat!"

No answer except the rustle and crunch of dry vegetation. Then a warning bark, followed by a throaty growl.

She had probably found a rat, but for some reason her growl lifted the hairs on my arm. I stood and walked to a better vantage point, hoping to spot her. "Abby!" I brightened my voice. "Want a treat? A cookie?"

Another bark, and then a sharp yelp, followed by a frenzy of rustling and crunching. Then Abby began to cry in a constant whine as she retraced her steps, moving faster this time. Had she found a snake? Venomous snakes were not common on the beach, but this was Florida. . . .

I flew down the stairs, drawn by the urgency in her tone. "Abs! Come here, honey. Come on, baby, come on out."

If she'd been bitten, I had only minutes to get her to a vet. My grandparents had left a car in the garage, keys on the ring by the door . . .

Abby appeared in the pathway. She lifted her head for an instant and wriggled her nose, parsing the air for my scent. Then she ran to me, barreling into my legs and knocking me onto the sand.

"Abs?" She was on top of me, thrashing her head while she

whined, and with great difficulty I managed to catch her jowls. "Abs, honey, let me look—"

My breath caught in my throat. Abby's panicked breaths fluttered over my face as I stared into what had once been gentle brown eyes but were now empty, blood-encrusted caverns.

Everything went silent within me, and I screamed.

My grandmother's expensive sofa had a flaw in its fabric, but I didn't think Safta had noticed. The tiny dotted pattern wasn't arranged in perfectly straight lines, resulting in a slight variation that must have caused a problem for the upholsterer. Then again, perhaps a machine assembled this piece, and most machines had no feelings.

Lucky machines. Apparently the deviation in this upholstery pattern had been enough to evoke a horrific nightmare in my afternoon nap. My heart pounded for ten minutes after I woke up, then I bent down and gave Abby a huge hug, relieved to find her alive and well. But the minute I put my head back on the sofa pillow, a lingering sense of dread enveloped me.

I released a pent-up sigh. I'd been at my grandparents' beach house for a full twenty-four hours, but being home hadn't helped me relax as much as I'd hoped. Being with family usually took my mind off my work, but my grandparents had taken their jet to Miami to attend a wedding, leaving me to examine patterns on the couch, watch the professor read, and suffer quiet nightmares.

"Andi?" As if he'd overheard my thoughts, the professor lowered his book and waggled a brow. "Your grandparents have anything to snack on around here?"

"I'm sure they do. Let's go to the kitchen."

I rolled off the sofa and led the way to the ultra-modern kitchen Safta rarely used. Because she and Sabba now lived alone in this big house, they tended to eat out a lot. But my grandfather liked to snack, so the pantry was usually stocked with goodies.

Like a hungry puppy, the professor followed me to the kitchen, then craned his neck forward as I opened the pantry door. "Almonds," I said, reading the labels on cans and boxes. "Matzo crackers, cheese crackers, chocolate cookies, Oreos, and pretzel sticks. Yum, and these." I reached for a bag of jalapeño chips, my personal favorite. "If you like hot and spicy—"

"I like almonds." The professor reached past me and grabbed a can from the shelf, then popped the top. Then he hopped on a barstool, picked up the book he'd been reading, and tossed a handful of nuts into his mouth.

I understood why he was hanging around—just as I understood why he'd been reading in the living room instead of the guest room. We were both still recovering from a harrowing experience in Port Avalon, and neither of us wanted to be alone.

"Nice place your grandparents have here," the professor said, his gaze moving to the wide sliding glass door with the ocean view. "Nice of them to let us hang out here for a couple of days."

"I know."

I crossed my arms and wished I could think of some way to dispel the creepy memories of Port Avalon. When I learned that the next stop on the professor's speaking circuit was the University of Tampa, I had invited my grandparents to come hear him, since they lived only a few miles away. They passed up the opportunity to hear the professor speak on the toxicity of believing in God in a postmodern culture, but insisted that the professor and I drive over to spend the next few days with them. Of course I'd said yes—how could I refuse the people who raised me?—but my dreams of lying in warm sand vanished when I woke up this morning and spotted the cloudy horizon.

Rain began to fall shortly thereafter, and the day had been melancholy, wet, and dismal ever since.

The professor didn't seem to notice the weather. This morning I found him reading one of my books on chaos theory, and even though I knew he disagreed with the premise, he seemed entranced by the topic. Occasionally he snorted as he read, sometimes he laughed aloud, and more than once I watched him scribble a note in the margin. When he finished, he'd probably quiz me on the topic, asking how I could possibly believe that the laws of science and order held room for any variation or exception.

I could answer him easily enough. All I had to do was remind him about Port Avalon, where few things had operated according to natural laws.

I walked to the fridge and dug around in the produce drawer, hoping to find something crunchy. I came up with a single scrawny carrot, which I carried to the sink. I'd no sooner finished washing it when Abby ran to my side, sat politely, and looked at me, her eyes plaintively asking for a treat.

Caught by the powerful undertow of memory, I had to resist a strong impulse to bend down and kiss those beautiful brown eyes.

I looked around for the old doggie cookie jar, but Safta's counters were now clean and bare.

"What do you want, Abs?"

The dog lifted a paw, politely asking for—what?

I followed her gaze and realized she was staring at the carrot. "You want a carrot?"

She whined.

"Okay, then." I pulled a knife from the cutlery drawer, chopped off the stub, and held out the rest. "Enjoy your vegetable."

Abby took the carrot between her teeth, then stood, wagged her tail in a polite thank-you, and trotted off to enjoy her prize.

"Well-trained dog," the professor remarked. "Probably heard the sound of the refrigerator drawer."

I shrugged. "She's always been smart. Maybe she knew that carrots were the only decent snack in the fridge."

The professor cast me a reproachful glance. "You shouldn't indulge in anthropomorphism, Andi. Assigning human qualities to animals is the stuff of children's tales and fables."

"But you're always telling me that humans are animals," I countered. "And in your speech yesterday you pointed out that human DNA is 98 percent identical to that of a gorilla."

"Another proof of our evolutionary history," the professor answered. "But though there is very little difference between man and the primates, what little there is, is very important. Man evolved in ways the gorilla did not, in language, social and emotional development—"

At that moment Safta entered the room, her bright orange caftan billowing behind her. "You two." She shook her head. "Always debating something. Always reading, always learning. Your brains should get tired, but do they? No."

"How was Miami?" I asked. "Nice outfit, by the way."

"This?" She made a face. "It's a nothing of a dress. And Miami is the same—hot, big, crowded. I could die happy never visiting again."

She looked at the professor, who seemed mesmerized by his view of the gray beach. "Professor," she said, her tone more pointed. "A woman could grow old and die waiting for you to notice her."

Something in her tone must have registered with him, because he turned his head and blinked. "I'm so sorry. Were you speaking to me?"

She laughed, once again the pleasant hostess. "Jacob and I are so pleased to have you in our home. We have wanted to talk to you about our Andi."

Alarm filled the professor's eyes. He shifted his gaze to me, so I stepped behind Safta and mouthed *humor her*.

"You know," Safta said, oblivious to the professor's discomfort, "we are people of the Book, so we love learning. Do you know what a Jewish dropout is? A boy who didn't get his PhD. But the girls—ah, the girls. Surely you know some nice Jewish boy who needs a beautiful wife like my granddaughter the genius?"

The professor's brows rushed together. "Andi wants a husband?"

"Not yet, I don't." I wrapped my fingers around my grandmother's soft upper arm. "Safta, I think I'm going to take the professor for a walk. He ought to see the beach while he's here."

Safta blinked. "Like they don't have a beach in California?"

"Not like ours, they don't." I took the can of almonds from the professor, set it on the kitchen island, and jerked my head toward the door. "Let's go, Professor. Everyone needs to see the Gulf at least once."

"When you come back, we talk," Safta said, waving us away.

The professor hesitated only a moment, then darted toward the door. Apparently he'd realized that a walk in drizzling rain was vastly preferable to remaining in the house with my plain-spoken grandmother.

CHAPTER 2

The rain had let up by the time the professor and I crossed the pool deck, but the professor insisted that we grab an umbrella from the old milk can by the door. "I'm not a tourist," he insisted. "I don't need to experience rain and sand to appreciate their existence."

Though he would have denied it, I had a feeling he grabbed the umbrella because he didn't want me to get wet. Though he was technically my employer, at times he treated me more like a daughter—making sure I got enough sleep, reminding me to eat fruits and vegetables, even offering to run background checks on the guys I dated—when I had time to date, that is. Several of my friends had lifted a brow when I told them I'd be traveling around the country with a man old enough to be my father, but within ten minutes of meeting him, they understood that our relationship was in no way romantic. He was my employer, I was his gofer/researcher. And sometimes, especially lately, a surrogate daughter.

By the time we walked past the wide beds of sea oats that separated my grandparents' property from the public beach, we could see a crowd near the water's edge. I was surprised to find so many people out in such bad weather—rain usually sent tourists to the shopping malls. Yet as far as I could see, clumps of people stood at the water's edge and stared at the sand.

The professor squinted toward the crowd. "Did someone drown?"

"Not likely. We'd see lifeguards and boats if they were searching."

When we drew nearer the water, we understood. The waterline was outlined with the narrow bodies of hundreds and hundreds of fish. Their silver bodies tumbled in the wavewash and carpeted the heaving surface of the gulf. The misty air felt heavy, permeated with foreboding.

When we stopped, I studied the fish at my feet and was horrified to note that something—disease or parasite—had removed the fish's eyes. Only round black holes remained.

I covered my mouth as déjà vu sent a shudder up the ladder of my spine. No eyes. Just like Abby in my dream.

I turned away, not wanting the professor to see the tumultuous emotions that had to be flickering across my face. I was not the sort of person who had prophetic dreams, but this could not be coincidence.

Anxiety swelled like a balloon in my chest, making it hard to breathe.

"Andi?" The professor touched my arm, then looked at my face. "What's wrong?"

How could I explain my premonition to a man who didn't believe in them?

"Um, I used to play on this beach as a child," I said, insignificant words tumbling from my lips. "And I've never seen anything like this. Occasionally my grandparents would point out an empty turtle shell or a bird that had become entangled in fishing line, but the beach always brimmed with more life than death. I saw jellyfish and stingrays and even an occasional tiger shark, but this—this is a monumental disaster."

I finally met the professor's gaze, hoping he might have a logical explanation, but in his eyes I saw a confusion that matched my own.

I walked a few yards down the beach and approached another group of onlookers. They were talking about pollution and red tide; one man insisted this disaster was the result of global warming. I was about to ask if he had documentation to back up his assertion when from the corner of my eye I spotted a man and woman approaching. The woman wore a blazer and skirt—definitely not beach apparel—and the man carried a video camera on his shoulder.

"This good?" The woman stopped in a deserted area and turned her back to the water. The cameraman retreated a few feet, then held up four fingers and began counting down. *Three, two—*

"Michelle Tybee here, reporting for Channel 13 news," the woman said, pulling back her windblown hair. "Residents of Indian Rocks Beach are out on the sand today, stunned and sorrowful to see evidence of a mass die-off on their pristine shores. As of yet there are no answers for this mysterious occurrence, but these Florida residents are dismayed to find themselves among the growing number of people who have stepped outside their homes and discovered hundreds, if not thousands, of dead animals on the streets and lawns of their neighborhoods. Are we witnessing the evidence of global warming? Are we unknowingly causing the deaths of the animals who share our planet? Is the government conducting secret experiments and wreaking devastation within our own borders? No one knows the answer, but the world waits for an explanation. As do these concerned beachgoers."

The cameraman nodded and the reporter flung back her hair

again, then bent to take off her shoe and shake out the sand. In search of an answer, I hurried forward. "Hello? May I ask you something?"

She gave me a polite smile. "I'm sorry, but we've finished our interviews for this piece."

"Um, no, I don't want to be on camera. I just wondered if anyone official has been out to investigate. Surely someone has done a necropsy on these fish to determine the cause of death—"

"I wouldn't know." The reporter shrugged. "But when someone comes up with an answer, I'm sure we'll report it. Check the news in a couple of days."

I was about to ask if she knew the names of any biological scientists in the area, but was distracted by something that fell at my feet. I stepped back and saw a red-winged blackbird dead on the ground. Like the fish, it had no eyes. I blinked, unable to believe I'd just missed being hit by the bird, then I heard another soft plop a few feet away. Another dead bird. Then another hit the arm of the reporter. She shrieked, lifted her hands over her head, and gazed at the sky. "What the—"

Like dark, oversized raindrops, a shower of dead birds fell onto the water and sand, sending us humans scrambling for cover.

The professor had come up with an explanation by the time we reached the beach house. "The weather." He pointed upward. "A storm front moved in, swept up a flock of birds, and exposed them to freezing temperatures or a sudden variation in barometric pressure. I'm no zoologist or meteorologist, but I'm sure the explanation has something to do with this bit of bad weather."

"Really? Then why doesn't every thunderstorm result in dead animals?" I stopped to open the sliding door, then faced him. "And what happened to their eyes?"

He blew out his breath in weary exasperation, then dropped the umbrella back into the milk can. "Ask someone who cares."

I watched as he walked through the kitchen and turned toward the hallway that led to his guest room. He wanted to be alone; maybe he would sleep. Maybe the weirdness on the beach had brought back too many troubling memories.

I, however, would not surrender to despondency. I found a note from Safta on the counter—she and Sabba had run to the grocery—then went into the living room and turned on the TV, switched to the local news, and opened my laptop. I did a Google search for "mass animal deaths," and within a couple nanoseconds I found several pages listing dozens of mass die-offs—of crabs, birds, fish, dolphin, starfish, whales, even cattle, elk, and sheep. I read about cows who'd been struck by lightning while standing under a tree, and sheep who had blindly followed the leader off a cliff and plunged to their deaths.

Then I read that mass animal deaths, even so-called animal suicides, had begun to increase at an alarming rate. I found a map labeled with the locations of mass deaths and saw that they were occurring all over the world, but the majority was being reported in "modern" countries. Scientists offered various explanations, of course—polluted water, algae blooms, submarine sonar experiments, global warming/climate change, or perhaps a combination of all those elements.

Staring at the global map with its heavy spattering of dots, I felt an odd tightening at the base of my skull. For some reason—or maybe a host of reasons—Earth's animals were perishing, and it seemed logical to assume humans would be affected next. Like the canaries coal miners kept below ground to signal a dangerous rise in toxic gases, certain species were dying because something was wrong with our environment. But what? And why had animals begun to die all over the planet?

I moused over the United States, then zoomed in to separate the dots that blanketed the map. The dots separated, so I enlarged the selection until the map of the United States filled my laptop screen.

Then I saw it: The gentle curve and swirl of the golden ratio. *Phi*, the formula said to govern the cosmos. The arrangement found everywhere in nature and purported to be the very definition of beauty.

I leaned back and closed my eyes, struggling to understand what I was seeing. How could these be natural events if caused by climate change? Was I seeing proof of chaos theory, or was a higher law at work? In either case, if the pattern continued, it would keep spiraling until every place was affected, until every animal species suffered. Each creature had its place in the food chain, and you couldn't eradicate one without affecting the entire ecosystem. . . .

My thoughts shifted as the professor entered the living room and dropped into Sabba's favorite chair. "Something I ate," he said, pounding his chest with his fist, "didn't agree with me. I just had the strangest nightmare, and I rarely dream in my power naps."

My pulse quickened. "What'd you see?"

"That kid—remember? Sridhar, the lucid dreamer from the Institute. He was calling to me, trying to say something. I couldn't understand him, but I had the distinct feeling that he was trying to warn me about something."

"That doesn't sound very nightmarish."

"You didn't see what I saw." He shuddered. "The kid had no eyes."

The professor went on, trying to imitate whatever sounds the dream Sridhar had been making, but my thoughts turned to Brenda and Tank. When we'd met Sridhar, he'd explained that the Institute had trained him to influence other people's dreams. . . . Was he trying to send a message to the professor? Was he also sending messages to me?

I lowered my hand and found Abby's head—she was on the floor at my side. She used to stretch out by my desk chair and take long naps, but now she lay with her head erect, her ears pointed forward, her eyes watchful.

I scratched her forehead, expecting her to close her eyes and groan in gratitude, but after only a second or two, she leapt to her feet, walked through the kitchen, and sat at the sliding glass doors, her attention fixed on something outside.

Even the professor noticed. "I thought Labs were mellow, but your dog seems unusually high-strung."

"She's not, usually." I got up and went to see what Abby was watching. Looking through the wide panes of glass, I saw nothing unusual—the sea oats, swaying in the breeze, the gentle surf, a bearded guy with a metal detector walking over the sand.

A low growl rumbled in Abby's throat.

"It's just a metal detector," I told her. "We see those all the time."

She continued to growl. When the bearded guy moved out of our view, I expected Abby to relax, but she stood, hair rising at the back of her neck. She barked in the deep, hoarse tone she used as a warning, but though I kept my eyes on the beach, I saw nothing that should have alarmed her.

But her apprehension was contagious. The dreams . . . Sridhar . . . the dead animals. Something was out of kilter in the universe, and, judging by Abby's reaction, the danger loomed right outside our door. The professor and I seemed to be in the middle of a verifiable mystery, and if we were, we needed the others.

"Professor?" I called over my shoulder. "Could you understand *anything* Sridhar was trying to tell you?"

I heard the soft sound of his loafers on the tiled floor behind me. "If I had to guess," he said, "he might have been saying 'prepare the eight.'"

I turned. "The *eight*? Eight what?"

He shrugged. "I have never been one to place much stock in dreams, let alone dream languages."

"Eight." I ran through the multiples. "Sixteen, twenty-four, thirty-two, forty, forty-eight—"

"Then again," the professor interrupted, "he might have said 'beware the rate.'"

I blinked.

"Or 'look there your fate.' Or 'aware the bait.'"

I groaned. He was toying with me now, making fun of my affinity for numbers and patterns.

"Thanks for your help," I told him, my tone frosty. "I'll take it from here."

He chuckled and went back to the living room, where he'd probably pick up his book or take another nap. And while he tried to take his mind off the bizarre occurrences that we'd encountered, I would think about Brenda, Tank, and Daniel. . . .

We had left Port Avalon feeling that we might not ever see each other again, but now I was beginning to believe we were meant to be together. But how was that possible? Brenda lived in California, and Tank—I couldn't remember exactly where he was living, but I knew he was playing football in the Northwest. Daniel was a resident at the Norquist Center for Behavioral Health. How was it even possible for us to come together again?

The impossible, Sabba always said, began with a single step toward the possible.

I bit my lower lip, then made a decision. Sabba had a jet, and he'd do anything for me. Even if it meant going to the ends of the earth to fetch my friends.

CHAPTER 3

Brenda?" I tried to keep my voice light, not wanting to frighten her with my theory of looming disaster. "Hey, it's Andi. Listen, something's come up, and I think the group needs to get together right away. I'm in Florida at my grandparents' beach house, and my grandfather is willing to send his plane for you—"

"I'd love to help you out"—I heard the crack of her gum—"but I have a tat scheduled for tomorrow. It's a five-hour gig, maybe more. I gotta pay the bills, you know?"

My heart sank. Until that instant, I hadn't realized how much I was counting on her. "Well—"

"Hang on a sec."

I waited, barely daring to breathe, and after a minute Brenda spoke again. "You're not gonna believe this," she said, a wry note in her voice, "but my client just texted me. He's canceling because his girlfriend threw a fit about the tat, but he's going to pay me anyway." She snorted. "So yeah, I guess I'm good to go wherever. Did you mention a private plane?"

"Yes." I sighed in relief. "I'll call Tank, too. And I have a feeling we need Daniel with us. I have *no* idea how to make that happen—"

"Leave it to me," Brenda said. "I took Daniel back to the hospital after our last little reunion, so those people know me. I'll pick him up."

I wasn't sure how she would get Daniel out of the hospital, but I had a feeling Brenda could manage almost anything.

"Okay. I'll give my grandfather your number so he can make the arrangements."

After hanging up with her, I dialed Tank's phone and was surprised when he answered right away. "'Lo?"

"Tank, it's Andi. I know you're probably in the middle of football and everything, but—"

"I'm not," Tank said. "Broke my toe last week. I'm benched."

"Wow." I paused to catch my breath. "Sorry about that."

"'Sokay. I'm third string, so it's not like the team's depending on me. Coach says I can use the rest of the season to lift weights and workout. And, you know, go to school."

"Can you walk?"

He laughed. "Sure. Just not very fast. And not very, you know, smoothly."

"Well . . ." I hesitated. "I hate to ask, with you being wounded and all, but I think the group needs to get together. Can you join us tomorrow?"

"Man, I hate to say this, but I promised the lady downstairs that I'd take her to the doctor tomorrow. She's old, so she doesn't drive. When I found out she couldn't get to the doctor, well—" he chuckled. "You know."

"Yeah." I tried to keep my disappointment out of my voice. "Brenda's coming, and she's bringing Daniel. And the professor's already here. So all we need is you."

"Sorry about that. I really am."

I waited, unable to accept that Tank wouldn't be joining us.

The idea was inconceivable, like imagining yin without yang, warp without weft . . .

I heard noise in the background—an increasingly shrill siren. "Where are you, Tank? Sounds like you're in the middle of a traffic accident."

"Maybe. I'm almost home, but there's an ambulance at my building. Hang on a minute."

I waited, staring at the ceiling, and heard muffled voices, sounds of movement, and the heavy thunk of something like a car door. Then I heard the siren again, even louder this time.

"Andi?"

I blew out a breath. "I thought maybe you'd broken something else."

"No, no—that was my neighbor. She slipped in her kitchen and fell, but someone heard her shouting and called 9-1-1. She's on her way to the hospital now."

Despite the worry in Tank's voice, my spirits began to rise. "So . . . you don't have to take her to the doctor tomorrow, do you?"

Tank hesitated, then laughed. "I guess I don't."

"So you can join us."

He hesitated again, then cleared his throat. "Gosh, Andi, I hate to be a bad sport, but I can't afford a plane ticket to Florida. I just—"

"My grandfather is sending his jet to get Brenda and Daniel, and they'll get you, too. Just let us know the nearest airport, and we'll have the pilot pick you up."

"Wow." Tank's pleased surprise rolled over the line. "Well shucks, how can I say no? I'll be there. Let me figure out where the closest airport is, then I'll call you back."

"Great. I'll see you tomorrow night."

I clicked off the call, even more convinced that the five of us were meant to be together—and together *here*.

CHAPTER 4

That night at dinner, Safta and Sabba listened in shocked silence as I described the dead, eyeless animals on the beach, then Safta shook her head. "Such a death shouldn't happen to a tadpole," she said. "All those birds and fishes. What could have done such a thing?"

"Do you really want to know?" The professor rested his fingers on the table and drummed them as he looked from Safta to Sabba.

Sabba lifted a bushy brow. "And you have the answer?"

The professor nodded. "It's no surprise—people have been talking about the situation for years now. Climate change is undoubtedly responsible for all the things we are seeing—the strange weather patterns, the animal deaths, the earthquakes. Mankind's damage to our planet has reached a critical stage, and the sentinel species are being affected. Very simple."

I dropped my fork and stared at him. I'd been working for the professor for nearly a year, and I liked him despite his tendency to be stubborn. The man was brilliant, unswervingly logical, and fluent in mathematics, physics, and chemistry, but for the first time in months, I didn't agree with him.

"Professor"—I folded my hands—"this afternoon I studied a map of places where mass animal deaths have occurred. I found another map of nations who have contributed the most to climate change. I might find your theory more believable if the patterns matched, but they're not even close. The animal deaths have occurred almost everywhere and there is no observable connection."

The professor looked at me a moment, thought narrowing his eyes, then he shook his head. "It's apples and oranges, Andi. Climate change isn't evidenced as strongly in the most polluting nations because it's in the more agrarian nations where the effects of climate change will be felt. In places where people farm for a living, a lack of rainfall spells disaster. And droughts happen because of climate change."

I didn't want to argue with him in front of my grandparents, but my gut told me I was right. I closed my eyes and saw both maps on the back of my eyelids—the map displaying countries with the most carbon dioxide emissions highlighted the United States, Russia, Australia, and Saudi Arabia. An accompanying map displaying countries most affected by climate change marked Saudi Arabia along with parts of Africa, South America, and the U.S. Neither map displayed any pattern resembling the golden ratio.

The map of mass animal deaths did not correlate with the maps of climate change. The United States and England had experienced dozens of animal die-offs, along with areas of Australia, South America, and the Arabian peninsula. But the Near East—Thailand, Japan, North and South Korea—had experienced several mass animal deaths, and those countries weren't featured on either of the climate change maps.

"Man not only has the power to change human life," the professor was telling my grandparents, "but for the first time in history we now have the power to change our planet. Unfortunately, most of our changes have been destructive because we haven't realized the significance of our actions. In the future, however, mankind will make great strides to preserve the earth and improve our standard of living."

"I blame it all on the Republicans." Sabba's face flushed as he leaned across the table. "For years they have refused to believe climate change was taking place."

"And should the Democrats get off scot-free?" Safta waved her fork at Sabba. "For years Al Gore has declared that the North Pole was going to melt—and I just read that it's getting bigger. The North Pole, melt?" She harrumphed. "Al Gore should live so long."

I slid lower in my chair and stirred my mashed potatoes, which were still hot from the KFC bag. Now that the conversation had turned political, my grandparents would argue with each other for another hour, forgetting all about me and our guest.

I glanced at the professor and saw that he was busy cutting up his fried chicken. He wasn't political, as far as I knew, but he could be as immoveable as Sabba and Safta. If he had his way, logic would rule the universe and chaos would be obliterated.

Of course, lately the professor had learned that logic didn't always win the day.

Over by the sliding door that opened to the deck, Abby was still sitting and staring out the window. Occasionally she pawed at the glass, then went back to watching. I tried calling her to my side, but each time I said her name, she looked at me, whined as if begging me to understand, and went back to her vigil.

Every whine pebbled my skin with gooseflesh.

My heart twisted as memory carried me back to all the days I used to sit with her on the deck before I left for college. She'd been my best friend in those days. When no one in high school cared to befriend the geeky girl with explosive red hair, Abby had been my constant companion and very best friend. She had guarded my secrets and listened to my dreams. She had warmed my feet while I studied and licked up the cookie crumbs from my bedroom carpet. My heart ached for her when I went away to school, but she was always waiting when I came home. We picked up where we'd left off, and for years I half-believed that time stopped for Abby while I was away.

Yesterday, however, Abby had given me an enthusiastic greeting, then gone straight to the sliding glass door to stare out at the beach.

Just like she was doing now. Just like she'd done in my dream.

I sank even lower in my chair and studied her, wondering what she knew that I didn't.

CHAPTER 5

Picking up dead birds wasn't my idea of a good time, but I figured someone had to do it. Sabba had kept his promise and sent his private plane to pick up Brenda, Daniel, and Tank. Until they arrived, I had nothing to do but play Mah-Jongg with Safta and her friends, watch the professor read, or venture out to the beach.

So I got up early, pulled a pair of shorts and a T-shirt from my old dresser, and slipped into a battered pair of sneakers I found in the closet. I smeared sunblock on my nose (redheads tend to burn easily, even in October) and pulled one of Safta's battered straw hats from a hook in the laundry room. I grabbed a couple of trash bags from a cabinet, then strode out across the deck and went down to the beach.

I wasn't alone. The beach was spotted with curious onlookers and social do-gooders. I smiled a "me too" smile at a girl dressed a lot like I was, then took a pair of rubber gloves from a table and read the sheet of instructions someone had posted:

1. Don't touch dead birds or fish with bare hands.

   No kidding.

2. Don't throw dead birds or fish back into the water. *Wouldn't that defeat the purpose?*
3. Place all dead birds and fish in a trash bag, then close securely. Leave bags by the lifeguard stand; someone from the Pinellas Fish and Game Department will pick them up later.

Simple enough. I powered on my iPhone, put the earbuds in my ears, then slipped my hands into the flimsy gloves and set out for a section of beach still littered with dead animals. The music carried my thoughts away as I knelt to clear the area around me. The fish's empty eye sockets seemed to accuse me—of what? If I'd known what killed them, I would have done something to help. Anyone would. Anyone who loved animals, that is.

After a while I stopped picking up fish one by one and began to gather them by handfuls. How many yards, I wondered, did this carpet of dead fish extend? And the birds—the tide had pushed most of them farther up the beach, but their little bodies littered the dunes several yards beyond the water's edge. If disease or climate conditions had caused their deaths, why had they fallen only here? Why hadn't they landed in my grandparents' front yard, or on the roadways? What had caused them to fall in this particular spot?

And most important, what had happened to their eyes?

The odor of decaying flesh was strong enough to overpower the tang of sea air, but after a while I grew numb to it. Numb enough that I was able to pick up a single bird, hold it in my gloved left palm, and bring it close to my face, using my right hand to probe its feathery little body. Like the fish, the bird had holes where his eyes should have been. In addition, this bird's little beak appeared cracked and some sort of brown liquid dribbled from its nostrils. The little body felt like a feathery bag of air in my hand.

When I heard the unexpected sound of a vehicle on the beach, I turned and looked behind me. A white van had pulled up near the lifeguard stand, and two men in hazmat uniforms had stepped onto the beach. Hazmats? Did these guys know something we didn't?

I dropped the little bird's body into my bag and went over to check out the new arrivals.

The van had no markings or identification on it, so for a while I simply watched the men dressed in white from head to toe. They walked over the sand as I had, but they used a long-handled tool to pick up the dead animals, then they put certain specimens into individual bags. After sealing each bag, they wrote something on it—probably date and time—and placed the sealed specimens in a cooler.

I gave them space to pick up a few corpses, then pulled out my earbuds and walked up to the closest guy. "Hi," I said, smiling. "Who are you and where are you from?"

He blinked at me as if I were a Martian who'd suddenly come up and introduced myself. For a moment he seemed taken aback, then he fumbled with his hazmat helmet and pulled it off. "Steve Laughlin," he said, his cheeks brightening as if he had suddenly realized how silly he looked in all that protective gear. "We're from the University of Tampa."

"Oh." I laughed. "I thought you were from the government."

He laughed, too. "Not by a long shot. The government's probably been here and gone already, leaving us to clean up the mess. This thing has made our biology department curious, and since it happened in our own backyard—"

"I get it. I'm curious, too." I felt the corner of my mouth rise in a half-smile. Steve Laughlin looked like a professional geek—my kind of guy. "Don't you feel a little overdressed? I mean, no one has even hinted that these animals died from contagion."

"No one has said they *didn't*." Steve smiled back at me, apparently recognizing a kindred spirit. "I've always found it better to err on the side of caution."

I nodded. "Listen, Steve—you got a pen?"

He pulled one from his pocket, and I took it. "I'm visiting the area with my boss, Professor James McKinney. We're keen to know more about this event, and if you learn anything, we'd appreciate it if you'd give us a call." I grabbed his gloved hand and pulled it toward me, then wrote on the back of his white glove. "This is my cell number. Will you call me?"

His eyes glinted with interest—more than a purely scientific interest, it seemed to me. "I'll call if you'll tell me your name."

"Andi." I released his hand and held out his pen. "Don't forget—I have friends who will be truly intrigued by whatever you learn."

His mouth curved in a slow smile. "Andi. Got a last name to go with that?"

"Maybe." I picked up my trash bag and waved. "Maybe you'll find out when you call."

CHAPTER 6

I'd gone maybe a mile down the beach when I turned to check the time. The sun stood about midway down the horizon, so Safta would nearly be finished packing.

Once my grandparents learned that I needed to invite several people to the house, they had graciously offered to leave us and spend a couple of days at their Manhattan apartment. Since Sabba had retired, Safta said, he didn't get to New York as often as he wanted to.

"I hate to put you out," I told them. "After all, I came here to see you."

"Listen, *bubeleh*," Safta said, "us you can see anytime. I see the shadows on your face, and I think your friends can help you now. Me, I will never understand the things you talk about, so you stay while we go. We will come back in a couple of days."

I reluctantly agreed to accept their offer.

Since my grandparents were leaving us alone in the house, I planned to put Tank in my grandparents' room, give the two guest rooms to the professor and Brenda, and bunk Daniel in Sabba's den, which was close to where Brenda would be sleeping.

I would remain in my old room, which still looked pretty much as it did when I left for college.

Now I squinted at people on the beach. Dozens of strangers were walking along the water's edge, but I spotted four familiar shapes coming from the house—little Daniel, Brenda, the professor, and Tank, who hobbled over the sand like a giant with a broken toe . . . because that's what he was.

I lifted Safta's sunhat and waved it, then clapped it back on my head and strode toward them. I felt as giddy as a kid, and I couldn't say why, but seeing the others made me feel a lot less melancholy.

I dropped my trash bag in the sand and ran to hug them—Brenda first, then Tank, and then Daniel. I grinned at the professor, who gave me a grudging smile as if he, too, were glad to be a part of this inexplicable team.

"Eew!" Brenda backed away, shaking her head. "I hate to say this, but you stink."

Tank was too much of a gentleman to say anything about the smell, but the strangled look on his face told me he was trying hard not to inhale.

"Andrea," the professor said, "I don't know how you can stand it out here. Come back to the house, take a shower, and let's talk. Your grandmother has ordered dinner, which should be arriving shortly."

"You bet." I grinned around the circle of friendly faces. "Just let me dump my collection bag at the lifeguard stand."

An hour later I was clean, perfumed, and sitting at the head of Safta's dinner table. She had ordered several Chinese dishes, which waited on a lazy Susan along with a selection of chopsticks and a note saying "Welcome to the Beach House."

"In a place this fancy, I know we're supposed to use good

manners," Brenda said, glancing around, "so I'll be good and not smoke in the house. But I'm starving, so if you'll pass your plates, I'll slap on some rice. Daniel, you want brown rice or white?"

Daniel shifted his gaze from the sliding glass door to look at her, but didn't respond.

Brenda nodded. "Okay, white rice it is. Cowboy, what do you want? A bowlful of everything?"

While Brenda served, I leaned back and studied her and Daniel. Something had happened between them since we were last together—the tenuous bond they established in Port Avalon was far stronger now. I could see it in the way her body curved toward him and in the way his eyes followed her as she served everyone else. Maybe he'd been afraid to fly this morning and she comforted him. Maybe he'd begun to see her as a surrogate mother. One thing I knew for sure—if the kid had managed to get inside her heart, he was the only one of us who had.

And Daniel—in Port Avalon, he had been accompanied by an invisible friend . . . a rather large friend who didn't care for the name *Harvey*. If Daniel's imperceptible protector had come along on this trip, apparently he hadn't joined us for dinner.

Brenda was watching Tank inhale a plate of Kung Pao chicken when I caught her attention. "By the way, how'd you get Daniel out of the hospital?"

She smirked. "You wouldn't believe it."

"Give us a try."

Brenda glanced around the table, then snorted. "Okay. So last time when I took Daniel back to the hospital, I had to explain why he was with me, right? So I told them that I was his aunt, and I was steamin' mad that they'd let that other couple sign him out without providing any kind of identification. I showed them a newspaper article about the murders in Port Avalon, and I told 'em Daniel had been in the middle of all that. Well."

She smiled. "They were so terrified by my threats of a lawsuit that they never asked to see anything from me. I had them put me down as Daniel's aunt, and I told them that if they ever released him to anybody but me, I'd sue the lab coats right off their pimply backsides. You should have seen 'em scampering to take care of the boy after that."

"That hardly seems logical." The professor smiled, but his eyes softened when he looked at the boy. "Surely his parents are listed in his file. I'm sure there are certain custody orders, medical releases—"

"That's the thing, Doc." Brenda leaned toward us and lowered her voice to a rough whisper. "That hospital is like the end of the earth. One look around and you know that nobody is comin' for any of those patients. I get the feelin' that Norquist is the kind of place where they put people nobody ever wants to see again."

A low rumble came from deep in the professor's throat.

"So this time when I went to get him," Brenda went on, "I sashayed right up to the desk and said I was Daniel's aunt and I'd come to take him out for a few days. The girl looked at me like I had a hole in the head, but then she called over some Deputy Dog security guard. I recognized him—he'd been on duty the last time—and he said, 'Oh, yeah, she's his aunt. She's cool.' And then the girl says, 'But I don't have her on his approved visitor list,' and the guard says, 'Then you'd better *get* her on his approved list.' So the next thing I know, I'm on some kind of list, and they're bringing Daniel out to me. The girl is watching me, though, probably thinking that Daniel will freak out or something if he doesn't know me, but he comes right over, slides his hand into mine, and off we go, just like Bonnie and Clyde."

The professor cleared his throat. "I'd choose another metaphorical paring, if I were you. Bonnie and Clyde didn't end well."

Brenda's eyes sparked with annoyance. She picked up her

fork, and for an instant I worried that she might lean across the table and stab the professor with it.

"Pinocchio and Jiminy Cricket?" Tank smiled, easing the tension. "They had a happy ending."

"Indeed." The professor nodded. "And the metaphor is more apt, considering the cricket served as the puppet's conscience. In a way, you are serving as the boy's window to the world."

Brenda lowered her fork and shot me a *is he for real?* look, and I shrugged. Being a professor, my boss often felt inclined to correct others, and Brenda didn't like being corrected.

Few people did.

"So, Miss Andi." Tank stopped shoveling food long enough to look over at me. "Why are we here?"

I bit my lip, hoping I could explain what I felt in my gut. "It all started when I had a horrible dream about Abby losing her eyes. Scarcely an hour later, the dead fish washed up and something had destroyed all their eyes. That was bizarre enough, but within minutes, dead birds started falling out of the sky, also without eyes. Then I got a strong feeling that the two events were connected—and when the professor said he'd had a dream about Sridhar and *he* had no eyes, I knew I needed you all to help me. I know there's a connection, but I can't figure out what it is."

"So what are we supposed to do?" Brenda asked.

"I have no idea." I raked my hand through my hair and propped my elbow on the table. "But I did some preliminary research and discovered that mass animal deaths are occurring all over the planet, and not only with birds and fish. Cattle, sheep, elk, crabs, oysters, honeybees, seals, starfish, puffins—"

"What's a puffin?" Tank asked.

"A kind of sea bird," I answered. "Cute little things."

Tank shifted in his seat. "Those other animals—did they lose their eyeballs, too?"

I shook my head. "I don't think so. They were just . . . dead."

"Yes, animals are dying." The professor folded his hands. "But mass animal deaths have occurred throughout the centuries. Look at what happened to the dinosaurs."

I blinked. I hadn't considered the dinosaurs, though I knew the cause for their extinction was hotly debated. Some scientists believed they died before the emergence of human beings when a meteor hit the earth; others believed the dinosaurs perished in an ancient flood. I didn't want to get into a debate about dinosaurs over dinner—the professor would certainly prevail, and we'd be distracted from the work we were supposed to be doing.

"Yes, the dinosaurs died," I admitted, "but now all kinds of animals are dying."

"Like the buffalo?" Tank asked.

I gave him a patient smile. "There's no mystery about why the buffalo nearly died out," I reminded him. "People killed them, and when they stopped, the buffalo herds came back. It's the same reason elephants and gorillas are dying now. But we don't understand why these other deaths are occurring."

"I'm sure there's a good reason," Brenda said, though she sounded anything *but* sure. "I'm no scientist, but don't they blame these things on pollution, red tides, stuff like that?"

"Sometimes they can find a reason for one situation," I pointed out, "but so many? And there's—something else."

I pressed my lips together, wondering if they'd laugh.

Brenda made an impatient gesture. "What?"

"A pattern," I said. "The golden mean. I was looking at a map of animal deaths, and there were dozens of dots all over the map. So I zoomed in and naturally the dots spread out. That's when I saw the curved spiral that looks like the inside of a sea shell—the golden mean. It occurs all over the place in nature, and it's nature's way of performing her work efficiently. Which means that if nature is killing the animals, she will efficiently meet her goals and we humans might be next."

"Whoa." Brenda held up both hands. "Step it back. I'm not getting this."

"Let me help." The professor leaned back in his chair and gave me a wry smile. "You know how Andi loves her patterns. But while the brain *does* tend to seek patterns in everything from clouds to breakfast toast, apophenia is not a true gift. We yearn for patterns because humans yearn for predictability."

"It *is* a real gift," I insisted. "I don't see the face of Jesus in mushrooms. I see . . . structures and schemes. And with all due respect, Professor, just because scientists debunk the idea of apophenia doesn't make it any less real."

Brenda and Tank shifted their gazes from me to the professor and then back to me, probably debating which one of us they should believe. Daniel just kept eating.

Brenda looked at Tank. "Maybe it doesn't matter," she said. "What matters is that next bit she mentioned—if she's right about all the animals dying and we're next, well, that's freakin' *interesting*."

Tank snorted. "Yeah. So—what *is* this mean thing?"

"The golden mean," I explained, "sometimes called the golden ratio. Philosophers consider it a definition of beauty; mathematicians call it *phi*. Fibonacci explained it as a series in which every number is the sum of the two numbers preceding it, like this: 1, 1, 2, 3, 5, 8, 13, 21, 34, 55 and so on. This series seems to be sort of a key for organisms in nature. For instance, consider flowers: the lily has three petals, buttercups have five, the chicory has twenty-one, the daisy has thirty-four, and so on. And seed heads, like sunflowers? In order to pack the seeds in so that no space is wasted and every seed receives an adequate amount of sunlight, nature needed to determine the perfect mathematical ratio for placing and positioning seeds.

That ratio is 0.618034—the ratio of phi, the golden mean. That ratio results in the spiral you see in pinecones, sunflower seeds, sea shells, even hurricanes. Artists and photographers use it in composition; architects plan buildings around it. It's perfection. Completion. It's the way nature gets things done."

"It's genius." Tank grinned. "And only a Master Creator could have figured that stuff out."

Brenda stared at me, a hard line between her brows. Clearly, she thought I was nuts.

"Let me show you." I stood and grabbed my laptop from the kitchen counter, then pulled up an illustration of the golden mean.

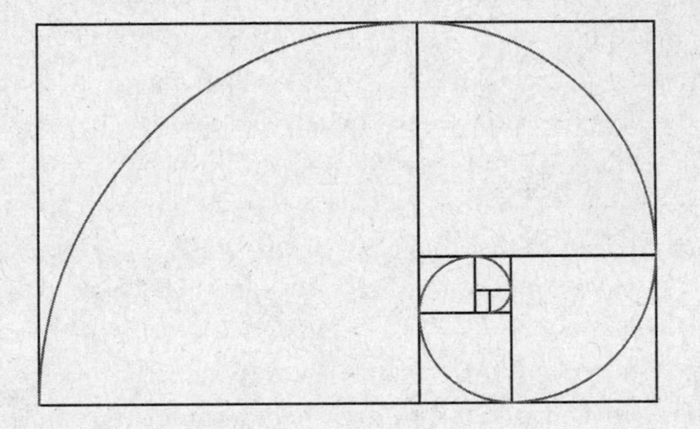

"Okay." Brenda nodded. "I may not understand all this, but it's enough that you do. But what makes you think these animal deaths have anything to do with pinecones and hurricanes?"

"Because of the pattern." On my laptop, I opened the map of animal deaths. Zooming in as before, I focused on a cluster in the south, then ran my finger over it, connecting the dots in the arch and resultant swirl.

I think even Tank was impressed.

Brenda tilted her head. "Cool."

"Is it? The golden mean is Nature in no-nonsense mode. What if she is killing the animals?"

"I wish you'd stop talking about Nature like it's a person," Tank mumbled. "Nature isn't a person, it's a creation. If someone is doin' something, it has to be the Creator."

"What if the operative force is mankind?" the professor said. "What if people have unknowingly triggered something that might result in the loss of all life on the planet?"

After a moment of heavy silence, Brenda laughed, Tank looked baffled, and the professor smirked. Even Daniel, who usually wore a blank look, seemed to have a small smile on his face. I guess that's what happens when ants look up at the rain and talk about how they might make it stop.

"We're not scientists," Brenda said, still snickering. "If what you're saying is true, what are idiots like us supposed to do about it?"

The professor stiffened. "I beg your pardon. *You* may not aspire to be an example of intelligent human life, but others—"

"Here we go," Brenda said, looking at me. "Just when I thought we were beginning to get along."

"Are we gonna be travelin' everywhere, checking out dead animals?" Tank asked.

I held up my hands, unable to handle all of them at once. "I don't know what we do next. I only know I was supposed to invite you here because Sridhar might be trying to reach us. Can we just leave it at that for now? Do you think we can spend a couple of days here without insulting each other?"

The others looked around the table, then Brenda's mouth curved in a smile. "I always did want a Florida vacation. Spending a couple of days in this big ol' beach house is all right by me."

The professor crossed his arms and lowered his chin, his way of capitulating. He was willing to humor me.

Only Tank seemed to think I might be on to something. He looked at me, his eyes shining with simple faith, then he nodded.

"All right, Miss Andi, I'm in. And I'm kinda excited to see what happens tomorrow."

I blew out a breath, hoping I hadn't brought them all down here for nothing. If I was wrong about seeing the golden ratio, or if I had misinterpreted what it meant, they'd never trust me again.

CHAPTER 7

The next morning, our agenda crystalized the moment Tank picked up a copy of the local newspaper. "Winter the Dolphin lives around here?" He grinned at me. "I saw both of those *Dolphin Tale* movies and loved 'em. Can we go see him?"

Brenda looked up, her eyes narrowed. "Who's Winter?"

"That famous dolphin who lost his tail," Tank said. "Now he wears a prosthetic."

The aquarium . . . that gave me an idea. I looked at Daniel, who was finishing up a bowl of Lucky Charms. "Feel like a trip to Clearwater?"

Daniel's eyes lit, and he looked to Brenda. I had a feeling that a local tourist attraction was the last thing on her priority list, but who could resist the look in Daniel's eyes?

"Why not?" Brenda shrugged. "Nuthin' else to do."

I knew the professor wouldn't want to go, but he'd finished the book on chaos theory and would be bored senseless sitting around the house. "All right," he said, sighing heavily. "As long as we stop by a store so I can pick up a raincoat. I don't want to get wet in one of those silly dolphin shows."

"Take one of the umbrellas," I suggested. "And don't sit down front."

The lines at the aquarium were longer than I expected, and the show every bit as wet as the professor feared. I'd been to the aquarium many times as a child, so I spent most of the hour looking around. Tank seemed entranced by the show, frequently grinning and applauding, while the professor appeared to be in danger of nodding off. Daniel watched the dolphin trainers intently while Brenda scribbled in her program.

It wasn't until the show was over and we stood to file out of the bleacher seats that I caught a glimpse of what Brenda had been doing. She'd drawn a face—a young man, probably in his early thirties, with stringy hair, round eyes, and a scorpion tattoo on his neck.

I elbowed her as we slowly inched forward. "That a client of yours?"

She glanced at the drawing, then quickly rolled up her program. "No."

"A friend?"

She shook her head.

"Someone you'd like to meet?"

She turned on me with the fury of a tigress. "It's nobody, okay? It's just a face. Don't make a big deal about it."

I put up both hands in surrender and made a mental note: *Don't ask Brenda about her doodles.*

When we finally threaded our way out of the mob, we walked over to talk to an aquarium staff member. I pulled out my university ID card and suggested that the professor do the same.

"Hi, I'd like to introduce Dr. James McKinney, PhD," I began. "I'm Andrea Goldstein, his assistant, and these are our friends. We're researching mass animal deaths and wondered if we could talk to someone on your staff who might be familiar with the animal die-offs at Indian Rocks Beach."

The girl who'd narrated the dolphin show glanced at my ID card, then jerked her head toward a nearby door. "Dr. Mathis, our marine biologist, has been following that story. Follow me, and I'll introduce you."

We walked through a doorway labeled *Employees Only* and found ourselves in a large room filled with aquariums and several in-ground pools. The aquariums housed turtles and stingrays, and in the pools I saw a small dolphin, a young shark, and a manatee. Several people in shorts and aquarium staff shirts sat on the concrete floor watching the manatee while a diver stood in the pool and stroked the animal.

"What *is* that thing?" Tank's eyes were in danger of falling out of his head. "I've never seen anything like that critter."

"It's a manatee," I told him as we walked over. "They're pretty common in Florida because they're freshwater mammals. According to legend, sailors used to see them and think they were mermaids."

Tank guffawed. "Beggin' your pardon, Miss Andi, but there's no way in the world I'd think that was a mermaid. That animal is—well, it ain't purty."

"Depends on who you ask, Tank."

An older man in a lab coat looked up as we approached, and when the girl introduced the professor, he stood and extended his hand. "Tom Mathis," he said, smiling at us. "Glad to meet you. So how can I help?"

I liked that he didn't add the word *doctor* in front of his name. "The fish and birds at Indian Rocks Beach," I said before the professor could speak and complicate our mission. "Do you have any ideas about what killed them?"

The professor crossed his arms and grinned. "Yes," he said, jerking his head toward me. "What she said."

Mathis took a deep breath and thrust his hands into his pockets. "Wish I did. They brought me a couple of specimens, but I haven't had time to examine them. We're currently facing a crisis with our manatee population—we've lost ten mature adults, several dolphins, and a half-dozen pelicans from a hotspot in the Indian River Lagoon. We don't know what's killing them, either."

"A hotspot?" Brenda crinkled her nose. "Is that anything like a hot spring?"

The marine biologist shook his head. "A hotspot is a dangerous location for wildlife. The entire lagoon used to be heavily polluted, but the river has mostly cleared. Except for that one spot—we still have animals dying in that area, and we're clueless."

"What about their eyes?" Brenda asked. "The animals from the hotspot—do they still have eyes?"

The scientist exhaled slowly. "Some of them have their eyes, yes. Others . . . well, we assume they're missing their eyes because decomposition takes place more rapidly in water."

I smiled at Brenda, grateful that she'd asked the question. She'd received a non-answer, but at least we knew that other animals were being affected in the same way as our birds and fish.

"I'm sure you see dead animals all the time," the professor said. "From predators, boat accidents, poisons—"

"Of course we do," Mathis answered. "But not all at once, and not overnight like some of these cases. You might find this interesting."

He gestured to a table covered with plastic bags. Inside each bag I saw a sizable fishing hook. Some of the hooks still had fishing lines attached.

"We pulled all of these from the stomachs of manatees or dolphins," he said, "but the hooks weren't the cause of death. We're still searching for that."

"Global warming?" Tank offered, leaning on a table to take the weight off his injured foot.

Mathis shook his head. "Doubtful. The entire lagoon would be affected by climate conditions." He looked at me and smiled. "I appreciate your interest, but I simply hadn't had a chance to do necropsies on the Indian Rocks animals. I'm sorry I can't be of more help."

"Thank you for your time," I said, pulling one of the professor's cards from my purse. "And if you have a chance to examine those fish or birds, will you give us a call? That card has Dr. McKinney's cell number."

Mathis promised to do what he could and slipped the card into his pocket.

Despite the small confirmations, I led the way out of the building feeling as though I'd led the team on a wild-goose chase.

At least Tank and Daniel had enjoyed the dolphin show.

CHAPTER 8

So we sat through that dolphin show for nothing," Brenda said, settling into one of my grandparents' deck chairs. She held a sweating glass of lemonade, complete with a paper umbrella, which I'd added as a festive touch. Brenda probably thought I was silly and frivolous, but I was only trying to keep her happy. If we were going to learn anything, we needed to cooperate.

"The trip wasn't a total washout," I insisted.

"Yeah, I got to see Winter the Dolphin," Tank said, grinning as he carefully lowered himself into one of the wooden deck chairs. "Man, he's a real inspiration, you know? I know athletes who get hurt and think they're gonna be benched forever, but if a big fish like that can lose his tail and find a way to stay in the game—"

"Your toe's gonna heal, big guy," Brenda interrupted as she fished a pack of cigarettes out of her purse. "Don't worry, you'll play football again."

"And it's a mammal, not a big fish," the professor added. He tilted his head. "By the way, Tank, I seem to recall that you . . .

did something to my leg when we first met. It was injured, but you touched it and then it wasn't injured any more."

Tank shrugged as a flush began to creep up from his collar. "Sometimes I can help."

"So why"—the beginning of a smile quirked the professor's mouth—"haven't you been able to repair your broken toe?"

Tank's flush deepened until the tip of his nose was glowing like Rudolph's. "Um . . . sometimes it doesn't work. So when I couldn't fix it, the team doc taped my toes together and told me to make the best of it."

"You're a good sport." The professor lifted his glass in a mock salute. "Here's to hobbling with dignity."

I looked at Daniel to see if he would smile or say something about the dolphin show, but he sat on the deck steps next to Abby. Both were staring out at the beach, their heads cocked at identical angles.

The sight sent the memory of my dream rushing through me, shivering my skin. But this was reality, and everything was okay. Abby wasn't growling.

"I know," Brenda said, exhaling cigarette smoke as she followed my gaze. "They look cute sitting together like that. I can't figure out if Daniel is copyin' the dog, or if the dog is copyin' Daniel."

I leaned forward to study the pair. When Daniel moved his head to the right, Abby did, too, almost as if they were connected by a string. "I don't know, either," I whispered. "But it is amazing, the way they mirror each other."

"You have to admit, Andi," the professor said, his tone flat and matter-of-fact, "Dr. Mathis was no help today."

"I think he was quite helpful." I straightened. "He gave us another piece of the puzzle, don't you see? He's dealing with bizarre animal die-offs, too, and he even gave us a term for an active location—a hotspot. For some reason, part of the Indian

River Lagoon is affected when other areas aren't, and maybe that's the same reason this beach is affected when none of the other beaches are."

The professor looked away and sipped his lemonade, a sure sign that he didn't have an answer. When some people met unanswerable logic, they raised their voices. The professor raised a glass. Fortunately, for the last few months his glass had contained only nonalcoholic drinks.

I was about to mention the manatees, but I stopped when Abby growled. The hair at the back of her neck had risen, and she was no longer looking at the beach, but at the sky. Beside her, Daniel stared upward, too, and his hands had curled into fists.

Brenda was saying something about how ugly the manatees were, but I cut her off with a flick of my hand, then pointed to Daniel and Abby. Tank and the professor must have seen my gesture because silence fell over our group as we watched the watchers without any idea of what we were seeing.

In Port Avalon, we had seriously entertained the idea that Daniel's invisible friend was real and the kid could see things the rest of us couldn't. Whether he was seeing into another dimension or a spirit world I couldn't say, but there he was, looking, watching something invisible to my eyes. . . .

A chill touched the base of my spine. Was Abby seeing . . . *had* she been seeing . . . the same thing?

"Abby?" I finally said, keeping my voice calm so as not to spook her. "Abby, it's okay."

The dog leapt to her feet, her hair bristling along her backbone as she stared up at the cloudless bowl of sky. Daniel stood beside her, his hands knotted so tightly that his arms trembled.

"Abby—"

In an instant, Daniel flinched and ducked and the dog leapt off the porch and soared over the steps. She landed on the sand and took off at a run, barking as though her life depended on being heard. As Abby ran, Daniel moved to the bottom step. For a moment I was afraid he'd take off after the dog, but Brenda took charge. "Daniel—stay with us, baby. It's not safe out there."

I don't know how she knew that, but Daniel trusted her. He stayed on the step.

The professor stood and stared out at the beach. "Do you see anything? Anyone?"

"Not a thing," I whispered, hoping Brenda was wrong about the beach not being safe. But my dream had warned me otherwise.

Tank shook his head. "Just water and waves. A couple of people walked by a few minutes ago, though."

"We're going to be all right," Brenda said, speaking in the tone a mother might use to soothe a child. I knew she was trying to keep Daniel from running off. We didn't know much about the boy, and though he'd been calm so far, I was pretty sure he could lose control if something flipped his switch. After all, there had to be a reason he was living in a hospital for the mentally ill. . . .

I moved to the lowest step so I could grab Daniel if he started to run. From there I saw that Abby had reached the beach, and through the path in the sea oats I could see her running back and forth, barking like crazy at something no one else could see. Then she fell silent and sat on the sand, as if waiting.

"Finally." Relief filled Tank's voice. "When our dog used to bark like crazy, my grandpa always said she was keeping the elephants out of the yard. I'd say, 'But Grandpa, there aren't any elephants,' and he'd grin and say, ''Course not. She does a good job, don't she?'"

Is that what Abby had been doing at the window? Keeping something evil away?

I whistled, knowing that the sound would bring her back. She'd come running, tail wagging, because she'd accomplished whatever she'd set out to do. Then I felt a trembling against my leg, and when I looked down, I saw that Daniel had gone pasty white. His arms were thumping at his side, beating against his thighs, and he looked for all the world like he wanted to turn and run back into the house, but loyalty or fear or something held him in place. I was about to take his hand and lead him up the steps, but Abby started barking again so I turned and saw her snarling and flashing her canines, then she ran into the water and started to swim toward the horizon. The sight was so unexpected and unusual that I forgot about Daniel and stared, watching Abby's bobbing head until it disappeared amid the swells and I couldn't see her anymore.

"Abby!" I screamed her name, my throat tightening. When she didn't answer and I still couldn't see her, I kicked off my shoes. "I've got to get her," I told the others. "I love that dog!"

I took three long strides toward the beach, then a shrill cry shattered my focus.

"*Nooooooo!*"

Something grabbed my arm. I turned, wondering what in the world could possibly make a sound that bloodcurdling, and to my horror I saw Daniel standing right behind me, his fingers clutching my sleeve, his mouth open and his eyes wide. "Don't go!" he yelled, his face reddening with effort.

Bewildered, I looked up at the others. They were all on their feet, staring at Daniel with confusion and bewilderment.

"Daniel?" Brenda flew down the stairs and fell to her knees in the sand. Her fingers fluttered over his head, his shoulders, his form as if she were afraid to touch him. "Are you okay?"

He closed his mouth and released my sleeve, then his eyes filled with tears. We waited, hoping he would speak again, but he simply lowered his head and trudged back up the steps and across the deck, then went into the house.

Tank, the professor, Brenda, and I stared at each other, not knowing what to say.

CHAPTER 9

We left Brenda at the house with Daniel, who had gone into Sabba's den and curled up on the couch, burying his face in a pillow. Since he was either asleep or pretending to be, we figured it was best not to disturb him.

"I'll sit out here and watch TV or something," Brenda said, sitting in the living room. "If he needs me, I'll be here."

"Do you think he'll talk again?" Tank looked from Brenda to the professor. "He doesn't say much."

"Unless he wants to," I said.

"At times of great duress," the professor added.

I pressed my lips together and led the way back outside. I didn't understand what kind of duress Daniel and Abby had been under, but now that Daniel was safe, I had to find Abby. Most Labrador retrievers are good swimmers and love the water, but Abby had been acting crazy when she took off. Plus, dogs weren't allowed on this beach, and I needed to find her before someone called Animal Control to pick her up.

The professor, Tank, and I spread out and walked south along the beach, stopping to ask people we met if they'd seen a chocolate Lab in or near the water. We got a lot of strange looks and head shakes, and one prim lady in a housecoat reminded me that dogs had their own beach in Pinellas County and weren't supposed to share the sand with people. "Worms, you know," she said, sniffing. "And all these people walking around in bare feet."

I didn't have the heart to tell her that barefoot people stood a greater chance of stepping on glass or being stung by a stingray than getting worms from a dog, so I thanked her with a smile and kept walking. After about thirty minutes of beachcombing, I whistled, caught the professor's and Tank's attention, and pointed north. "Let's head back," I called. "She wouldn't have gone this far south."

As we moved north, Tank drifted from his center position and hobbled a few feet away from me. "I wouldn't worry about the dog," he said, obviously trying to ease my anxiety. "Labs are great swimmers. And dogs can find their way home pretty easily."

I looked over at him, grateful for his concern. "Thanks, Tank. I really appreciate your help, by the way. Not many people would agree to come out here and help me scour the beach, especially if they had a broken toe. The professor came only because I threatened to surprise him by translating his next speech into binary code."

"Shucks, Andi, I'm from a place where there ain't no beaches, so this is a treat for me. In fact"—he lowered his head so I couldn't see his face—"being with you is a treat, too. All week, most weeks, I'm with a bunch of rough, rude football players, and none of them can hold a candle to—well, none of them are much fun to be with after practice. So I'm glad you called. I'm glad I'm here."

He looked at me then, and in the golden glow of sunset I saw hope, happiness, and sincerity shining in his eyes. I'd seen that look in his eyes before, so maybe I realized what he was up to even before he did. If you took one innocent, good-hearted lug, added in a decent-looking girl of the right age, and multiplied the mood with mystery, danger, and a gorgeous sunset, you ended up with a guy who didn't know the first thing about having a girlfriend but was awfully eager to learn.

I knew one sure way to nullify this equation before things got out of hand.

"Tank." I stopped and met his open gaze head on. "I appreciate you so much. I've never had a brother, so I think I'm going to like having you around."

I gave him a sweet smile, punched his rock of an upper arm, and strode toward the house, leaving him and the professor on the beach.

CHAPTER 10

Dr. Mathis?"

We looked up from our pancakes when the professor raised his voice. His cell phone had rung during breakfast, and he hadn't bothered to leave the table.

I felt a tingle in my stomach as the professor listened to the marine biologist.

"Are you quite certain? . . . Um-hmm. Nothing else could have done that? I mean—"

I grinned when the professor fell silent. Judging from the disgruntled look on the professor's face, Dr. Mathis was standing his ground.

"I see," the professor said. "Well, we appreciate the information."

He disconnected the call, slipped his phone back into his pocket, and picked up his knife and fork.

"Well?" I leaned toward him. "What did Mathis have to say?"

The professor began to cut his pancakes. "He necropsied the birds and fish last night. He could find no reason for the fishes' demise, so the man is obviously not very good at his job. Apparently your aquarium needs a more qualified marine biologist."

I bit back my impatience. "Professor! Is that all he said?"

Finally, he met my gaze. "Though he did not know what killed the fish or removed their eyes, he did determine that the birds died from blunt trauma. He believes the impact may have forced the eyes out of their sockets." He lowered his knife. "May I eat my breakfast now?"

I shifted my gaze to Brenda. "Blunt trauma? Like someone hit them?"

"Or they hit somethin'," Brenda said, thought working in her eyes. "Maybe they hit a jet."

I shook my head. "There were no jets overhead. Flights coming into Tampa International circle Tampa Bay, not this beach. Believe me, I've flown into Tampa enough times to know."

"It could have been a small plane," the professor said. "Any small plane could have been buzzing around and flown through a flock of birds. You have to admit, Andi, there's nothing strange about that. Airplanes and birds are always colliding in midair."

"A flock," I said. "A flock is what—twenty birds? A hundred? *Thousands* of birds fell on our beach, Professor. I heard one of the guys from UT say there had to be at least ten thousand dead blackbirds. That's a big flock."

"Maybe they hit, like, a thunderhead." Tank lifted his orange juice. "That's up in the sky, isn't it?"

The professor opened his mouth, but I kicked him under the table, knowing he was about to remark on Tank's intelligence. The big guy couldn't help it if he spent more time in the locker room than in his books.

"A thunderhead," I explained gently, "is a cloud. It may be dark, it may have winds and lightning, but I don't think birds could kill themselves by running into one."

"So maybe this marine biologist guy is wrong," Brenda said. She poured two sugars in her coffee, then closed her eyes and breathed in the aroma. "Fresh ground coffee in the morning. I tell ya, I could get used to livin' like this. What do you think, Dan?"

I looked at the boy. He had gotten up to eat breakfast with the rest of us, but he kept glancing toward the sliding doors as if he expected to see Abby at any moment.

"I know, Daniel," I said. "I'm waiting for her, too."

"Did you check the SPCA?" Tank asked. "Someone might have taken her to the lost and found."

"I'm going to call this morning. I'm also going to go out again and talk to people who live near the beach. She's such a nice dog, she'd have gone with anyone. But she's wearing a collar and tag, plus she's microchipped, so I'm hoping someone will call. I'm sure she'll turn up soon."

Brenda shrugged. "I hate to tell you this, but where I'm from? A good-sized dog like that would end up in the center of a fight pit as a bait dog. I have to say, though, last night your dog looked like she could give those fighting dogs a run for their money."

I stared at Brenda, horrified by the thought of Abby in a dog fight. I knew Florida had its share of such horrible crimes, but this was Pinellas County, home to thousands of retirees. None of our neighbors would be involved in something so despicable, but you never knew who might be strolling down a public beach.

"So . . ." I pushed away from the table and tapped my fingers on the edge. "We're stuck, huh? We don't know what killed the fish, we don't know what killed the birds, and we've lost Abby. This weekend is turning out to be an unmitigated disaster."

My cell phone jangled. I pulled it from my pocket and stared at the unfamiliar number, then pressed Receive. "Hello?"

"Andi? Are you ready to give me your last name?"

I blinked, caught off guard by the question. But the voice evoked a distant memory, and suddenly it all came back: the white van on the beach. The hazmat guy.

"That all depends," I said, glancing at the professor. "Were you able to learn anything about why those animals died?"

"Do I get a name if I tell you?"

"You've already got my number," I reminded him. "So let me hear what you have to offer."

"The fish—unknown cause of death," he said. "The birds—COD is blunt trauma."

I closed my eyes. "So what caused the trauma?"

"I wish I could tell you, darlin'. But truth is, that's all I've got. That's all anybody's got right now."

I heaved a sigh. "Goldstein," I told him. "My name's Andrea Goldstein. And thanks for the answer."

I put my phone on the table and folded my hands. "Dr. Mathis's opinion was just confirmed by a guy from the University of Tampa's biology department. The birds died because they ran into something solid, and from the sheer number of dead birds we can surmise that the thing they ran into must have been huge. But there are no jets, wind turbines, or skyscrapers along this stretch of the beach."

"Okay, then." Tank slapped out a *ta-da-boom* on the table. "We have a confirmed fact. We're making progress."

Brenda snorted. "Dial it back, CSI. We got a big pile of nothin'."

The professor lifted his coffee cup as if to say *touché*, but even though we had another piece of the puzzle, I had never felt farther from the truth.

"Andi, I appreciate your intellect, I am grateful for your technological assistance, and I admit you're pleasant company, but I simply cannot believe that you would ask us to go door to door like encyclopedia salesmen."

"Ease up, Professor," Brenda drawled. "The last encyclopedia salesmen died years ago. Nobody goes door to door anymore, especially in Florida." She turned to me. "Isn't this the state where people can shoot you if you knock on their doors without an invite?"

"No one's going to shoot you." I lifted my chin, struggling to overcome my rising irritation. "All I want you to do," I said for the fourth time, "is go up and down the beach and ask people about two things: have they seen Abby, and did they see anything odd on the day of the fish and bird kill. Is that so hard?"

The professor grumbled under his breath, but he didn't speak again. Once he left the house, though, I knew he'd fill someone's ear with complaints.

So I'd have to go with him.

"Brenda"—I pointed south—"why don't you and Tank go that way? You can take Daniel with you. The professor and I will head north."

Disappointment filled Tank's face for an instant, but he smiled at Brenda and stood back as she and Daniel went down the stairs. The professor merely lifted his brows when I looked at him. "Ready?"

"You are a clever girl," he said, leading the way over the deck. "Pairing that lovesick boy with Brenda."

I nearly laughed aloud. "Tank is not lovesick," I said, grabbing an umbrella from the stand near the back door. "He's just infatuated or something."

The professor snorted. "Be careful, Andrea. Inside the biggest men reside some of the softest hearts."

"Did you make that up?"

"I would never write something so maudlin. I probably read it on a Hallmark card."

We walked the fifty or so yards to the closest house, then approached the back deck. All the beach houses in this area had welcome mats at the front and back doors, since residents spent so much time on the beach. The professor remained a good ten feet behind me, undoubtedly embarrassed by the possibility that someone might think he was some kind of solicitor. Dressed the way he was, in long pants and a tweed sport coat, complete with elbow patches, he *did* look like a guy who might be peddling Dyson vacuum cleaners.

"Hello?" I knocked on the screen door. "Anybody home?"

A moment later an older woman approached, a wide smile beneath her curious gaze. I searched my memory for her face, but she must have arrived after I left for college. "Hello?"

I introduced myself, said I was staying with my grandparents next door, and asked if she'd seen Abby. The woman was distressed to hear the dog was missing and promised to call if she spotted her.

"One more thing," I said. "Did you notice anything unusual the day the fish and birds died?"

The woman blinked rapidly. "They died right in front of us, isn't that unusual enough? I called 9-1-1 the day it happened, but they wouldn't send the police until we were practically suffocating from the stench."

"Did you see anything else unusual? Did you, for instance, see anything in the sky?"

The woman tilted her head, then opened the screen door and joined us on the deck. "I didn't see anything," she said, "because it was raining and I tend to stay inside when it's damp and cold outside. But my nephew was out here that morning, and he said he saw something. He sounded crazy, though, and then the birds and fish started dying so I forgot about what he said."

"Is your nephew around? I'd love to talk to him."

The woman's smile faded. "Of course he's around. He's unemployed, lazy, and he sleeps until three o'clock because he stays out drinking with his pals all night. He's around, all right." Her face brightened. "Want me to wake him?"

"He wouldn't mind?"

"Of course he'll mind. But I won't." She winked. "Just a minute, let me get the lazybones out of bed."

She went back inside the house, her slippers shuffling over the tile floor, and I turned to study the horizon. The professor stood facing the water, too, his arms folded, his eyes intent on the sky.

"I know what you're thinking," he said, his voice flat. "And you know it's preposterous."

"Nothing's preposterous, Professor. What is it Sherlock Holmes always says? 'When you have eliminated the impossible, whatever remains, however improbable, must be the truth.'"

"You haven't ruled out a small plane, a weather balloon, and a fireworks display. Those birds could have run into any number of things within a few miles of this place. The storm gusts could have picked up their bodies and dropped them here. Stranger things have happened before."

"Yes, but let's hear what the nephew has to say."

A few moment later I heard the slap of bare feet on the tile, followed by the squeak of the screen door. "Yeah?"

I turned. The nephew—in his early thirties, stubbled, bed-headed, and wearing only a pair of cargo shorts—squinted at us, his round eyes bleary and bloodshot. On the side of his neck I saw a tattoo—a scorpion.

For a split second, the world seemed to sway on its axis, then I grabbed at the strings of reality and held them tightly.

"Sorry to disturb you," I said, knowing that the conversation would be significant, "but your aunt mentioned that you saw something odd the day of the mass fish and bird kills. Would you mind telling us what you saw?"

"Why?" He leaned against the doorframe and crossed his arms. "Nobody believes me."

"I'll believe you," I said, looking steadily into his eyes. "I've found myself believing a lot of unusual things lately."

He looked at me for a moment, then the corner of his mouth quirked in a smile. "It was early," he said. "I'd been out partying and I'd had a few drinks, if you know what I mean. I walked up to the house this way, 'cause I didn't want to wake Aunt Edna. The sun was just coming up behind the house, so I dropped into a chair to chill out for a minute. That's when I saw them."

"Who?"

"Balls of light. Orbs, I think they're called. Three of them were bouncing around near the waterline. It looked like they were playing tag or something, but they never went far, just in and out, up and down. Then one of them zoomed right up here and hovered next to the porch railing. I was more than a little freaked. I couldn't move, so I just sat there while it sort of hung in the air and studied me. Then suddenly, zip! It flew out over the water and disappeared. Its buddies went with it."

"Did you hear anything?"

"Don't think so. Maybe a little varooming sound, like the light sabers in *Star Wars*. Or maybe I just I *thought* I heard that. I don't know."

"How long did the orbs stay around? Five minutes? Ten?"

He shook his head. "I don't know. It was like time stood still, you know? When I shook myself out of my daze, the sun had come up and everything looked pretty normal, except for the rain. I thought I must have been dreaming or somethin', but when all those fish started washing up right after, I wondered if those orbs had anything to do with it."

"They were only balls of light?" I asked. "Nothing tangible? You didn't see metal or wood or vinyl?"

"Nothin' like that. Just light. But not mindless light, if you know what I mean. They knew what they were doin'. The one came over and studied me like I was some kind of specimen in a jar."

I slipped my hand into my pocket so he wouldn't notice that I had begun to tremble. "So they were autonomous."

"Yeah, whatever." He scratched absently at his chest, then looked at me. "You think they had anything to do with all that stuff dying?"

"I don't know. I wish I did." I nodded, then smiled. "Thank you."

"No problem." As the professor and I turned to walk away, he followed us to the edge of the porch. "Hey, if you need something to do tonight, we'll be gathering down at the corner bar. We got everything we need for a party—"

"Thanks!" I waved, then joined the professor on the beach.

CHAPTER 11

An afternoon shower sent all of us scrambling back to the house. "I thought Florida was supposed to be warm and sunny," Brenda groused.

"It is," I assured her, "but this is October, so you never know what you're going to get. It can be hot one day and cool the next—and it can rain almost any time."

After drying off, we went into the kitchen to make coffee and hot cocoa. I had to admit, the warmth of the liquid in my cup took the edge off the chill I'd felt ever since meeting Edna's nephew and hearing about what he saw on the beach.

The professor shared the nephew's story with the others. "But he was clearly drunk, and probably delusional," he finished, "so his story is not credible."

"I disagree," I countered. "He may have been drunk, but drunks still see things." I lifted a brow and lowered my voice. "With all due respect, Professor, you should know that."

The professor pressed his lips together, then looked over at Brenda and Tank. "I'm not sure what you've picked up, but you might as well know that I am a recovering alcoholic. And Andi is correct, of course. Drunks do see things. Sometimes they see things that are actually present."

"I would have believed him if he said the moon was made of green cheese," I said, then made a face. "Well, not really. But I knew he was going to tell us something important the minute he walked out on that deck."

"Because you noticed another pattern?" the professor said, softly mocking.

"Because I'd seen him before—on Brenda's aquarium program."

Brenda sputtered into her coffee mug, then set it down and wiped her mouth with the back of her hand. "You're kidding."

"It was the same guy, down to the scorpion tat. You *saw* him."

Brenda didn't answer but stared at her mug.

"The guy saw *orbs*?" Tank made a face. "Somebody better fill me in."

"Technically, an orb is a sphere," I said. "Lately the term has caught on with ghost hunters and UFO researchers. When they speak of an orb, they are talking about a ball of light that moves independently and shouldn't be part of the scene."

"It's poppycock," the professor said, sipping his coffee. "And those people are kooks. There's absolutely nothing scientific about their so-called investigations—it's all hocus-pocus performed for television cameras or YouTube videos."

"I don't know." Brenda shook her head. "I've always had respect for people with mysterious gifts. A witch once worked a root on my aunt—sent Auntie to the hospital until some church women came and prayed over her."

I made a face. "A *root*?"

"A spell." Brenda gave me a one-sided smile. "My world has mysteries, too. Some that science can't begin to explain."

"Actually," I said, leaning against the counter, "an alien craft *is* a logical explanation. It could emit heat or sound or some substance that poisoned that particular variety of fish. The birds could have run into the craft, suffering blunt trauma and dying from the impact."

"Maybe it didn't have to be big." Brenda frowned. "Maybe they were small but there were a lot of 'em, so that's why so many birds died." Her frown deepened. "That makes sense, though the thought of outer space creatures scares me spitless."

"Then why didn't anyone else see this improbable fleet of space ships?" the professor asked.

"A cloaking device." Brenda smiled and lifted a brow at Daniel. "Anyone who watches *Star Trek* knows about cloaking devices."

"Why didn't anyone *hear* this fleet?"

"It could have made sounds above or below the range of human hearing," I pointed out. "After all, dogs can hear things inaudible to the human ear—"

I froze as my thoughts crashed into a wall. *Abby heard it.* The birds, the fish . . . the dog heard everything. Ever since I'd arrived, Abby had been sitting by the sliding glass door, listening, watching, whining. But she ran off to chase some invisible something *after* the birds and fish died. So whatever had done the damage . . . was still around.

Without saying another word, I set my mug on the table and walked to the wide glass doors. Gray clouds hung low over the sea, heavy with rain, and mists skirted the surface of the sand. Clouds were the perfect camouflage for anything . . . or anyone . . . that might be patrolling the earth.

Or spying on us.

In Port Avalon, the professor had made enemies who escaped. A man and a woman, he said, who had taken Daniel out of the hospital and worked with A.J. Van Epps to test the boy's supernatural abilities. We had good reason to believe the man and woman were affiliated with the Institute for Psychic Studies, which we'd pretty much trashed before we all found ourselves in Port Avalon. . . .

I pressed my hand to the glass and peered past my reflection into the gathering darkness. Was Abby still out there? Were other things—aliens or spies—out there? Were they hovering nearby, maybe watching us now?

I startled when I heard the click of the latch on the door. I looked over and saw Daniel standing next to me, his gaze focused on something beyond the glass. Without speaking, he grabbed the handle, pulled the door open, and stepped into the storm.

What?

I turned to look at Brenda, but she and the others were already out of their seats and hurrying toward me. "Daniel," Brenda called softly, not wanting to frighten him. "Daniel, kid, come on outta the rain."

If he heard her, he gave no sign of it. Instead, he walked forward, crossing the deck, stopping only when he reached the railing. For a moment, I was afraid he'd continue down the stairs and make a run for the water as Abby had, but he stood motionless, his hands at his sides, as if he were waiting. For what?

"Never thought I was signin' on to be a babysitter," Brenda grumbled good-naturedly, but she went after the kid, ignoring the rain pelting her head and shoulders. "Danny, come on in before we catch a cold."

"He's not budging," I remarked to anyone listening. "I don't know what has mesmerized him, but he's not going to move."

"Let me take them an umbrella." Tank pulled one from the milk can and opened it, then crossed the deck in three giant hops. Like some kind of overgrown butler, he held the umbrella over Daniel and Brenda.

"What are you all looking at?" I called through the open

door, crossing my arms in a halfhearted effort to ward off the cold breeze. "What is Daniel looking at?"

"Something," Tank answered, an edge to his voice. "Something evil. I can feel it."

"There's *nothing* out there." Pushing his way through the space between my shoulder and the edge of the door, the professor went outside, too, and peered into the darkness. "There's nothing here," he yelled, glancing back at me. "Just sand, sea, and a pack of fools."

Then Tank tipped his head back and called out, his voice loud enough for all of us to hear above the wind and rain: "Open our eyes."

Before I could draw another breath, the air between my friends and the beach seemed to shimmer, then a glowing shape filled the space. The shape was vaguely spherical, but the edges were soft and translucent. The outline glowed big and round like an odd golden moon, then it began to spin, slowly rotating until I saw an opening—a window?

I didn't realize I had walked onto the deck until I felt the splash of rain on my cheeks. A rough fabric brushed my elbow, and I knew the professor had joined me at the railing, all of us drawn forward by the object . . . or our own fascination. I opened my mouth to say something, but I couldn't speak. My lips were as dry as paper and my tongue as heavy as lead.

The opening—the window—shifted and shimmered, then a covering peeled back, like skin from an orange. From within the sphere, a form appeared—round, soft body, stick-thin neck, circular face. Long nose topped with a red rubber ball. Clown-like smile exaggerated and painted red beneath black eyes, with no white, no shine, no life at all.

Long fingers extended from a wrinkled hand and seemed to invite us closer, then one of the fingers waggled back and forth like a scolding schoolteacher's. The eyes blinked; the head turned. And then I heard a scream—not a human scream, but the sound of an anguished dog in pain.

Daniel's agonized howl mingled with my own. With my senses reeling and my gaze still fixed on the horrible caricature in the orb, I reached out for the touch of something—anything—solid, and caught Tank's arm. Beside me, Daniel stiffened, reached into the darkness, and collapsed.

The window closed, the orb spun and zipped toward the water, then it vanished.

CHAPTER 12

I closed my eyes as a scream clawed in my throat. That cry—surely that wasn't Abby. That couldn't be Abby. Why would anyone want to hurt her? She had never done anything but love me and my grandparents. She was the personification of love and faithfulness, so why would anyone—anything—want to hurt her?

This time Brenda couldn't stop herself. She ran forward and drew Daniel into her arms until he came to, then she kept holding him as he flailed, slapped at her head, and kicked her legs. The professor finally pulled Daniel away and helped him stand—alone in a corner, trembling and staring at nothing—until he could regain control of himself.

Brenda crumpled in a heap on the deck, burying her face in her hands as her shoulders shook with soundless sobs. Tank positioned himself in front of the steps in case Daniel decided to run down to the beach, but after a few minutes the professor succeeded in persuading Daniel to go inside the house. The professor went with him, but I stayed on the deck, my hands gripping the railing, rain dripping from my nose and hair.

Tank held the umbrella over me, sheltering me from the

percussive *plops* of fat raindrops. "Miss Andi," Tank said, his voice urgent, "what you saw out there—it can't hurt you. What we saw, what we heard—"

"The professor says we should only believe in what we can see and hear and touch," I answered, my voice shaking. "Well, I saw and heard, and I'll never forget it. We all saw and heard it—"

"Andi—" Tank hesitated. "There are more things in this world than you know."

A wry chuckle slipped from my lips. "This isn't the time to be paraphrasing Shakespeare."

"I'm not paraphrasin' anything," Tank replied. "But surely you know—I mean, look at us. Look at this group and think about the odds against us ever comin' together. We've been given special gifts, and I know there's a powerful reason for those gifts, just like I know there's a reason we've been brought together."

I pressed my hand to my head and turned toward the house. "I need to get inside. I need . . . light."

I made my way back to the kitchen, where the professor handed me a clean towel. When he saw how my hands were trembling, he wrapped the towel around my shoulders, then went back to keep an eye on Daniel.

Tank stayed outside with Brenda, urging her to get up, even slipping his arm around her thin shoulders. I don't know how he did it, but he got her to come back inside, though the woman he escorted through the doorway looked nothing like the confident, sassy woman I'd come to know. Her eye was partly swollen—probably the result of a collision with Daniel's elbow—and her face was wet with tears and rain. Tank guided her to a chair, then handed her a clean towel as well.

"Let me turn on that fancy hot drink machine," he said, hobbling into the kitchen. "I think I can set us all up with coffee or somethin'."

A few minutes later, we were all sipping from hot mugs and

sitting around the fireplace in the living room. Daniel lay in a huddle on Safta's bearskin rug, the professor had taken Sabba's easy chair, and Brenda perched on the edge of the oversized ottoman. I sat on the floor by the fire and watched as Tank finally took a seat next to Brenda. Only after a few minutes had passed did I realize that he had picked up a book on his way to the living room.

"I think"—my voice trembled—"we need to talk about what just happened. We need to compare notes from our varied perspectives."

"Nothing happened." The professor crossed his arms. "The boy had a breakdown, that's all."

I stared at the professor, but he refused to meet my gaze. Instead, he set his jaw and stared at the flickering fire.

I understood. His mind was still trying to sort through everything he'd endured in Port Avalon. Asking him to absorb all this, too—it was too much.

"I saw . . . an orb," I said, turning to Brenda and Tank. "For lack of a better word, I guess that's what I'll call it. It had a window, and I saw this . . . clown-like creature in it. And then I heard Abby scream."

Brenda, Tank, and the professor turned their heads sharply, looking at me with incredulity.

"You heard a dog?" Brenda said. "I heard a child."

"Sounded like a lineman to me," Tank said. "Like the guy I hit last season and broke his leg. I didn't mean to hurt him, but accidents happen. At least that's what Coach told me."

I looked at the professor and waited. Finally, after several seconds had ticked away on the mantel clock, he shook off his false indifference. "All right, I saw it," he said, his jaw tight. "I don't know what it was, but it was exactly like you described, so I have obviously been influenced by the power of suggestion."

"And what did you hear?" Brenda asked.

The professor clamped his lips together.

"Professor?" I tilted my head to meet his gaze. "We all heard something. What did you hear?"

A muscle worked in his jaw, then he glared at me. "I heard myself, okay? I heard myself screaming like someone had set me on fire. And while self-immolation is not something I aspire to, the experience was entirely too much like what I felt in the House in Port Avalon. So I do not wish to discuss it further."

"It's as if someone"—Brenda paused as if choosing the right word—"knows us well. They're messing with our minds."

"If someone is messing with our minds," I said gently, "then who is that someone?"

Silence stretched between us as we considered the possibilities. We had seen strange forces at work in the past few weeks, and the fact that we kept finding ourselves together had persuaded us—or at least some of us—that someone kept bringing us together. If the uniting force was good, and the destructive force evil . . .

The professor would insist that life was rarely so black and white.

Tank broke the heavy silence by picking up his book. "Listen to this, guys: 'Therefore the land mourns, and everyone living there languishes, wild animals, too, and the birds in the air, even the fish in the sea are removed.'"

I looked at him, bewildered. "What are you reading?"

Tank shrugged. "I found this book on your grandfather's nightstand. I was flipping through it when I saw this bit about the birds and fish."

"Let me see that." I stood and went to Tank, then recognized the book. "You're reading from Hoshea. This is Sabba's copy of the Tanakh."

"Really." Cynicism lined the professor's voice. "Bad enough that we've all shared a mass hallucination due to the suggestions of the drunken fool next door, but to follow it all up with religious nonsense—"

"It's all here." Tank lifted the book. "The birds dying, animals, fish—it's all predicted here. The earth is mourning. The birds and fish and wild animals are dying, but no one wants to recognize the truth. Andi has seen the pattern, and she knows what it means."

"Tank." Brenda glared at him from beneath her dreadlocks. "What we saw out there had nothing to do with God."

"You're right about that." A small smile lit the big guy's face. "But what if God has an enemy, and his time is running out? He could be feelin' the pressure, and be determined to destroy as much as he can in the short time he has left. He's sent his minions out to destroy and confuse people—"

"That's it." The professor shook his hands as if washing them of everything we had seen and heard. "I'm going to bed. I'll see you all in the morning, when I expect we'll all be eager to get back on the jet and head home." He turned toward me. "Be sure to thank your grandparents, et cetera, et cetera. This hasn't exactly been a relaxing time, but it has convinced me that I am as susceptible to mass hallucinations as anyone else."

One by one, they headed toward their rooms—Brenda and Daniel left after the professor, and soon only Tank and I remained by the fireplace. I missed Abby. The heaviness of grief was like a dead body strapped to my shoulders, weighing me down, draining my energy and my joy.

I knew Tank sensed my sadness. Anyone who knew me had to realize that if someone took Abby, they'd stolen something vital and precious from me.

"I . . . miss her," I said, my voice breaking. "I don't know if you can understand, but for years, she was the only friend I had. I was a misfit, but never around her."

Tank remained silent, letting my words hang in the space

between us. And then, just when I thought he hadn't been paying attention, he reached out, caught my chin, and lifted my face to meet his gaze.

"God doesn't lie," he said simply, his gaze shifting toward the sliding doors as if that gruesome caricature of a clown might return at any moment. "And He's more powerful than anything out there."

"Then why," I asked, "couldn't He keep Abby safe?"

I got up and went to my room, too, leaving Tank alone to guard the fire.

CHAPTER 13

We ate breakfast—or Daniel did, anyway—in a thick silence. None of us wanted to talk about the night before, but every other topic felt silly and stupid in comparison. How could we talk about the weather or travel plans after what we'd seen? How could we talk about *anything*?

As shaken as we were, I didn't feel uncomfortable. For some reason I felt weirdly connected to everyone at the table. Despite our differences and our disagreements, I knew I would rather be miserable with them than indifferent by myself.

Brenda made coffee, then filled four mugs and passed them out. Like automatons, we poured in cream and sugars, then sipped and stared at the polished surface of the dining room table.

I never would have believed that Daniel would be the first to speak.

"They were real," he said, making eye contact with me for the first time in—well, ever. "I see them all the time."

I blinked at him, then looked at the others, who were also watching Daniel. The boy didn't seem inclined to say anything else, though, and went back to eating his cereal.

"The kid is right, but I don't think they were aliens," Tank said. He spoke slowly, as if carefully considering each word. "I don't think that clown thing and his buddies came from another galaxy. They might have come from another dimension, and I'm pretty sure they've been on earth and around earth since the birth of this planet. I think they were demons, just like the ones we saw in action at the Institute for Psychic Studies."

I couldn't have been more surprised if Tank had begun to sing opera at the breakfast table. The big guy was usually two steps behind us, yet there he was, offering a theory that sort of made sense. But was it our answer?

"Demons?" Brenda looked at him with bleary eyes. "You're telling me I couldn't sleep last night because I saw a *demon*?"

Tank shrugged. "Fallen angels, demons—call 'em whatever you want. But they're real and they meddle in people's affairs . . . even though most sophisticated folks don't want to admit they exist."

"And that explains why you believe so devoutly," the professor said. He twisted in his chair. "So what's the point, Tank? What are we doing here? If these events are caused by supernatural forces, we mere humans may as well go home."

"No, because we have gifts. And we have power." Tank flashed a grin bright enough to be featured in a toothpaste commercial. "The power's not in us, but God can give us the power to fight them and the people who work for them. And more important, I think God's the one who brought us together. We're supposed to cooperate and warn people. We're supposed to interpret the signs."

"I didn't get a call from God," Brenda said, "I got a call from Andi. And God didn't fly me here, Andi's grandpa did. As I recall, you were on the same jet."

"Why did you come?" Tank asked quietly. "And don't tell

me you came because you wanted a few days in Florida for vacation. I know better."

Brenda glared at him a minute, then looked at Daniel. "Don't matter why I came, and what happened yesterday don't matter, either. All that matters now is that we get Daniel back to—well, get him back for some help. This trip has stressed him out, and they're not gonna let me see him again if I don't take him back so he can get better."

"Wait." I looked around the table, frustrated that the others appeared to be giving up. "Aren't we going to investigate this further? We didn't solve anything. The animals—the planet—is still in danger."

Brenda set her coffee cup down. "Nothin' I can do about that. Like I said, I have to earn a livin'."

"I'm done here, too." The professor pushed back from the table. "My brain can only tolerate so much madness."

I waved my hand, about to suggest that talk some more, but a blur of movement outside the window distracted me. People on the beach were running toward something in the water.

My stomach tightened for no rational reason. Leaving the others at the table, I went to the sliding doors and stepped out, then ran down the stairs. From there I could see something tumbling in the wavewash, something dark, with straight legs like a table. Something brown, like *chocolate* . . .

I broke into a run.

By the time I heard someone shout, "It's a dog!" I was already approaching the water's edge. I splashed into the shallows and gripped Abby's collar, then pulled her onto the sand. Rigor mortis had already set in. Her legs were splayed straight out, as if she'd died in a standing position. Her brown eyes were missing, the empty sockets encrusted with sea salt.

I fell to my knees and balled my hands into tight fists, struggling against the sobs that welled in my chest. Soft murmurs from bystanders wrapped around me, and a moment later I heard the pounding feet of Daniel, Brenda, Tank, and the professor. They stood silently, watching me weep in the tide, then Daniel knelt beside me, too, bending to press his forehead to Abby's.

"Why did this happen to her?" I asked, glancing up at Tank. "You know who did it—I heard her scream. They are evil, and they did this because they hate. I never understood hate until this minute, but I understand it now. They hate us, so they hurt and destroy and inflict pain on the ones we love. . . ."

In a flash, I remembered how my grandparents spoke of the Nazis, and the people they knew who had lost mothers, fathers, siblings, and families in the Holocaust. Hatred—pure and simple and evil—had gripped Hitler and spurred him to blind his people with hostility and contempt. Whoever had tortured and killed Abby would do the same thing to a child, a family, anyone. That kind of hatred was elemental; it did not discriminate, but it loved to destroy innocence.

I lowered my head, too, and dared to place my hand on Daniel's shoulder. I needed to touch him, and in that moment I think he needed to be touched.

The bystanders peeled away, probably uncomfortable with our open grief. When we were finally alone, Tank knelt across from me and Daniel. I thought he was going to help me carry Abby's body up to the house, but instead he placed one hand on Abby's side and the other over her ravaged face.

A rush of gratitude flooded my heart. He was silently telling me that he understood, and he was sparing me the sight of her awful wounds.

I placed my hand on Abby's belly, next to Tank's. "It's okay," I whispered, my voice as ragged as my emotions. "If you'll help me carry her, we can find a spot to—"

I stopped, suddenly aware that the fur next to Tank's hand

felt *warm*. His hand had reddened, and Abby's body seemed to grow warmer with every second. Tank's eyes remained closed, but I could feel *energy* flowing from his hands, over the dog, even tingling my fingertips—

Abby whined. I righted myself so suddenly that I fell on my butt in the wet sand. Daniel laughed as he buried his fingers in Abby's soggy fur, and Tank finally opened his eyes. He lifted his hands, releasing the dog, and Abby bounded up, then turned and shook herself off, her brown eyes sparkling above an enthusiastic grin.

I looked at the professor, who was speechless, probably for the first time in his life.

"Cowboy"—Brenda began, turning wide eyes upon Tank—"when did you become a superhero?"

Tank stood and brushed sand from his hands. "I dunno. Doesn't always work. But I figured that God wouldn't want the other to have the final word here, so I gave it a try."

He extended one of his healing hands toward me and helped me up, then gestured toward the house. "Guess we'd better go give that dog a bath."

Abby had not only been restored to me, but she seemed to have the energy and spunk of a pup. Tank and I knelt by Safta's huge bathtub as my girl splashed and alternated between trying to eat the soap bubbles and kissing our chins. I was exhausted by the time Tank hauled her out of the tub and toweled her dry.

I watched, amazed, as my rejuvenated Abby ran through the house, then sat prettily and offered her paw to everyone, even the professor.

Not once did she go to the window. Not once did I hear her growl.

We were in the living room when I finally gathered the

courage to ask Daniel the question uppermost in my mind. "Abby saw the evil, too, didn't she?"

The boy slowly turned and met my gaze, then he nodded.

My heart thumped at the confirmation.

"And that evil—is it still out there?"

One corner of Daniel's mouth lifted in a small smile, then he shook his head.

I felt my shoulders relax. I could leave now, knowing that Abby would be safe with Safta and Sabba.

"So what did we accomplish here?" Brenda asked, looking from me to the professor. "This wasn't much of a vacation."

"You got to see a dolphin show," Tank offered.

The professor snorted.

"I think"—I paused to gather my thoughts—"I don't think we did anything to that thing out there, but I think it did something to us."

Brenda made a face. "Speak for yourself. I'm fine."

"Not like that. I think it did something *in* us. We saw something horrible, and then we saw a miracle. The yin and yang, good and evil. And for now at least, the evil's gone and we're all here. Together."

The professor pressed his lips together, displaying his disagreement, but what could he say? He'd seen everything we'd seen, and he had no explanations for any of it.

"I'm done with that kind of crazy stuff. For now, anyway." Brenda stood and gestured to Daniel. "Let's go get your bag packed, okay? It's time to go home."

After Daniel stood and followed her, so did the professor and Tank.

I sighed and did the same.

EPILOGUE

Sabba and Safta arrived as we were packing. I gave my grandparents a hug, thanked them for their hospitality, and promised that I'd check in after I got back to my apartment.

"Did you have a good time with your friends?" Safta wanted to know.

"I don't think the word *good* really does it justice," I told her.

Before I left, I gave Abby a good brushing and thanked her for being so vigilant in her protection of us. "I see what you were doing," I whispered in her ear, "and I love you for it. Take good care of the folks, okay?"

We were lined up outside the house, waiting for the car Sabba had hired to take us to the airport, when a kid on a bike rode up and handed an envelope to Brenda. "For you," he said, then he grinned and rode off.

"Secret admirer?" Tank asked, winking at her.

Brenda snorted. "I'm not likely to find one in this neighborhood. This is probably a citation for trampin' through somebody's sea oats."

She took out the paper, read it, and frowned.

"What's it say?" I asked.

She shook her head. "This makes no sense to me, but maybe you guys can figure it out."

She handed me the paper, which I read aloud: "'Likewise you, human being—I have appointed you as watchman. Yechizk'el.'"

I glanced at the back of the paper to see if I could find any clues as to who had sent it, but the page was blank.

"Forget it," the professor said, turning to search the road for any signs of our cab. "Someone's idea of a joke."

But it wasn't. With everything in me, I knew it was another piece of the puzzle.

THE GIRL

ALTON GANSKY

CHAPTER 1

Snow

JANUARY 1, 7:10 A.M.

"You're gonna love being a cop, Tank. Yes sir, you'll fit into the sheriff's department just fine."

I wanted to slap my forehead but I had too much respect for Uncle Bart. Instead, I kept my eyes directed out the passenger side window of the patrol car and took in the scenery.

"You don't even have to finish college, boy. Of course, that doesn't hurt nuthin', but I'm just sayin'."

That made me take my eyes off the snow-covered fields. "Momma wanted me to go to college, Uncle Bart. I gotta go. I *wanna* go. I like it."

"Hey, no problem, son. There's no rush. I could use you up here with me. I might just be a small town sheriff, but that doesn't make the work no less noble, does it?"

"No, sir. I admire what you do. I just don't know if I'm cut out to do it."

Uncle Bart—Sheriff Bard Christensen to everyone in Dicksonville, Oregon, and the other small towns that make up the county—directed the car around a bend. I could feel the tires slip some and heard snow crunch beneath the treads. The tail end of the patrol car did a little fishtail.

Uncle Bart chuckled. "I love driving in this stuff. I wish we got more snow around here. Not enough to shovel, you know, just enough to keep life interesting."

I released my grip on the door handle. To tell the truth, I had enough "interesting" stuff happen to last me a lifetime, and I had a feeling more was coming.

"I didn't scare ya, did I, boy?"

"No, sir. I was just makin' sure the door didn't open. It might get dented or somethin'."

Uncle Bart smiled big. "Sure ya were, son. Sure ya were.

A few moments later, Uncle Bart turned serious. "I think that's him up there." He nodded to a man standing on the side of the road. He looked to be in his early seventies and wore a heavy wool coat over what I guessed was denim overalls. We pulled to the side and exited the car, then walked to the old guy. Yep, overalls.

"Sheriff." The man nodded. He had an accent. Maybe from the northeast. Maine?

"Mr. Weldon." Uncle Bart extended his hand.

"You can flush all the 'mister' stuff, Sheriff. Just Chuck. That's what everybody calls me. Chuck."

"Yes, sir." Uncle Bart smiled. "Chuck, this is my nephew, Bjorn Christensen, but everyone calls him Tank."

"Ayuh, I can see why. You're a biggun', aren't you, son?" He looked puzzled. "Wait, ain't you the one who plays for the Huskies?"

I didn't know how to answer. Thankfully, he moved on.

"Not much of a college football man, myself, but the sheriff here was telling everyone about you gettin' that football scholarship. He's real proud of you, he is. I hear that he'd lock up anybody who didn't want to listen." He followed the comment with a chuckle.

Uncle Bart came to my aid. "You called about something strange on your property, Mr. W—, um, Chuck."

"Ayuh, that I did. Could be real important so if yer done yappin' I'll show it to you."

"If *I'm* . . . yes, sir. Of course. Lead the way."

"Follow me." Chuck talked as he walked. "So, Tank, you gave up football to become a deputy?"

"No, sir. I'm just visiting." I was about a step and a half behind him. "Football is over for my team. We didn't have our best year."

"We watch the Rose Bowl together most years." Uncle Bart acted casual but I could tell he was scanning the ground. I knew why. When Mr. Weldon called he said there were some strange tracks Uncle Bart should see. "Probably just a three-legged rabbit," he had said. That was Uncle Bart's way. He made light of things. Everything.

"It ain't far, maybe another hundred yards or so. I was out this morning checking on my animals. I don't have many no more. Too old to take care of them. Too much arthritis. My feet ain't much good anymore. Sugar in the blood, don't ya know."

"Diabetes?" I said.

"Ayuh. I should've taken better care of myself, but I was always more concerned about the ranch. Ain't always been in the condition it is now. We used have a good number of cattle and other livestock. . . ."

A sadness seemed to trip him mid-sentence.

"They give you pills for the diabetes?" It was none of my business, but I couldn't help asking. Uncle Bart cut me a hard look. I shrugged.

"Stuff's expensive. The insulin is worse, and all I got these days for income is my Social Security check, and there ain't much of that."

The sadness that seized Mr. Weldon turned on me. I felt like I should say something but couldn't put the right words together. Poor old guy had everything working against him: age, disease, and poverty.

"I got three things to show ya. Here's the first. I ain't gonna tell you anything about it. I'll let you jump to your own conclusions."

"Let me guess." Uncle Bart was smiling again. Maybe he was trying to lighten the moment. "Bigfoot came to visit."

"If he had, he'd be lying dead in the snow. I'm old, but I can still shoot straight." He slowed. "Now watch yer step."

I had noticed that he stayed close to the tracks he had made when he walked to the road.

Mr. Weldon pointed. "As you can see, Sheriff, these ain't Bigfoot tracks. If anything, they're Littlefoot tracks. If you catch my drift."

I stayed close to Uncle Bart and looked at what Mr. Weldon was pointing at.

A chill rose inside me. It didn't come from the snow, or the stiff breeze coming off the nearby mountains. This cold started inside my bones and clawed its way to the surface. No heavy coat can keep out a chill that starts on the inside.

Uncle Bart swore.

"Yep. My sentiments exactly," Mr. Weldon said. "You see now why I called so early?"

I'm not one of those people who frightens easily, and Lord knows I'd seen some pretty chilling stuff over the last few months. During football season, I faced some pretty big guys. I'm big. Six-foot-three and a solid 275, but the guys I played against last season were bigger and meaner. There were several players on my University of Washington team who made me look small. Still, they don't frighten me. I like to think my faith has something to do with that, but this—

"Tell me what you see, Tank." Uncle Bart was testing me. For a moment I thought about giving a dumb answer—people are used to that from me—but this seemed too important. Besides, I didn't like the idea of trying to fool Uncle Bart. "Stop thinkin', boy; give me your first impressions."

"It's a footprint." I raised a hand. "I know, that part is obvious." It took me a moment to get the words to flow. "It's no animal. It's a human print. Small and—" The next part was difficult to say. "I can see toe prints."

"What does that mean to you, son?" Uncle Bart raised his gaze to me. Maybe it was my imagination, but he looked almost as white as the snow on the ground.

"They're the footprints of a child. A child without shoes." I inhaled a lungful of cold air. "Uncle Bart. The kid is going to freeze his feet off."

He turned to Mr. Weldon. "Give me a sec, then I want to see what else you have to show me."

Mr. Weldon answered with a nod.

Uncle Bart raised the portable radio mic that hung from his shoulder to his lips, pressed the microphone key, and reported what we had found. "I want everyone on this, Millie. I also want the helo up in the air. You know who to call for that."

I'd met Millie several times. She's a nice fifty-something-year-old woman who has been the lead dispatcher for as long as I can remember. She always took holiday duty. I felt sorry for her at first, but now I was glad she was on the job.

"Chuck, how far did you follow the tracks?"

I could see a set of larger footprints running side by side with the kid's. The prints were not only larger but deeper, and I didn't have to be a detective to see the sole prints of the walker's boots. No doubt they belonged to Mr. Weldon.

"About a quarter mile, I'd say. Like I said, my feet ain't real good. I hate to admit it, but if I'd kept going I might be out there facedown in the snow. Thought it the better part of valor to call you."

"Yes, sir. You did the right thing." Uncle Bart looked in the direction of the tracks. "Mr. Weldon—sorry, Chuck—I think me and Tank can move a little faster on our own. You've already been out in this stuff too long. If you don't mind, we'll go it alone."

"I had two other things to show you, but I appreciate it. Just follow the tracks. You'll come to a fence. You'll see what I saw. A little farther on you'll come to a barn. Take a moment there."

"We will, Chuck. We'll keep you posted."

Mr. Weldon started to go.

"Hang on a sec, Mr. Weldon." I stepped to him and placed a hand on his shoulder. "I'm sorry you're having a rough time. Maybe God will bless you for what you've done this morning."

He looked puzzled. "Um, okay, if you say so, Tank. I'm just doing what any man with a heart would do. . . . Why is your hand so warm? It feels like you been holding a potato fresh out of the oven."

I shrugged. "Thank you again, Mr. Weldon." I released him and followed after Uncle Bart, praying all the way that we could find the child before frostbite had turned bare feet black.

CHAPTER 2

"This Ain't Right"

7:20 A.M.

We hadn't taken more than a dozen steps when the gray skies began shedding more snow. The wind picked up, too. I was wearing an extra police jacket, nylon on the outside and stuffed with whatever they put inside to keep a body warm. It kept the wind out but couldn't protect my face. Snow and tiny bits of ice nibbled at my skin, and the cold wind was pushing through my jeans and trying to freeze the hair of my legs. I didn't focus on the discomfort much, not with some kid out here tromping through the snow with no shoes. Images fought for my attention and none of them were good. They all ended the same way: a dead child frozen in the snow. *Help us find the child, God. Please, please help us find the kid.*

Prayer is natural for me. I'm not from a religious family, and I'm the only one of my friends who goes to church. Most just tolerate my beliefs; others poke fun at me. It makes no difference.

Truth is truth, and it remains that even if I'm the last one alive to believe it.

Uncle Bart, a man who could talk the ears off a statue, had gone silent and glum. I guess he had images flashing in his brain, too.

"You're worried about the snow covering the tracks, aren't you, Uncle Bart?"

He grunted. "It ain't making our job any easier. That's a fact." He didn't look up when he spoke. His eyes were glued to the impressions.

I walked on the left side of the small trail; Uncle Bart trudged along on the right. Like my uncle, I had trouble tearing my eyes away. Still, from time to time, I scanned the white land in front of us, hoping, praying to see a small figure still upright and moving. All I saw was a thickening blanket of white and split-rail fence sixty or so yards ahead. As we neared, I could see the tracks continued on the other side.

We stopped at the fence. Uncle Bart squatted near the tracks and studied the ones closest to the fence. He rose and looked over the other side, careful not to touch anything. "This ain't right, Tank. Not by a long shot, it ain't."

"What ain't right?"

He started to say somethin' but held up. "You tell me."

"Uncle Bart, I don't think we should be wasting time testing my detective skills. I don't have any."

"Just look, boy. Look here." He pointed at the last two tracks closest to the fence. I did. "Now look at the ones on the other side. Do they look the same?"

I had no idea what he was getting at. All I could think of was the lost kid who was gonna need his feet amputated. Of course, I'd do what I could, but my gift is a little iffy. Sometimes it works, sometimes it doesn't. "They look the same to me, Uncle Bart. What am I missing?"

"Should they look the same?" he pressed.

"I don't know, Uncle Bart, but I do know that if we don't find that kid—"

"I know what's at stake here, Bjorn. I don't need to be reminded. Just look."

He used my real name, something I hadn't heard him do since I was in kindergarten. So I looked. And I looked. The prints on the west side of the fence looked identical to those on our side.

Then I looked at the top rail of the fence. Two, maybe three inches of snow rested on the rail. The same amount on the rail to the north. The top rail to the south was different. Much of the snow had been knocked off. I could tell from Mr. Weldon's tracks that that was where he crawled over. The disturbed snow on the other side was proof of it.

"Do you see it?"

I nodded. "How is this possible?" I'm not the brightest crayon in the box, but I'm not stupid, no matter what anyone else thinks. "If the kid climbed the fence, the snow on the rail would have been knocked off. Even if the snow continued, the amount on the rail would be less than that on the others."

"Right."

"So maybe the kid just crawled through. . . ." Dumb thought. Crawl through or climb over left the same problem. The snow on the rails would be very different than the snow on the rest of the fence. I moved closer and looked over the top rail. The tracks were unchanged. No sign of someone disrupting the snow by crawling through it or jumping down from the fence. It was as if the kid had just walked through the fence—no, as if the kid had floated over the barrier.

"What's your take on this, Tank?"

I shook my head. All I could do was repeat Uncle Bart's words. "This ain't right." Then a second later I said, "We're not giving up, are we?"

He narrowed his eyes but still managed to look disappointed. "Of course not, Tank. It's my job to gather information as I go. Who knows what will be important later?"

He scaled the fence and I followed by climbing the rails right in front of me. An easy job, but my foot was reminding me that I was still nursing a bad toe. A lineman showered his attention on me by pivoting his three hundred pounds on that toe. I'm good now, but sometimes the toe likes to remind me it's there.

"I can't believe Weldon trudged all the way out here, not as old and sick as he is." Uncle Bart shook his head. "I have to admire the old coot."

"He's worried about the kid. He has a good heart."

"Yeah, I saw through that grumpy act pretty quick." Uncle Bart followed the tracks with his eyes. "There's the barn he mentioned. Let's pick up the pace, Tank. That toe let you jog?"

"I'm good to go."

We set off in a jog. Man, my foot hurt.

We reached the barn. It was an old building but someone had taken pretty good care of it. The wood was painted brown and the roof looked in good shape—at least, it didn't bow any. The blanket of snow concealed the roofing material beneath—

What?

I blinked a few times, then turned to face Uncle Bart, but he was rounding the barn. He reappeared a few moments later. "The tracks continue on the other side. You know why that's impossible, right?"

I didn't answer; I backed away from the building.

"What's wrong, Tank?"

I pointed to the top, to the snow, to the footprints walking up the slope of the roof.

Uncle Bart followed my example and stepped back from the barn. He stared at the tracks on the roof, then looked at me. At first he said nothing. He returned his gaze to the roof, then the tracks on the ground. More silence, then a string of curses lit up the air. I didn't interrupt.

I no longer felt cold. I no longer noticed the wind or my almost-healed broken toe. I was numb, not from the freezing air but from being forced to face the impossible—again.

"This is a joke, Tank. It has to be some kinda sick joke. And when I find out who's behind it, I'm gonna kick his butt from here to Mexico and back. . . ." He went on like that for a couple minutes. He got hotter and his language got worse. I used the time to restart my brain.

The fence with the undisturbed snow was too much to take in, but this, well, this almost shut me down. From the looks of things, the kid we were tracking had flown over a fence and, apparently, onto a roof. Maybe Uncle Bart was right: This was all a gag, a joke played on the sheriff. If so, then I could understand Uncle Bart's reaction. Of course, I wouldn't help him kick the perpetrator's butt up and down the west coast, but I probably wouldn't stop him from doing so. The way I felt at the moment, I'd be willing to sell popcorn at the event.

"Now we know why Mr. Weldon told us to take a few moments here." My voice sounded strange to me. I hoped I sounded normal to Uncle Bart. "I'm gonna check out the other side of the barn." I had to assume that there was still a kid missing. If Uncle Bart was wrong and we turned back, then we could end up finding someone's kid dead and alone. Before I rounded the corner, I saw Uncle Bart remove his smartphone and start taking pictures.

On the other side of the roof was the same kind of tracks descending the slope. They went right to the eave, then picked up on the ground as if the hiker had twenty-foot-long legs with tiny childlike feet. The image would have been funny if I wasn't standing in ever-increasing snow with a missing kid on my mind.

I looked at where the tracks on the ground picked up. I had

learned a couple things from Uncle Bart's insistence that I study the fence. This time I didn't need his encouragement. I did my best to look for clues, but the only thing I saw was the same set of tracks as we had been following. The stride was the same. The impressions the same. No sign that someone jumped from the roof. If this was a gag, then the guy pulling the joke was good. Really, really good.

I heard an electronic squawk, then a voice. Uncle Bart was on the radio. He rounded the barn, then looked up beyond the roof to the slate gray skies. First came a thumping sound like rhythmic thunder, then I spotted the sheriff's helicopter.

"We'll have answers soon." Uncle Bart watched the craft sail overhead, directly over the tracks.

"Did he see anything on the way in?"

Uncle Bart shook his head. "They disappear two miles up the trail. Just disappear in the middle of a snow-covered field. I have him looking for other tracks. Didn't make much sense to the pilot, but I told him nuthin' about this makes sense."

He was right about that.

Found and Lost

7:52 A.M.

The warmth of the patrol car felt good even though I worked up some internal heat jogging back with Uncle Bart. The helicopter pilot had told us the tracks we were following ended two miles farther on from the barn. That was too far to trudge in the snow. Driving made more sense. Under Uncle Bart's order, the 'copter kept searching. Maybe the kid transported or whatever to a place nearby. I would have thought that was a stupid idea if I hadn't seen what I had seen.

"You okay, Tank?" My uncle steered the patrol car down the slick road, moving faster that he should. Earlier he said he loved driving in these conditions. He didn't look like he was having as much fun now.

"I'm worried about the kid." I didn't look at him. I needed to keep myself together for Uncle Bart—for the kid in the snow.

"You always did have a big heart. Maybe too big."

"You're not worried?"

He pushed his lips in and out a couple of times. "Yeah. I'm worried."

I believed him. I could hear it in his voice. Truth was he had a pretty big heart himself, especially when it came to children. He and Auntie June never had kids. It wasn't talked about in the family, but it was assumed that they were just one of the couples who couldn't have kids. All that love he would have had for a son or daughter got lavished on other people's children and me. Lord help anyone who hurt a child in Uncle Bart's presence.

He let off the gas and let the car slow under its own weight. A couple of moments later he tapped the brakes. Anyone who hit their brakes on an icy road like this was looking for an expensive tow home. As the car slowed, he flipped on the light bar. Red and blue splashes of light danced on the snow and the trees that lined the south side of the road. He pulled onto the shoulder facing oncoming traffic—if there had been any—and let the car slide to a gentle stop.

"Let's go."

He was out of the car before I could unbuckle my seat belt.

I had to jog a few steps to catch up to him. He plunged into a small stand of trees, the one the 'copter pilot told us about. He slowed, glanced around. "I'm going south, you go north. Maybe the kid ducked in here to get out of the snow."

The logical thing for me to say was "But the kid's tracks stop in the middle of the field. The pilot told us so." I didn't say that. Why would I? I had seen the fence. I had seen the barn. For all I know, the kid flew to the moon. Once you cross over into the world of the impossible, you learn that anything can happen. I've been in a house that came and went as it saw fit, seen thousands of eyeless dead fish wash up on shore in Florida and equally eyeless birds fall from the sky. I've seen and been attacked by evil beings in a place that was supposed to be a school for gifted kids. These days I can believe the impossible without raising a sweat.

"Got it." I looked at the ground. I searched behind trees. I peered under bushes. The good news: I didn't find a body. The bad news: I didn't find anything. The stand of trees was not large, just the leftovers from when some farmer cleared an area for his crops. That probably happened decades ago. Some farmers and ranchers left trees up for a wind block.

I wove my way through the trees, ignoring the snow bombs they dropped on me, and saw nothing. The whole time I prayed for help, but I couldn't seem to get prayers above the tops of the trees. Once I reached the edge of the tree stand, I turned and worked my way back, taking a different path. When I got to where I started, I found Uncle Bart waiting for me. His expression told me he found no more than I had.

"I wanna take a look at those tracks in the field. I don't know that it'll do any good, but I don't want to overlook anything."

There was little more that he could do. The helicopter was still searching and every deputy in the region was driving the roads and lanes. I even heard Uncle Bart ask Millie to call up the volunteer search-and-rescue team. They would soon be searching using horses, dogs, and off-road vehicles.

We slogged through the snow, leaving a set of our own tracks behind us. Ours and the kid's were the only tracks visible. The kid's steps just ended in the middle of the field. He had disappeared.

"It's like the kid just evaporated into thin air." Uncle Bart was sounding discouraged and angry. "I see it with my own eyes and I still don't believe it. This is impossible. I'm starting to question my sanity."

Before I could offer any encouraging words, his radio crackled to life. It was Millie from the station house.

"Sheriff, you need to return to town."

He keyed the mic. "I'm not coming back until I have found this kid."

"That's just it, Sheriff. We found her. She's in town. Standing in the middle of Main Street."

"How do you know it's the same kid?"

"Well, she's a kid and she's barefoot."

"I'm on my way. Get an ambulance. She's gonna need medical care."

"We can't get close to her, Sheriff. She goes nuts if anyone approaches."

Uncle Bart paused, then, "You try, Millie. Maybe she'll respond to a woman."

"I thought of that, Sheriff. She doesn't like me or any other woman any more than she does men."

"I'm on my way. Keep people away from her. I'll come up with a plan."

We sprinted, as much as the snow would allow, back to the car. Uncle Bart added a siren to the lights and had us motoring down the road in moments.

"She's alive," I said. "Thank God, she's alive."

"I got a strange feeling about this, Tank. I don't know why."

I had a guess, but I kept it to myself.

The drive back didn't take long, but even with traffic pulling over for us, it seemed to take a day and half. Time is funny that way. We pulled into Dicksonville and onto Main Street just a few blocks past the sheriff's station.

The first thing I noticed was a patrol car pulled across the center line of the street in a one-car roadblock. Made sense. If the girl was in the middle of the street then someone had to stop traffic. I assume another deputy had done the same farther down the road.

The presence of the deputies was no surprise. Uncle Bart had ordered them to return to town. He wanted eyes on the girl. Slowly, Uncle Bart pulled around the parked patrol car and crept forward. People in the street stepped aside for him.

A short distance away, I saw a circle of people surrounding a child. My heart broke. Being surrounded had to be terrifying. "No wonder she's upset. She's like a trapped animal."

"I was thinkin' the same thing, Tank."

We exited the patrol car. A uniformed deputy approached. "Hey, Sheriff."

"Hey, Wad. Fill me in."

Deputy Waddle—everybody called him Wad, which I don't think he liked but put up with—was tall, wiry, and had an inflated Barney Fife ego. He wasn't the nicest guy I've met. Uncle Bart once told me that Wad was a pimple on most people's butts. I've had trouble shaking that image.

"Hey, Tank. How's college life—"

Uncle Bart cut him off. "Focus, Wad."

"Yes, sir. I was first back from the field. Someone reported a child in the street. When I arrived I tried to move her to the sidewalk. Didn't work out so good."

"What do you mean you tried to move her?"

"You know, Sheriff. I tried to pick her up and carry her to the side. She went ape on me. I had to back off."

From the look on Uncle Bart's face I could tell he had a few words for Deputy Wad, but he swallowed them whole. "Let's get the crowd back. They're making me nervous, and if they make me nervous they gotta be terrifying the girl. Move 'em back, Wad. Let's give the kid a little room to breathe."

I followed Uncle Bart but stayed well back of the kid. She didn't need a mountain like me towering over her. Once the crowd cleared I could see the little girl. She looked to be about ten, had blond hair that parted down the middle and hung to her shoulders. Her hair was wet, which made sense since she had been in the snow. She wore a white, short-sleeved blouse, the kind with frill on the sleeves. I'm sure women have some name for it, but I don't know what it is. She also wore jeans. They were soaked below the knees.

It took a moment for me to muster the courage to look at her feet. A glance told me she wore no shoes, but I needed to look closer. I expected to find red skin on its way to frostbite black. I didn't see that, but then I was several yards away. I knew she had been in the cold long enough to need medical care. A short distance down the street sat the ambulance. The EMTs were near the vehicle, waiting to be called in.

The little girl watched as gawkers backed away. She made no attempt to flee. Instead, she stood on the blacktop as if she had grown roots. She seemed free from pain and the effects of the cold wind swirling down the street. She did, however, look concerned, eyeing everyone in her line of sight. Uncle Bart smiled at her. He was a man with a friendly face and nonthreatening manner. If anyone could gain her trust, he could.

Or so I thought.

He held out both hands, showing that he held nothing that could hurt her. He took a step forward and for a moment I thought she would scream. Uncle Bart stopped. "Okay, okay, little one." He took a step back, then dropped to one knee. "Nobody is gonna hurt you. I'm your friend." He pointed at his badge. "See, I'm a policeman. Children can trust policemen." He spread his arms like a parent calling for a hug. The kid didn't move.

She stayed put, her gazed fixed on him. She raised one arm across her chest. At first I thought she was mimicking Uncle Bart's movement when he pointed at his badge, then I noticed she was holding something. I couldn't make it out. It reminded me of a scroll. A scroll of brown paper.

"Maybe I should go around behind her." It was Deputy Wad. He was moving in Uncle Bart's direction.

Uncle Bart smiled at the little girl, held up one finger, and turned to Wad. He spoke softly but his tone was as sharp as a razor blade. "I told you to get back."

Wad retreated, looking like a scolded dog.

Uncle Bart turned back to the girl. "My name is Mr. Christensen. What's your name?"

Nothing.

"I'm the sheriff here, sweetie. That means it's my job to take care of people. Especially little girls like you."

No response.

"Do you know where your mommy and daddy are?"

Nothing doing. I was beginning to think that she might be one of those special kids—special needs kids, they call them. That thought broke my heart all the more. This little girl needed a friend.

It was a standoff in the streets of Dicksonville, with the sheriff on one end of the street and a ten-year-old girl on the other. The girl was winning.

A motion caught my attention. While we were watching the drama in the street unfold, Deputy Wad had worked around the crowd and pressed through the citizens until he was behind the youngster. His intention was clear: He was gonna rush the girl.

Uncle Bart saw him about the same time I did. His eyes went wide for a moment, then his brow dropped like a guillotine.

"Wad, I told you—"

Wad charged for all he was worth, which isn't much, but it would have been enough to hurt the girl had he caught her. He didn't.

She was gone.

Then she was back, standing twenty feet in front of me. She glanced back at Wad, who had slipped on the ice and executed a perfect, five-star face-plant on the snow-covered pavement. I'm ashamed to admit this, but it was a good thing to see.

The girl turned to face me. She looked into my eyes, and something hot, scorching, flooded my soul. I felt weak, confused, and a bit dizzy, the kind of dizzy I get when I crack helmets on the field. It kinda made my bones go soft.

I cocked my head to the side. She did the same.

Then she was in my arms.

I don't know how. Don't ask. I didn't see it coming. Didn't see it happen. One moment we were staring at each other; the next she was in my arms, her tiny arms wrapped around my neck.

It was the best hug I ever had.

"Um, hi, little girl."

She remained silent.

"People call me Tank. What should I call you?"

She tightened her grip around my neck. I got the feeling she wasn't afraid of me, she was just giving me another hug. She buried her face in my neck. I knew then and there, I'd move mountains for her.

"That's all right. You can tell me when you're good and ready. Until then I'll call you . . . what?" My mind jumped back to our conversation with Mr. Weldon when Uncle Bart was joking about Bigfoot. He said something like "More like Littlefoot." I chuckled. "How 'bout I just call you Littlefoot because of all the tracks you left in the snow?"

Another hug. I took that to be a *yes*.

The next bit of business scared me the most. "I need to look at your feet. I won't hurt you. I promise."

I did my best to examine her feet, best I could while holding her to my chest. I saw enough.

Perfect.

No injuries. No cuts. No damage from the snow. Her feet

looked like they had never touched anything more harsh than a plush carpet. There was great joy in that.

Uncle Bart approached but kept some distance between so as not to spook the girl. "I'm not sure what I just saw."

"Me neither." I gave the girl a little squeeze. "This is my Uncle Bart. He's a real good guy. I trust him, and I hope you'll trust him too."

She turned her head so she could see him.

Uncle Bart removed his uniform hat and bowed, bending deep at the waist like he was bowing to the queen.

"Uncle Bart, this is Littlefoot. At least for now."

"A pleasure to meet you, Your Highness."

Then a real miracle happened.

Littlefoot smiled. It might be my imagination, but when she did the sun came out and a spring breeze rolled down the street.

CHAPTER 4

I Almost Failed French

8:45 A.M.

We returned to the sheriff's substation, me walking with the little girl in my arms, and Uncle Bart driving. It wasn't a long walk, and I found it easy to carry her. After the heavy weight of worry I had been living with since I first saw her bare footprints in the snow, she seemed light as a feather. She hung on me for all she was worth and kept her face buried in my neck. I could feel the rolled-up paper rub against my skin. I wondered about it, but it was a wondering that could wait.

The paramedics followed Uncle Bart to the station. I know it would have made more sense to examine Littlefoot for injuries in the ambulance, but she made it clear—real clear—she wanted nothing to do with it. I suggested the station because it would be warmer there and out of view of the rubberneckers who seemed to come from nowhere and everywhere.

Millie was waiting for us, holding down her spot at the dispatch radio.

The station was larger than most expected for such a small town. There were four jail cells in the back. Uncle Bart told me people don't stay there long; they were just holding cells. The front office had several desks, the largest ones near the middle of the room where a deputy was assigned to deal with walk-ins. Uncle Bart had a private office in the back. There was a small kitchen tucked away out of sight, and a small lunchroom. Of course, there were a couple of bathrooms. The walls were covered with dark-wood paneling, something my uncle called "early '70s crap."

Deputy Wad showed up a few moments after we entered the station. He had a decent-sized scrape on his right cheek and his nose looked a tad swollen. One paramedic, a woman named Beth, took a look at him, examining his cheekbone to see if he busted it up. I know that had to hurt, but he gave no sign of it. If I was into gambling, I'd put money on the fact that if the paramedic had been a guy, Wad would have been swearing like nobody's business. In football, I've taken a few shots to the head and can't say I liked it.

The second paramedic, a middle-aged man Uncle Bart called Jim, examined Littlefoot, or least *tried* to examine her. She pulled away every time he tried to touch her. The female paramedic gave it a try, which I think should have been the way to start the whole thing, but she had the same bad luck.

"Let's try this," I said. Littlefoot was sitting on my lap. I gave her a little hug and a big smile. She blinked a few times, and I felt her body relax some. As gently as I could, I took hold of her right ankle and lifted her foot. The paramedics stared at it, shining a beam from a small flashlight on the skin. We did the same thing with her left foot.

"No cuts and no signs of frostbite." Jim shook his head.

"Skin is not even red. You sure she's been hiking through the snow?"

"Several miles," Uncle Bart said. "Tank and I followed the trail for over a mile before . . . before returning to the car to check the roads."

I wouldn't have mentioned the strange way the tracks disappeared myself.

"Her feet are fine," Jim said. "I need to take her temperature, Tank. Any ideas how I do that?"

I had an idea. "Take mine first."

Jim nodded as if he thought it was a good idea. He removed one of those new thermometers they rub on your forehead. I was glad to see that. I gave Littlefoot's shoulder a little squeeze and leaned forward. Jim ran the device over my skin, then showed the readout to the girl. "A little low, Tank, but considering you've been tromping through the snow, I'd expect your skin to be a little cool."

He handed the device to me and looked at Littlefoot. She studied it for a moment, looked at my forehead, cocked her head again, then seemed to come to some understanding. She tilted her head back and let me run the digital thermometer across her forehead. I handed it back to Jim.

"Normal. Interesting. It's right on the money." He looked puzzled. "Well, that's good." He removed a small blood-pressure tester, the kind that fits on a person's wrist. I held out my arm. He looked at my wrist. "Um, I hope this fits."

It did, but not by much. It ran its test giving my blood pressure and pulse rate. He handed it to me, and Littlefoot immediately held out her free hand but kept the one with the scroll close to her chest. That kinda trust can bring a tear to a man's eye.

Jim looked at the message while Beth jotted down the info. "Normal." He grinned and tried to pat Littlefoot on the knee, but she pulled away. He jerked his hand back, then sighed.

He rose, picked up his medical kit, and turned to Uncle Bart. "That's about all I can do, Sheriff. She's responsive, I see no injuries—"

"Why doesn't she talk?" Uncle Bart asked. The question carried unspoken companions with it.

"I can't say, Sheriff. She could have a learning disability, or she might be mute. She seems to track with our voices and other sounds, so I doubt she's deaf. She looks well fed—not fat, but not starved. Skin tone is good. I don't have answers. She needs to be tested in a hospital by doctors."

"I assume you'll be calling child protective services," Beth said.

"Of course. Somebody somewhere is probably worried sick about her."

Millie broke her silence. "That's the thing, Sheriff. No one has reported a missing child."

"It's still early. Maybe her parents are sleeping off last night's party."

"If that's the case, CPS is going to raise a real stink." Uncle Bart thanked the paramedics.

"Glad to help." Jim glanced at Littlefoot again. "I hope you get it all straightened out. She's a cutie. Gotta love those blue eyes. I'm afraid, though, that someone may have abused the tyke. I don't like saying that."

"It occurred to me," Uncle Bart said. Unfortunately, it had occurred to me, too.

The paramedics left the office, closing the door behind them.

I was thankful for their help, but blue eyes? I looked into the face of the angel sitting on my lap. She looked back at me through her big brown eyes.

Under Uncle Bart's order, Millie called Child Protective Services. It was New Year's Day so the process was moving slowly.

I set Littlefoot in my seat and pulled up another straight-backed chair so I could face her. Her blond hair, big brown eyes, and round face made her appear angelic. I don't know if I will ever have kids. I like the idea, but who knows what the future holds. If I do, I hope God will give me a little girl like the one staring at me.

"My name is Tank," I said and pointed to myself. Maybe I could get her to open up. I doubted she had a learning disability, although I'm certainly not qualified to say that. Call it a feeling if you want.

I repeated myself and tapped my chest: "Tank." I pointed at my uncle: "Uncle Bart." I probably should have called him Sheriff Christensen, but that seemed like too much of a mouthful. Then I pointed at her. Nothing.

I tried again and then another time. Nothing. No name. No words. Still, I felt certain she understood.

Uncle Bart inched closer. "What about the paper, Tank? You think you could get that from her?"

"I dunno. It seems real important to her, Uncle Bart."

"I noticed. She hangs on to that thing like your Aunt June hangs on to a dollar."

Wad cleared his throat. "You want me to just grab it from her, Sheriff? It would only take a moment."

Uncle Bart turned. "Deputy Waddle, I assume that comment came because of the injury to your head. If I were you, I wouldn't argue with me about that."

"Yes, sir." Wad didn't sound all that genuine.

I gazed at the paper, then motioned to it. To my surprise, she held it out to me. Uncle Bart stepped forward and tried to take it, and she pulled it back just as quick. When he backed away, she held it out again.

I took it. "Thank you, little one."

The scroll was a single piece of brownish paper rolled into

a tight tube. I opened it slowly and with great care. No telling what she would do if I tore the thing. The page was about the size of a legal pad. There were letters, or pictures, or picture-letters, I didn't know what to call them.

"Doesn't look like anything I've ever seen." Uncle Bart was looking over my shoulder. Wad came close, too. "What about you, Tank? Seen anything like it in those college classes you take?"

"No, sir, but then again I almost failed French. I have enough trouble with English, let alone a foreign language." I tapped the odd paper. "Especially something as weird as this."

Wad weighed in. "Maybe it's an alien language."

"You mean like from Canada." Uncle Bart was good with sarcasm.

"Of course not, Sheriff. That's ridiculous. I mean like from outer space. You know, like a UFO or something."

"Yeah, that makes much more sense that an alien is from Canada." If Uncle Bart's tone wasn't so dark, I'd think he was having fun with Deputy Wad.

"I bet Tank agrees with me, don't ya?"

I glanced at Wad and shrugged. "After this last year, I've stopped ruling things out."

Uncle Bart straightened. "What's that supposed to mean?"

"Long story, sir." I looked back at the girl and smiled. She didn't respond. I looked back at the weird paper with the odd markings. "I know who might be able to help. Several someones."

My cellphone chimed. A text:

On our way. Will be there in the morning.

It was from Andi. The sight of her name made my heart trip. I replied with a text of my own: *How did you know?*

Another chime. *I will explain when we get there.*

I assumed by *all* she meant Dr. McKinney, too. Before I could ask, another text appeared on my smartphone. *We're all coming. Daniel too.*

I was already pretty freaked out by the day's events, but knowing my friends were coming without a clue as to why I needed them kinda shook me. Still, I couldn't wait to see Andi—and the others.

Uncle Bart was staring at me. "Judging by that befuddled look on your face, I assume that the message was unexpected."

"Yeah. Help is on the way, Uncle Bart."

Wad asked, "What kinda help? The Feds?"

"I don't know any Feds." I put my phone away. "These guys are better than the Feds."

CHAPTER 5

A Burger and a Shake

10:30 A.M.

"A priest?" Uncle Bart sounded stunned. "What's a good Lutheran boy like you doin' hanging with a priest?"

"Well, he used to be a priest," I explained. I reached for Littlefoot's hand. She didn't hesitate to take it. That made me feel good and so did the warmth of her touch. For the life of me, I couldn't figure out how she could have been walking through the snow and wind without feeling like a bag of ice water. "He gave that up."

"He left the priesthood?"

I followed Uncle Bart into the small break room. "Yep. He gave up on God. Decided to be an atheist. He thinks that's what smart people do." I lifted Littlefoot into one of the chairs and pushed it close to the battered table. I guess the table is older than half the town.

"You know me, Tank, I ain't much on churchgoing, but I

don't think I've turned my back on God. I may not be as religious as you, boy, but I still got my beliefs."

I started to tell him that faith and religion weren't the same thing, but it didn't seem the time to have that conversation.

"Who are these other people?" Uncle Bart took a chair at the end of the table. No matter what table he sat at, he sat at the head. I suppose it was a control issue. No one complained, but then it would have done no good to do so. Uncle Bart did whatever Uncle Bart wanted to do.

"I'll introduce you to them when they get here. They're good people, but they're a little—different."

"Different? How?"

The best I could do was shrug. "I'm not sure I can explain it. I'm not sure I understand it all. I trust them. I've had to."

"Now, boy, you're gonna have to explain that. There's gotta be a story behind that statement."

A story? As old man Weldon would have said, "Ayuh." Except I didn't say it out loud. A story. How could I tell him about the unusual people I'm hangin' out with these days? A professor, a tattoo artist, a kid who sees strange people, and a young lady with a mind that chews information like a computer.

"Uncle Bart, have you ever seen anything you couldn't explain?"

He leaned back. "Well this thing with the girl qualifies, but I've seen a thing or two, yes."

"Do you tell people about it?"

"Not really."

I nodded. "It's not that I don't want to tell you, but I just don't know how, not in a way that you'd believe. Maybe the others can do a better job than me."

I heard the door to the station open and close. The sound of it came with the smell of cooked meat. It was a tad early for lunch, but we were up early and hadn't eaten. Add to that the fact that we hiked a long way in the snow and endured some real emotional strain, so we were beyond hungry. We also needed to make sure Littlefoot had some food. She had to be hungrier than us. We also wanted to be able to tell CPS that we had done right by the little girl.

I smiled at her. She didn't smile back, but she did blink those lovely eyes—hazel? Weren't they brown? I remembered the paramedic calling her eyes blue.

"Chow is here, guys." Wad walked into the break room struggling to carry several bags of food and a tray of drinks. "Burgers and shakes."

My stomach did a couple of flips of joy.

"Thanks," Uncle Bart said and reached for one of the drinks.

Wad sat at the foot of the table. Littlefoot eyed him for a moment, then looked at the bags of food. I removed a small cheeseburger, unwrapped it, setting the wrapper on the table like a napkin, and then set the burger on top of that. She looked at the burger as if she expected it to get up and move. I took a chocolate shake and inserted a straw, then placed that near the cheeseburger. I felt a bit of guilt about giving her this kind of food. I probably should have asked for something healthy. That's me. I have tons of great ideas; I just have them about a half hour after they're needed. Besides, what kid doesn't like a burger and a shake?

I took a sip of my shake, placing the business end of the straw in my mouth and watching Littlefoot. It's hard to say why, but I had a feeling that all of this was confusing her. I took another sip, smiled, and said, "Yum." I pointed at her shake. She pulled it close, lifted it from the table, put the straw in her mouth and waited. Of course, nothing happened.

"You gotta suck, kiddo." I showed her again, exaggerating the way to use the thing. She got it on the second go around. I watched the chocolate ice cream rise in the clear straw.

She set the cup down and frowned, then she smacked her lips and stuck out her tongue a few times like a dog trying to get peanut butter off the roof of its mouth.

"No doubt about it," Wad said, "the kid is missing a few marbles."

I may play football, but I don't believe in violence. Not usually, anyway. Wad was giving me a reason to change my point of view.

Uncle Bart was staring at him. "I need a favor, Deputy."

"Sure, Sheriff, what can I do for you?"

"You can keep your opinions to yourself. Eat your burger, then get back on patrol."

"All I'm saying is . . ."

Uncle Bart's expression made Wad trail off.

"I think I'll go eat with Millie." Wad rose from his chair and left.

Uncle Bart didn't try to stop him. I saw no reason to insist he stay.

Littlefoot repeated her actions: sip, frown, followed by tongue gymnastics. I don't think it tasted bad to her. It was as if she had never seen a milkshake or burger. She tried the sandwich, first licking the bun, then the edge of the meat patty.

It broke my heart. Littlefoot was as innocent as any child I had ever seen. Where had she been living that she didn't know what a burger and milkshake were? A vision of the child locked in a closet for years invaded my brain. A stew of emotion boiled in me. I was glad she was safe; I was pleased she was unharmed; my heart ached at her simplicity and confusion; and I was furious that anyone would let a child grow up this way.

I think Uncle Bart was reading my expression or something because he spoke in a tone softer than I was used to hearing from him. "You've been a big help, Tank."

"I ain't done much. Just showed the kid a little kindness."

"Don't sell yourself short, boy. The world can use a little more kindness, especially the kind you've got. That little girl took to you when she'd have nuthin' to do with anyone else. She sees you as a friend."

"Well, I'm not wearing all the police gear you are. I'm just a big teddy bear."

Uncle Bart laughed. "Is that what they call you on the football field?"

I looked away. I didn't want to talk about football. Littlefoot watched me bite into the burger. Man, the cafeteria made a good cheeseburger. She cocked her head, then picked up the food and nibbled a bit of the bread. She set it down while she chewed as if examining some strange object. She picked it up again and this time took a bigger bite. She was getting the hang of it.

"What's going to happen to her, Uncle Bart?"

"You can't keep her, Tank. She's not a puppy."

"I know that. I'm just worried about her. She's so innocent."

"Social services will be here soon. They'll get her set up all nice and comfy. Soft bed, warm covers, toys, whatever she needs." He paused. "You think she'll go along with them easily? I hate to think of them picking her up and putting her in the back of the car. I've seen it before—some kids refuse to leave a place even if it's for their own good."

"I hope so, Uncle Bart. I don't think I could stand to see that." The image made my appetite disappear, and it took a lot to do that. "I can't figure her out. Somebody's gotta be looking for her."

"Unless they just dropped her off and drove away. I've seen worse."

Just hearing the words twisted my guts inside out. "I don't know how you live with what you see. I'd lose my mind."

Uncle Bart studied the table. "I've lost my composure a few times." He was seeing something in his head.

He snapped out of it. "After CPS gets here I'll drive you back to the house. You've had a full day and it's not even noon. You can rest and watch the Rose Bowl. I wanna follow up on some things."

"If it's all the same, I'd rather hang out with you."

Uncle Bart smiled. "I knew there was a cop somewhere in you."

I didn't correct him. Didn't seem the right time to do such a thing.

He carried on. "I've got Millie making calls to the other LEOs. Maybe someone in some other county knows something."

"LEOs?"

"Law Enforcement Officers. Other cops in other departments."

"Oh. Thanks for letting me help, Uncle Bart."

"As I said, Tank, I'm thanking you."

We ate in silence for a few moments—even Littlefoot—then Uncle Bart said something that nearly knocked me off my chair.

"I know about what happened, Tank. I know about your football."

CHAPTER 6

Back to the Tracks

3:02 P.M.

The rest of the morning and the first part of the afternoon passed slowly. I continued to worry about Littlefoot although she showed no signs of distress. She had eaten half of the cheeseburger and downed about a third of the milkshake, doing her dog-licking-peanut-butter-from-the-roof-of-its-mouth after each sip thing. On one hand it was funny, but on the other kinda sad. Nonetheless, she seemed to enjoy the meal.

Still, she never spoke and never moved from any chair I placed her in. She didn't show much reaction to events around her. I continued to study the paper she'd given me but I could get nothing out of it. It was gonna take someone a lot smarter than me to figure it out, and a part of me worried that even the smartest man or woman would walk away as confused as I was.

The paper fascinated me, but even more fascinating was the girl's response to it. When we first saw her, she stayed away from everyone but me; then, once we were in the station and asked for the paper, she handed it over. She showed no interest in it after that. None. One moment she seemed to guard it with her life; the next she no longer cared. It was as if I was meant to have the message and once she delivered it, she was done with it completely.

The problem was, I had no idea what I was looking at or why she would want me to have it. As is often the case in my life, I had more questions than answers.

I had something else on my mind: Uncle Bart's revelation that he knew about me and football. I didn't know what he meant, but I could guess. He didn't bring it up again. I had the feeling he was leaving that up to me.

At two thirty or so, two women from Child Protective Services showed up. One looked fresh out of college, probably a sociology major. She looked to be about my age. Maybe a couple years older. The other woman could have been the young social worker's mother. She was maybe fifty-six, round in the face and in the belly. She had the look of a grandmother, and I thought that was perfect. It's easy to trust grandmothers. Grandmothers stood for milk and cookies, pies, hugs, tickles, and kisses on the top of heads. They say there is no love greater than that of a parent. Grandmothers may be the exception.

They came into the station, showed some identification first to Millie, then to Uncle Bart, who came out of his office when he heard them arrive. Littlefoot showed no fear, and when the grandmotherly woman held out a hand, she slipped from her chair and took it. My heart shriveled in my big chest, a raisin alone in an empty warehouse.

I stood just outside the station's doorway and watched as Littlefoot crawled into the backseat of a county sedan. The grandmotherly woman joined her; the young woman slipped behind the steering wheel. I took a few steps closer and waved good-bye. Littlefoot bent forward, and I could see her pure face.

She was staring back.

With green eyes.

The image was still playing in my mind when Uncle Bart pulled the patrol car to the side of the road, to the same place in front of Old Man Weldon's spread. During the drive he told me what he was up to. He wanted to follow the tracks again, this time in the opposite direction.

"Since we know the tyke is safe, we can take a little more time with our search. She had to start her hike from somewhere, and I want to know where."

That made sense. "Couldn't the helicopter do this faster?"

He nodded. "It was needed elsewhere. Once we found the girl, the pilot had to move to some other pressing issue in the county. Besides, we can get a better feel for things walking the ground."

That made sense, too.

We exited the car and followed our own tracks from earlier to the spot where Weldon first led us. Snow had filled in things some, but not as much as I had feared. Oddly, the snow filled our tracks more than Littlefoot's. I'm not sure how that can be, but then none of this made much sense to me.

"Okay, son, let's see if we can't find out where this journey began. If we can find the where, then we might find the why. Police work often works that way. You'll learn that in time."

At some point, I was going to have to break Uncle Bart's heart.

We started backtracking Littlefoot's journey. We encountered another fence, and the tracks looked as if she had either walked straight through the split rails or levitated over it. Both ideas were impossible, yet that's what the tracks showed.

We continued on, mostly in silence. I worried about Littlefoot and decided to distract myself with a different kind of unpleasantness.

"Uncle Bart, what did you mean when you said you knew about my football?"

He was slow to answer. He took a breath, then blew it out like a smoker emptying his lungs. "Straight up, Tank?"

"I think that's the best way to go."

"I know you were cut from the team."

And there it was. "Dad?"

"Yeah, he called about a week ago. Figured he should let me know since you were going to be up here. I gotta ask, Tank—is that why my brother didn't come up to watch the game this year?"

A wave of shame washed over me. "I hate to say it, Uncle Bart, but yes. He's—angry with me."

"Angry?"

"Furious, really."

Uncle Bart chuckled. "He's always had a short fuse. The stories I could tell."

"I haven't seen him since I moved from Southern California to Washington. He was proud as he could be of the football scholarship. I've let him down. Big time."

"Mind if I ask what happened?" He didn't look up from the tracks. "I'm not trying to butt in, son, just trying to be a good uncle. Was it the injury?"

"No, not really." How did I explain? I'd reviewed everything in my mind time and time again, and it was all so weird that I barely believed it myself . . . and I lived it. "Players get injured all the time: concussions, broken bones, hyper-extensions; I guess there are as many possible injuries as there are body parts, so a busted toe is nothing new. I was third string anyway, being new to the university and all. I was still learning the plays the team uses."

"So it wasn't your toe—how is it by the way?"

"Okay. It hurts, especially in the cold, but the doc says it's healing up pretty good. I should be back to normal in a couple of months."

"And here I've been dragging you through snow."

"No problem, Uncle Bart. It's just pain. I'm not making things worse."

We walked on another dozen steps, our gaze fixed to the tiny prints. "So, if not the toe, then what?"

This was the difficult part. "I needed to take a trip. Since I couldn't play, I asked if I could travel to Florida."

"Florida?"

I didn't look at him. It took all my focus to keep talking. "You know the friends I mentioned, the ones coming to Dicksonville." He said he did. "They needed me in Florida for something. Coach said I could go. What he didn't say was that a real football player wouldn't leave his team even if he couldn't play. He didn't say so, but I think he wanted me to prove my loyalty. Leaving told him I wasn't committed to the team."

Talking about it hurt, but I continued. "I should have realized that, but I'm not real good with subtlety. I blew it as far as the coach was concerned, and an injured, third-string guy isn't all that valuable."

"He should have been more upfront with you, Tank. He handled that wrong. All wrong." He paused for a moment as if he were trying to scoop up some memory buried in his brain. "Can they cut you like that, Tank? Wouldn't they wait 'til next year to cut you? It seems a little strange to me."

It seemed strange to me too. Rules were being bent if not broken, but what did it matter? The coach wanted me gone and he made it happen.

"Maybe, but it wouldn't have changed anything. I would have gone anyway. I had to make a choice."

Uncle Bart stopped and stared at me. "Let me get this right, Tank. You had a full football scholarship to the University of Washington and blew it all off to go party with friends in Florida. That is the dumbest, most selfish—"

"It was no party, sir. No party at all. We weren't there to hang out."

"Then why were you there?"

I was getting frustrated. "Uncle Bart, you wouldn't understand."

"Try me."

I started walking again. "I've got a feeling you'll understand when this whole thing with Littlefoot is over. Strange things happen, and for some reason, me and my friends get pulled into it. I think it's a God thing."

"A God thing? You blame God for flushing your scholarship?"

"No, sir. I don't blame God for anything." This time I stopped and looked him in the eyes. "Weird things are happening. Don't ask, because I don't have many answers, but let me ask you a question. When was the last time you tracked a little girl walking barefoot in the snow who can pass through fences and levitate to the top of a barn? Have you seen anything like that before?"

"No, not exactly."

"Not exactly?

He looked away. "Okay, never anything like that."

"We don't have answers, Uncle Bart, but somehow, some way we are all tied together in this and there isn't much we can do about it. I just know that it is the most important thing I've done or can ever do. I blew it on the football thing, but I'd do it again if my friends needed me. I'd go to them, just like they're coming here—and I didn't call them. I was going to, but they were already on their way."

"How could they know?"

"Beats me. We'll find out when they get here."

We continued our hike in silence, then Uncle Bart said, "Just so you know, boy, I love you like my own son. You need to know that. I'm here if you need me."

My eyes grew wet. "Thanks, Uncle Bart. I love you, too." A few moments later I asked, "Is that why you said I didn't need to go to college to get a job as a deputy sheriff?"

"Maybe."

We chuckled. The chuckles stopped ten steps later. We had found the end of Littlefoot's tracks, or rather the beginning of the tracks. The first steps were surrounded by a wide, circular depression in the snow. I figure it was thirty feet across.

Uncle Bart was the first to speak. "Maybe I was too quick to nix Deputy Wad's UFO idea."

I think Uncle Bart was right.

We both turned our eyes upward.

CHAPTER

7

The IT

JANUARY 2, 3:33 A.M.

IT was closing on Littlefoot. She ran. Screaming. Cold air pushed her hair back. Tears ran from her face. Her face. Her face. Dear God, her face. The fear. The shock. The panic.

I ran toward her. Through the snow. Pushing my bare feet through the snow to the frozen ground beneath. Shards of ice bit my feet, cutting them, jabbing them, shredding the skin. I couldn't stop. I wouldn't stop. I had to get to her first, before . . . before . . . the Thing did.

The Beast. The Animal. It was fuzzy, indistinct. I could hear its demonic yapping, like it was laughing. It found joy in Littlefoot's terror. I saw white teeth. I saw thick, black fur.

The IT was closing. Every stride moved it a couple of feet closer to its prey, to its evening meal, to my friend, to tiny, innocent, ten-year-old Littlefoot.

She screamed and dear God it burned my soul like acid.

Faster. I had to move faster. I could not allow the IT to catch her, shred her, dismember her. . . .

Tears wet my face. The white field disappeared. The trees that lined the perimeter of the farm faded from existence. Only Littlefoot existed. Littlefoot and the Beast.

"Taaaaank!"

Her first word to me was born out of terror. Her first word a cry for help. A plea. A first word that could be her last.

I've never wanted to kill anything in my life, but I would rip the spine from the Creature, the IT, the Beast, the Demon, the Spawn of Hell. I would make sure it never chased a child again.

My blood ran like lava through my veins; my heart was an airplane piston and my fury beyond description. My vision narrowed until I saw nothing but Littlefoot and the Predator. Something or someone was going to die tonight, and it wasn't going to be Littlefoot.

I pumped my legs and for the first time wished I was smaller and faster. I needed speed now more than bulk.

Littlefoot fell. Facedown. In the snow. She rolled to one side, glanced at the Sprinting Death, then turned to me.

She held out a hand, and I was still too far away.

The Hound closed the distance. So did I. It leapt, its fierce gaze fixed on the little girl. It soared low, cruising toward the helpless child.

She screamed.

So did I.

It opened its jaws and snapped them shut.

On my hand.

I didn't care. The thought of her dying in this thing's mouth brought me more pain than I could process—I could feel nothing else. A powerful, violent bite was nothing in comparison. There were greater pains to worry about.

The Beast had my right hand in its jaws and was shaking his

head as if trying to tear my hand from my arm. I found its throat with my left hand and squeezed. Harder. Harder until I felt its windpipe fold, until I felt my fingers press deep into its neck.

The IT bit harder. I couldn't feel the pain. I felt only fury—fury and fear for Littlefoot. Each second brought more anger, more hatred, more—

I screamed again and closed my left hand like a vice. Another scream—

I scrambled from my bed in Uncle Bart's guest room. Sweat covered my body, and my muscles were more tense than I'd ever felt them. A sheen of tears covered my face. My tendons strained to hold constricting muscles in place. I took in air by the bushelful, my fists granite stones. My heart bounded in my chest like a caged ape trying to escape.

The dark room was lit by moonlight reflecting off the snow one floor below. I wondered if anyone heard me. Were my screams just in my head? I hoped so. I prayed so. I strained my ears to listen for footsteps, voices, or a knock on the door. Nothing. The animal part of my brain listened for the Beast.

"A dream. Thank God. Only a dream."

I was thankful. I didn't want anyone checking on me. I wanted to be alone—needed to be alone. I trembled like a captured mouse. I dropped to my knees, leaned over the bed, and wept.

It was an hour before I could pray.

At 5:15 I noticed the smell of coffee. There would be no more sleep that night and, truth be told, I wasn't sure I ever wanted to sleep again.

I dressed, hit the hall bath, then walked quietly down the stairs. A light from the kitchen splashed on a figure in the dining room. The figure's wide shoulders told me it was Uncle Bart. He sipped from a cup, set it down, and stared at the table. He hadn't heard me. I didn't want to startle him so I cleared my throat.

"I heard you coming down the stairs, Tank. I ain't young anymore, but my hearing is as good as ever."

"Sorry, Uncle Bart. I hope I didn't wake you."

"Wake me? No, I've been up for a little while. Can't sleep." He looked up. "What are you doing outta bed? I figured I'd have to drag you out around ten or so."

I faked a laugh. "I've never been good at sleeping in." I moved to the table. "I used to do extra work in the gym before classes."

"Get yourself a cup o' Joe, Tank. A man doesn't like to drink alone, even if it's coffee."

I did. I like coffee, and this smelled better than any I'd had. I assume that's because it reminded me that all I had seen was just a dream. I found some dry creamer, doctored my coffee, then moved back to the dim dining room. I preferred it dim for now.

Uncle Bart sighed like he was depressed or something.

I took a guess. "Bad dream?"

"Yeah, something like that." He took another sip. "You?"

"Yep. A doozy."

"Wanna talk about it?" He was trying to be a good uncle, but I could tell he didn't want to hear it.

"Nah. I'd rather forget the whole thing. You wanna talk about yours?"

He chortled. "Not in the least."

There was a catch in his voice and, dim as the light was, I could see his eyes were tinged with red. I assumed mine were, too. "Littlefoot?"

"Yeah. You?"

"Yeah."

It was all we needed to say. We'd talk it about someday, but not now, not before the sun was up and we had been well lubricated with hot coffee.

We were on our third cup before we spoke again. It was a simple conversation.

"You hungry, Tank?"

I worked up a good smile. "I don't know what it's like not to be hungry."

After two three-egg omelets and more bacon than I should admit to, we both felt better. Auntie June helped herself to the leftovers, glad she didn't have to fix breakfast on a Monday morning.

Thirty minutes later I was showered, shaved, and dressed for the day. I almost felt human again, and the sharp edges of the dream had dulled some. I found Uncle Bart in uniform and strapping on his Sam Browne service belt. "Gotta hit the mean streets of Dicksonville, Tank. You wanna go or stay here and help June clean house?"

"Let me get my coat."

Where yesterday had been gray and stuffed with snow, today was bright and sunny. I imagined much of the white stuff would melt by the end of the day, except in the foothills where we saw Littlefoot's tracks. That snow would probably hang around for a couple of days, maybe a week. Still, it was a good thing we retraced her steps yesterday. It gave us an opportunity to talk to some of the other ranchers, not that it did any good. They knew nothing of the girl and saw nothing.

Uncle Bart pulled onto Main Street, drove about a mile, slowed and began swearing. I followed his gaze. In the middle of the street, at about the same place as yesterday, stood Littlefoot, still barefoot, still in the same clothes. The sun was up, but the air was still cold.

"I don't believe this." Uncle Bart slapped the steering wheel. "I'm gonna have someone's head."

A car pulled around the little girl and slowed. I could see the driver's side window lower and a head poke out. Someone was checking on her. Uncle Bart turned on his emergency lights and the other driver saw it, waved, and slowly pulled away.

Uncle Bart had a little more rant left in him. "There's no way the girl could have walked back here. The CPS home is over thirty miles away."

"I'm not sure that's a problem for her."

"That's too weird, Tank. I know what we saw yesterday, but thirty miles? Really?"

"Weird is the new normal, Uncle Bart. Stop here. We don't want to scare her."

I glanced at him. Despite his outburst I could see that he was glad to see that she was safe. I know I was.

I exited the car and gave the girl a little wave and big smile.

No response. Just as before. I walked toward her. She looked up at me. Never had I seen a sweeter face. Her gaze was almost enough to erase what I saw in my dream. Well, almost.

I held out my arms and she reached for me. "Let's you and me go somewhere it's warm. I'll bet you're hungry. Do you like eggs?" Of course, there was no answer. Sometimes I can touch sick or injured people and they get well. I wish I could tell you it works all the time, but it doesn't. I don't know why. If it worked all the time, I'd spend my days walking through hospitals. Maybe that's why it doesn't. Maybe that's not my purpose. My hope was that my gift might work on Littlefoot and fix the reason she didn't talk. Maybe she didn't need fixing. I just didn't know.

It was only a two-block walk to the sheriff's station, but in those two blocks I came to realize two things. First, I grew more depressed with each step. I don't get depressed too often and never for long, but I was feeling it today. There was a weight on my heart, like a car being dropped on a soda can. Maybe it was the dream. Maybe it was the shock of seeing Littlefoot back here, impossible as it was. I had no idea why I felt this way, but I started wishing the ground would open and swallow me. Take me away from all the misery in the world—

I shook off the idea. I had the little girl in my arms. That was my second concern. I didn't notice at first, probably because I was so glad to see her, but she was different. Littlefoot was smaller. She didn't *seem* smaller, she *was* smaller. I carried her yesterday. I spent hours with her. She was different today: tinier and lighter.

Impossible. But what about Littlefoot hasn't been impossible?

My feet grew heavier. My heart slowed. Strength poured from me as if there were an open faucet in my ankles. I was bleeding energy.

When I reached the sheriff's station, Uncle Bart held the door open. The girl buried her face in my neck as I heard a growl behind me . . . a familiar growl. I spun on my heel, ready to cover Littlefoot's body with my own. From the corner of my eye, I saw Uncle Bart reach for his weapon. He left it holstered and I saw nothing. No Predator. I shuffled in, made my way to one of the chairs where Littlefoot sat yesterday, and set her down.

"You okay, boy? You look spent."

I bent and rested my hands on my knees as if I had just finished a set of wind sprints. "I'm okay. Must be your cooking."

He took me by the arm and sat me near Littlefoot. "You rest there. If you're not better in five minutes, I'm calling the doctor."

"I'll be fine."

I saw Uncle Bart look at Littlefoot. "I'm gonna call CPS and find out who let a ten-year-old . . ." He stared at her for a moment. "Um, Tank—"

"I know. She's shrinkin'."

CHAPTER 8

Reunion

9:03 A.M.

I was sitting in one of the holding cells in the back of the building. All of them were empty, they usually were, so I thought it might be a quieter, less frightening place for Littlefoot. Because she had changed since yesterday, I was tempted to call her "Littler-foot," but it was too hard to say and it might just confuse her. It was quiet back there. We were away from deputies and citizens coming and going.

The cell also had a bed and I was hoping my little friend would take a rest. She didn't look sleepy and I wondered, in light of all I had seen so far, if she even needed to sleep. I scolded myself. Of course she did. She had a body, right? She ate food, didn't she? Why wouldn't she need sleep?

I picked up the paper plates that had, moments earlier, held our breakfast. Yes, my second breakfast for the day. I wasn't the least bit hungry, but I feared that Littlefoot wouldn't eat unless

I did the same. I introduced her to scrambled eggs, rye toast with jelly (she really liked that), and bacon. She avoided the plastic fork and used her hands to shovel the food from plate to mouth. To my surprise she ate everything and not once did she do the dog-peanut-butter thing with her tongue.

Uncle Bart had placed a call to social services to advise them that one of their charges was missing. He used colorful language and spoke loudly enough that the phone was probably unnecessary. That's when it occurred to me that things might be better back here in the cells.

"Tank." It was Uncle Bart. "You got visitors."

He stepped to the side, and the tall, gentlemanly figure of Dr. McKinney entered. "I knew you would come to no good, my boy." He said it with a smile. It took me a second to get the joke.

"Dr. McKinney!" I was on my feet and out of the cell. He raised both hands as if he could stop my approach. He wasn't much for hugs. I didn't care. I wrapped my arms around him and lifted him off the ground for a moment.

"Careful, Tank, he's old and frail." That voice sent electricity through me. Andi stood a step or two back from the professor. Her face was just as gorgeous as it had been a couple of months ago in Florida when I last saw her. Her red hair was still as bright and still defying gravity. I set the professor aside and gave Andi a big hug. I may have held the hug a little too long. She started to pull away. I don't know how to judge such things. I could see joy and humor in her eyes.

"Oh, sure, the white girl gets a hug."

I looked over Andi's big hair and saw Brenda's face. One corner of her mouth ticked up. It was the closest thing to a smile I had seen from her. Brenda was tough, streetwise, and at times, a little scary. She was quick with a cut and was a great tattoo artist. I have some of her work on my arm, although I don't remember much about getting it. I took her in my arms.

She hugged back. She could pretend to be as hard as nails, but I knew about her softer side.

"I didn't expect to see you here, Miss Brenda," I said.

"Yeah, and don't think I'm not put out by that, Cowboy."

Something touched my leg. A small person stood by my right leg. "Daniel!" I scooped the kid up like a bundle of laundry. Daniel doesn't like to be touched, but he lets me get away with it. I set him down. "Secret handshake." I held out my hand and we went through a series of slaps and bumps. It takes about fifteen seconds, but the kid enjoys it. Me too.

Uncle Bart cleared his throat. "You gonna play patty-cake all morning or are you going to introduce me?"

"Oh, sorry, Uncle Bart. This is Brenda Barnick. She's a tattoo artist and a good one. This little guy is Daniel Petrovski. He's amazing in his own way. Brenda takes care of him some."

"Some?" Uncle Bart said.

"I'm his aunt."

Uncle Bart looked at her black face then at Daniel's white skin. "His mother know he's here?"

"He's got no mother. I'm the only adult in his life—well, me and this crew." She paused. "He lives in an institution most of the time, but me and the professor, here, we been pullin' some social service strings gettin' him to stay with me more and more. We go on trips and stuff when we can."

I could tell Uncle Bart had a million questions, but he kept them to himself, his way of trusting me.

I took a step closer to Andi. "This is my good friend Andrea Goldstein."

"Please to meet you, Deputy." She held out her hand.

"It's Sheriff, thank you." At least he smiled when he said it. He took her hand, stared at her for a minute, then looked at me. I hate being transparent.

"Sorry." Andi looked amused.

"And Uncle Bart, this is Professor James McKinney. We just call him Professor."

"Ah." Uncle Bart held out his hand. "You the priest?"

"No, I'm the used-to-be priest. I travel the country and lecture now. Andi is my assistant."

Uncle Bart eyed the professor like he was checking him for a hidden gun. "What do you lecture on?" I cringed at the question.

"I help people get over the crippling belief in God and the supernatural."

My uncle's face hardened. "The crippling belief."

"Yes, sir. You see—"

I had to nip this in the bud. "How did you guys know I needed you? I was gonna call—"

"Which you didn't," Brenda snapped. "We ain't much of a team, Cowboy, if we don't stay in contact."

"I know. Sorry. It's been a strange few months. I still wanna know how you knew to come."

Brenda, who was wearing an old leather jacket two sizes too large, pulled a piece of paper from an inside pocket and handed it to me. I unfolded it. The paper was thick and I guessed she had taken it from an artist's pad. She had folded it three times, as if by doing so she could keep it safe and secret. Brenda was cautious. She didn't trust anyone and asked no one to trust her—present company excluded, of course.

I stared at the image. She had sketched it in pencil then traced it over in ink. I recognized myself. She had captured Littlefoot to a T, and—

My knees went weak and my spine turned to Jell-O.

"Blessed Jesus."

I swayed for a moment. No one spoke, but I did hear Andi gasp. A hand grabbed my right arm. The professor. Another hand seized my left arm. Uncle Bart.

"You okay, son?" Uncle Bart sounded worried.

"He's scared." It was Brenda. "I ain't never seen him scared before. Ease up, Cowboy. You're with friends."

I was going to lose my breakfast. Both of them. I've trembled before, but only after I've over-exerted my muscles during practice or a game. Never for any other reason. I couldn't stop quivering.

Something grabbed my leg. Correction. *Someone* grabbed my leg. It was Daniel, and he held my leg as if he could hold me upright.

"Talk to me, boy." Uncle Bart spoke in a steady tone, a lawman's tone, but there were several gallons of fear hidden in his words.

I straightened, took several deep breaths, then handed the paper to Uncle Bart. He looked at it, then said something that made me want to apologize to Andi and Brenda. Of course, I had heard Brenda use the term a few times myself.

"This was in your dream?" Uncle Bart's words were more than a question; they were a demand for information.

"Yeah. You?"

"Yeah."

"Again with the dreams," the professor said. "What's with this group and dreams?"

Uncle Bart snapped his gaze to the professor. "What's that supposed to mean?"

"It's hard to explain, Sheriff, and I don't believe in such things anyway."

"You don't believe in anything," Brenda snapped. "You've seen everything we have; you're just too stubborn to believe your own eyes and experiences."

"I'm not stubborn, I'm analytical."

Andi reached for the drawing. "What is that thing?"

I willed my heart to slow to a sprint before it unraveled in my chest. "The IT."

It took a full five minutes before I could stand on my own. "I'm okay now." I turned to Brenda. "When did you draw this?"

"The day before yesterday. Well, the night before yesterday. I was working late. I was inking a client's back. I drew that afterward."

I processed that for a moment. "You did this as a tattoo first?"

"That's how it works sometimes, Cowboy. You know that. I didn't even know I was doing it until I was done. I figured the client was gonna go ballistic since she came in for a Scottish castle. I lucked out. She was a Goth girl and loved what I did, which is a good thing since tats are impossible to erase."

"Some girl out there has this tattooed on her back?" Uncle Bart asked.

"Yeah. Turns out, it's not the strangest skin art she has."

The professor crossed his arms. He wore a tweed coat with elbow patches. Real scholarly like. I hoped he had a heavier coat. What he was wearing looked good inside but wouldn't do much outside after dark. "Tank, we've been traveling most of the day. Even with a flight to Medford, we still had a long drive out here. Maybe I could bother you to tell me why we're here."

I nodded. "Sure, Professor. First, there's someone I want you to meet, then I need your permission to let Uncle Bart—I mean, the sheriff—know about us. He's into this pretty deep, and he's family."

We didn't have any rules about secrecy, but we didn't much talk about our gifts and adventures. No one would believe them. I led them back to the cell where Littlefoot was waiting.

"Everybody, I want you to meet the greatest little girl in the world. This is Littlefoot."

"Littlefoot?" Brenda always came with a large stock of sarcasm. "Really? Littlefoot?"

"You'll understand when I explain things." I turned to the little one. "Littlefoot, these are my friends. They're here to help you."

Littlefoot slipped from the edge of the bed where she was sitting and walked forward. She looked at each one, then ten-year-old Daniel pressed through to the front and stepped in front of Littlefoot. They stared at each other for a moment: two silent children, two kids who didn't fit this world.

Then the miracle. Littlefoot smiled. I waited for angels to start singing. Daniel smiled, too.

Then Littlefoot's eye color turned silver.

"Um . . ." Andi began.

"Yes, we saw." The professor sounded stunned. Another miracle.

CHAPTER 9

It's All Greek to Me

11:15 A.M.

We sat in the break room. Uncle Bart had Millie put a sign on the door telling people not to disturb us. The privacy was appreciated. It took the better part of an hour to fill everyone in on all that had happened. None of my friends seemed stunned. The professor kept his detached skepticism alive, but it was part of his personality and I was used to it. At times he seemed like a swimmer being pounded by the waves but refused to believe there was any such thing as an ocean. We got along. I knew he thought I was a big, dumb jock, but there were days when he seemed less smart than me.

I told them about the tracks in the snow. Hearing that Littlefoot had been walking in the snow with no shoes made Brenda's hard crust crack. I saw her look away. Since I had been bawling like a baby in the wee hours of the morning, I wasn't inclined to judge.

I even told them of my dream—our dream, 'cause Uncle Bart admitted to having had a similar nightmare. Except in his dream he failed to save Littlefoot. I didn't think my dream could be worse. Turns out I could have had Uncle Bart's.

It took some time to explain our group to my uncle. I told him about Andi's ability to see patterns in almost everything and make sense of things none of us could see; of Brenda's ability to see a bit of the future but only through her art; our belief that young Daniel saw people, angels, things that we couldn't. Of course, I admitted to my sometime-gift of healing.

"What about the prof, here?" Uncle Bart asked.

The professor lifted his chin. "I see reason where they see foolishness. I'm their ballast."

"Ha," Brenda said. "I see you more as a dead weight."

"And who was it, young lady, who paid for your airline ticket? You'd still be hitchhiking up Interstate 5. It's a long way from Southern California."

Andi took over. "That's enough, Professor." Andi was the only one who could handle the man, although he never made it easy.

"Let me see if I got this right." Uncle Bart leaned back in his chair. His leather Sam Browne belt squeaked with the movement. "A crazy school in Southern California with a well that reaches to the spiritual world; a house that haunts instead of being haunted; birds dying mid-flight and hitting the ground with their eyes missing—"

"And other animals too," Andi said.

"And that was in Florida." Uncle Bart scratched his chin. "Where Tank resurrected your dog." He went from scratching his chin to rubbing his eyes. "All I wanted to do was watch the Rose Bowl."

"I know it's hard to believe, Uncle Bart—"

"Hard to believe? That ain't the problem, son. I saw what

turned out to be a little girl's footprints on the snowy roof of a two-story barn. You could tell me Martians landed just outside of town and I'd believe ya. I just gotta process it. That's all."

I looked at Littlefoot. Millie had run to the diner and picked up a couple of milkshakes for the kids. You know, to give them something to do while the big folks talked. Littlefoot took a sip, then did the peanut-butter-dog thing again with her tongue. Daniel took a sip and did the same. It was good to have something to smile about.

We batted around some of the weirdness involved with Littlefoot, then the professor made a request. "All of this is well and good, but you said you had a document you wanted me to examine."

Uncle Bart rose from his chair, then exited the room. The sound of a metal file drawer opening and closing rolled through the open door. My uncle reappeared with the small scroll. "Here ya go, Professor. See what ya make of that. Lord knows I've got no idea."

The professor opened his mouth to speak, most likely to make a wisecrack about Uncle Bart's use of "Lord knows," but a sharp jab from Andi's elbow changed his mind. The others leaned in to take a look, too.

"Don't just sit there, Professor," Andi said. "Share your thoughts."

"He just handed the thing to me. I don't have any thoughts."

That made Brenda laugh.

Andi pressed her lips into a line. I expected something snide to come out of that mouth. Instead I heard, "We all love the way your mind works, Professor. Share your thinking."

Okay, maybe that was snide.

The professor cut his eyes her way, then turned them back to the document. He rubbed one of the corners like a man feeling the fabric of a fancy suit. "Doesn't feel like paper, at least the kind we're used to." He held it up to the overhead lights, then frowned. "Sheriff, I need a flashlight and a magnifying glass." He then added, "Please."

"I can do that." Uncle Bart disappeared from the room again and returned a couple minutes later. "This do?" He set a heavy, metal-case police flashlight on the table. It was the kind that could be used as a baton as well as a light source. I knew I'd hate to be hit with one of those. He also set down a magnifying glass, the kind with a rectangular head and a small light.

"Yes." The professor first set the flashlight on its base. "Andi, hold this so it doesn't fall over." She did. He turned the light on and a spot of illumination appeared on the ceiling. The professor stood and set the paper on the business end of the light so the beam shown through it. Starting with the upper left corner, he moved the paper back and forth over the light, his eyes fixed on it, often bending close as if looking at a tiny bug.

"Interesting."

"What's interesting?" Brenda asked. Patience wasn't one of her virtues.

"Hang on . . . Hmm." The professor repeated his actions. "No watermark."

"What's a watermark?" I asked. I don't mind appearing ignorant, so I ask a lot of questions.

"On some papers, especially fine papers, the manufacturer places its watermark. Sometimes you can identify the source of a paper. No help here. Of course, not every paper has such a mark. In fact, I'm not sure this is paper."

"Not paper?" Uncle Bart said. "It sure felt like paper to me."

"With all due respect, Sheriff, could you tell the difference between typical paper, vellum, and parchment?"

"Probably not."

"It isn't difficult, really, once you know the difference. Paper is made from plant material; vellum and parchment are made from animal skins."

"So that paper is made from an animal?" Uncle Bart said.

"I doubt it." The professor sat again and moved the flashlight to the side. He used the magnifying glass to study the document. "No fibers, no sign that it was once an animal." He leaned back. "I don't know what to make of the material."

"And the writing?" Brenda shifted in her seat. She was getting antsy. When I first met her she was a smoker. She'd been trying to quit, but for people like Brenda, quitting was a long slog up a steep hill.

"That's another mystery." The professor leaned over the paper and put the magnifying glass to work again. "It's live ink—"

"What's live ink?" Brenda snapped. "You screwing with us, Professor?" Yep, she was antsy.

The professor didn't snap back. Not that he was a patient man. He wasn't. He wasn't a perfect man, either. When we were at Andi's grandparents' home in Florida, he admitted to being an alcoholic. I guess alcoholics believe they will always be an alcoholic. Anyway, he was one who no longer drank. I have yet to get the whole story on that. Perhaps he recognized his own symptoms in Brenda.

He continued to study the images. "It means it was written with ink by hand, not printed on a press or by a computer printer. A real hand wrote with real ink. Live ink."

"Does the ink tell you anything?" Uncle Bart asked.

The professor shook his head. "That's beyond my education and experience. To get real answers the ink and paper need to be analyzed by experts." He rubbed his chin. "The writing is a puzzle. At first I thought it was a form of ancient Hebrew. Not too old. Not paleo-Hebrew, something more recent, but I doubt my first assumption. It seems to be based on an early pictograph or logogram—um, characters that are based on pictures. Like Egyptian hieroglyphics. It's an interesting form of writing but has many shortcomings. Most writing that began as pictures became more alphabetic over time. As language grows, so does the need for ways to communicate through writing. I suspect that's what we have here."

"Can you read it?" Andi asked.

"Oh my, no. I can't even identify it. I've never seen anything like it." He passed the paper to Andi. "Do your magic, Andi."

She pulled it close, studied it for a few moments. "I can't tell much. It has forty-two lines, each line has twenty-one characters. Twenty-one, that's half of forty-two. The space between the lines is even. I can't see any variation. It's almost machine-like, which contradicts your idea that it's handwritten."

"Maybe," the professor said. "Keep going."

Andi was a wonder to watch. She saw what no one else could. I once saw her staring at a kitchen floor of fake-marble tile. In a few moments she determined that the tile had been manufactured with six different patterns. She also knew that the tile layer had followed a pattern that kept him from putting identical pieces next to each other. "I could marry a man like that," she had said.

That made me a little sad.

"The kerning—the space between letters—is just as uniform," she went on. "To be honest, I can't tell if I'm supposed to read this from left to right, right to left, or up and down." She kept her eyes on the document. "Okay, there are 882 characters or symbols or whatever they are. There are . . . fourteen different characters each repeating on an average of . . . never mind, that kind of average doesn't help. One character repeats 126 times—oh, that's three times forty-two—and one character that repeats only six times. Hmm. Six goes into forty-two seven times."

Uncle Bart looked at me. I shrugged.

"Forgive me for saying so," Uncle Bart said, "but I'm not sure what to make of all this."

The professor answered. "Well, neither do we. Not yet. I suppose it's like you investigating a crime scene. You don't start with the answers—you start with evidence. Some of that evidence will be useless, some of it will lead to a conviction. At the time you gather it, though, you have no idea what's valuable and what's not."

"Okay, I'll give you that."

Someone knocked on the door. It was firm yet somehow polite.

"Come." Uncle Bart said.

Millie poked her head in. "Social services will be here in about ten minutes, Sheriff."

"Thanks, Millie."

I caught Brenda looking at the children. I wonder how Daniel would respond when they took Littlefoot away.

"I want to try something." The professor pulled the paper away from Andi. "I need your help, Tank."

"Sure."

He picked up a pad of lined paper from a stack on the table. "Mind if I use this, Sheriff?"

"Help yourself."

He rose and rounded the table to where Littlefoot and Daniel sat on the floor, their milkshakes apparently gone. The professor sat on the floor in front of them and offered the first genuine smile I had ever seen him give anyone. "Come sit with me, Tank. I want our new friend to feel safe."

I did, lowering myself to the thin carpet that blanketed the floor.

The professor set the paper facedown on the floor in front of Littlefoot. He turned it several times, then waited. He smiled at her. She didn't smile back. It seemed those smiles were reserved for Daniel. Littlefoot looked at the blank side of the paper, then at the professor. He motioned for her to take it. He was relaxed and seemed to enjoy interacting with the girl. I had a feeling he had been a good priest.

We waited a few moments. I wasn't sure what the professor was up to, but I trusted him. The room grew quiet as a tomb.

Littlefoot looked at what had been her scroll, then picked it up and turned it around.

"Well, at least we know which edge is the top of the page."

That was clever. And simple, too.

The professor patted his chest. "James." He did it again, then wrote his name on the pad. He pointed to the word he had just written, then at himself. Littlefoot watched as if she found the whole thing as interesting as a television show.

He pointed at me. "Tank." Then he wrote my name on the pad. "Tank."

She blinked a few times. Looked at the paper and then pointed to the first four letters on the first line. "Hel-sa."

Her first word. It sounded like music to me.

The professor laughed and clapped. Littlefoot—I mean Helsa—did the same. Even Daniel looked pleased. The professor held out his hand and she returned the paper. He then gently took her hand in his and gave it a little kiss. Another first. The girl giggled.

The professor rose and returned to his seat. I did the same.

"And what did that accomplish?" Brenda asked.

"Several things." The professor worked his smartphone. "First, we now know where the top of the document is, something we need to know if we are to decrypt it. We also have sounds we can attach to the first few letters. And . . ." he studied his phone, then raised an eyebrow. "We also know Littlefoot, as Tank likes to call her, is really Helsa. The name sounded familiar. It's Hebrew. Now, don't go crazy on this"—he looked at me when he said it—"but it sounded familiar because Hebrew has a similar name that means 'devoted to God.'"

Devoted to God. I liked that.

CHAPTER 10

A Knife to the Soul

JANUARY 3, 6:30 A.M.

I was walking through the snow with no shoes on. Just like Littlefoot . . . Helsa. I was alone, trudging against the icy wind. If I came to a fence I would rise above it and gently settle on the other side. If I encountered a building—a farmhouse, barn, any structure—I simply floated over it. It made no sense to walk around when I could sail over with no exertion on my part.

My feet were cold. Colder than I had ever felt them. Even my nagging, almost-healed toe was numb. Still I moved on to a destination I didn't know for a reason I couldn't understand.

There was the sound of the wind and nothing more.

At first.

Then there was another sound. Dark, close, evil. I stopped to look around. Nothing but white fields and my footprints trailing behind me in a straight line. I turned my face to my destination, whatever that was. All I knew was I had to keep going forward.

The growl startled me.

The smell unsettled me.

The presence was similar to . . . to what? To my dream. Was *this* a dream?

Something touched my shoulder. I turned. Teeth. Black fur. Black eyes. Rancid breath.

Heart stopped.

Breathing seized . . .

"Hey, boy. Wake up."

The hand was still on my shoulder, but my surroundings had changed to something familiar. The snarling had turned into a human voice. Uncle Bart's.

"You okay, son? You were thrashing like nobody's business."

I took a deep breath. "Wow. Oh, my aching soul." I sat up in the bed and swung my feet over the side of the mattress.

"Another nightmare?" Uncle Bart was already in his uniform.

"Yeah. I was about to have my face chomped off. I wasn't looking forward to that."

"Ya think?" He studied me a moment. "Good news is, you have the same ugly face."

"Hey!"

"Jus' razzing you, boy. Nothing like a little laugh to scare away the dark thoughts."

"Right. I appreciate it." I didn't have the heart to tell him it wasn't working. "I don't suppose you had the same dream."

"Nope. I woke up at four and decided to drink massive amounts of coffee. I didn't want to risk going back to sleep."

"You are a wise man, Uncle Bart." I stood and winced.

"What's wrong? Toe actin' up?"

"No." I sat again and turned on the nightstand lamp. I hoisted up a leg and looked at my feet. They were red and a little tender.

"Let me see, son."

"I think I'm okay."

"I said, let me see."

There was no arguing with Uncle Bart.

"I could be wrong, but that looks like the beginning of frostbite."

"I haven't been outside." I thought of the dream. Couldn't be.

"Let me see your other foot."

I did as I was told.

"Looks about the same. Just red. No damage that I can see. You wanna see the doctor?"

I shook my head. "It doesn't hurt that much. Just caught me off guard."

His cell phone rang. "And so it begins." Uncle Bart answered and listened. "I'm on my way."

He turned, and for a moment I thought someone had stabbed him in his heart. "That was Wad. It's Helsa. She's back in town."

I didn't want to believe what I heard. Social services had picked Helsa up yesterday afternoon. I watched them drive away with her. I don't forget pain like that. We spent the rest of the afternoon getting the team settled in one of the few hotels in Dicksonville, having dinner, and trying to figure out what was happening.

"I'll get dressed in a flash. I wanna go with you."

"Tank—"

"I'll be quick. I'll get breakfast later."

"Tank."

His somber tone frightened me more than the monster in my dream. "What? What's happened?"

"She's hurt. She's been . . . she's been stabbed. Wad called for an ambulance. We'll meet him and the girl at the hospital."

I wish I could tell you what I thought, the worries I had, the anger I felt, but my brain shut down. All I remember of the next few moments was praying, one of those very short prayers repeated over and over: "Dear Jesus, dear Jesus . . ."

Uncle Bart wasted no time getting to the hospital. County Hospital was an extension of a larger facility in Everett, near the coast. It was small by comparison, but it had great facilities and doctors. I think Uncle Bart told me that to comfort me. It's what people shared to make the worried worry less: "Oh, that's a great hospital. Your loved one is in good hands." I could appreciate that, although I admit I was in no mood to be comforted.

A little girl had been stabbed. Stabbed! Who stabs a little girl? Normally, I am balanced. My emotions seldom get out of control. Sure, I know worry. Sure, I know anger, but they have never taken over. I wasn't sure I could say that five minutes into the future.

The drive took ten minutes longer than eternity. Cars pulled to the side of the road as Uncle Bart, still mindful of the patches of snow and ice, stomped the gas, emergency lights flashing around us.

"You know we won't be able to do much when we get there, right?"

"I know, Uncle Bart. Maybe."

"Maybe . . . oh, your gift." He fell silent. "Shoot straight with your old Uncle Bart. Have you ever healed anyone? I know Andi says you resurrected her dog, but that's a tad hard to believe. You're not Jesus."

"It's true, Uncle Bart, and what you believe or don't believe makes no difference." My conscience gave me a sharp punch in the gut. "I'm sorry. That sounded harsher than I meant it to."

"I understand, son. I'm scared, too."

Tears made it hard for me to see. "I don't have many answers. I don't know why this gift only works sometimes. I tell myself that it has something to do with God's will, but I can't be sure." I looked out the side window and tried to focus on the passing terrain, illuminated by blasts of lights from the light bar. "I busted the leg of a lineman in a game. That was my first year at the junior college. Shook me up pretty good. I could see one of his leg bones trying to push out of his uniform pants. The guilt ate at me. I dropped to my knees and laid a hand on him. He was screaming. The pain was too much for the guy. I prayed and he stopped screaming. I was afraid he'd died or something, but when I opened my eyes, he was staring at the sky. I couldn't see any pain in his expression. The trainers arrived moments later and pushed me away. I took a couple steps back, looked at his leg again. The ragged lump where the bone had been trying to bust through was gone. Only a patch of blood remained."

I took a deep breath. "They cut away his uniform. I guess the blood told him his leg was busted, but the leg looked fine. He walked off the field."

"Tank . . . that's too amazing to believe."

"I know. I don't talk about it much. It confuses me. Still, have I ever lied to you?"

"No, but you did keep secret the fact that you had been cut from the team."

"I've been feeling like a loser of late. I didn't want to relive the whole thing over."

"I guess I can understand that." He drove for another mile before speaking again. "When you said you wanted to carry Littlefoot the last couple o' blocks to the station—"

"Yep. I was hoping that God would heal her feet and whatever else might be bothering her. Turns out she didn't need healing . . . then."

A quick look at Uncle Bart told me he was thinking a big thought. "When this whole thing began and we were talking to Old Man Weldon—"

"Yes. I prayed for him."

"I wonder how he's doing."

Another mile passed.

"Tank, I'm gonna say something, and I want you to let me get through it before writing me off. This is gonna seem bad timing on my part, but I gotta say it."

"Okay."

"When we started this little adventure, I was trying to talk you into becoming a cop. I was trying to help you by giving you a goal after losing your spot on the team. I still think you should be a cop, but now I have a different reason." He cleared his throat as the next sentence got caught in his throat. "This is tough business and it's easy to lose perspective, to avoid getting close to those we help. You have the biggest heart I've ever seen. Cops everywhere could use a reminder of why we do this work. You have relationship skills that can't be taught. Let's say you do have the gift to heal—"

"Sometimes. I can't control it."

"Okay, you *sometimes* have the gift of healing, but your real gift is something greater. You see the good in everyone. I can only see the bad. You are a tonic, son. A real shot in the arm."

"I can't commit to anything now, Uncle Bart."

"I know that. I know it. I have one more thing to say. I don't know what to make of your friends, your team, whatever you consider yourself, but I think you got something waiting for you. Something to do. A mission. Yeah, that's it, a mission."

I didn't know what to say. I sensed he was right, but at that moment I couldn't think about life missions because Littlefoot was in trouble. Fear had me quaking on the inside. Portions of my brain were shutting down as if my mind wanted to keep things from escaping. Dear God, I was lost.

We rounded a corner and the hospital came into view. It was a two-story structure common in small towns. It looked new and modern, and I did my best to convince myself it was a place of healing and not a great big crypt.

We pulled into a parking place near the emergency room and parked next to another patrol car. I assumed it belonged to Deputy Wad.

The next thing I remember was standing in the waiting room of the ER. Uncle Bart was next to me and Deputy Wad stood in front of us. His uniform was covered in blood.

"Deputy Waddle," I said. "You're hurt."

He looked at me, his eyes wet. Something about him was different. "It's not my blood, Tank."

I began to shake.

CHAPTER 11

Hospital Rounds

1:10 P.M.

I thought time had passed slowly in the patrol car. Time in the hospital oozed by.

I'm no good at science or math, but I did have to take a couple of science classes in high school. One of my teachers told a story about Albert Einstein. Someone asked what he meant when he said time was relative: "Time spent with a pretty girl seems to go faster than time spent sitting on a hot stove." That's all I know about his theories, but at least that part made sense to me. We had been at the hospital over six hours, but it felt like we'd spent a decade in the waiting room. Relative time.

They wouldn't let me see Littlefoot. I thought about pushing the doctors and nurses aside. Not one of them was big enough to stop me, and I was highly motivated.

But an invisible hand held me in place. At least that's how it felt to me. Reason came back. God could save her whether I was there or not. I'm not indispensable. I'm just one tool in

God's tool kit. Not every tool is right for the job. So I did the tough work. I waited. And waited.

Deputy Waddle—I couldn't call him Wad after what he did for Littlefoot—filled us in on what he knew. He had been on graveyard shift. It was his week. He left the station to do another patrol before the day crew came in. He heard a scream. Looked down the street. Saw something a couple blocks away, the same place we first saw Littlefoot, and something blurry. He rushed in her direction. He found her . . .

Sorry, it's a hard story to tell. I wasn't there but I could still see it.

Waddle found her lying in the snow, bleeding. He called for backup, found the worst wounds and tried to slow their flow—with his bare hands. Another deputy arrived to help and the ambulance came shortly after that. Then he called Uncle Bart from his cell phone.

To me, Waddle looked like a hero—a pale, blood-splattered, shaky hero.

"Seeing her lying in the middle of the street, in the dirty snow . . ." He swore. Shook. Then wobbled. I took him in my arms, bloody uniform and all, and held him. He cried, not like a child, but like a man who had seen brutality he would never forget.

We tried to get what information we could, but only learned that emergency surgery was needed and the doctors would talk to us later. I knew they weren't brushing us off, but it sure felt like it. Uncle Bart decided to go back to town and take Waddle with him. The deputy seemed too shaken to drive. "Give Tank the keys to the patrol car in case he needs them. You know, to get a bite to eat or somethin'."

I wasn't going anywhere.

Uncle Bart also wanted to check out the scene of the crime. Maybe there was something to be learned. Maybe.

The triage nurse in the ER directed me to a surgical lobby, a place where friends and family did the impossible work of waiting. I found a seat in the middle of a row of padded chairs, closed my eyes, and began to pray. It was the least I could do; it was the most important thing I could do. There weren't a lot of words, just a wounded soul crying out for help.

Several hours had passed when I heard the shuffling of feet. I couldn't, didn't want to open my eyes. Big as I am, some things are too heavy for me to lift, like swollen eyelids over red-rimmed eyes.

A gentle hand reached under my arm at the elbow. It was small. It was warm. It was tender. A moment later I felt the weight of someone's head on my shoulder. It was Andi. I recognized her scent, a scent I longed for many times. Uncle Bart must have told them where I was.

A larger hand rested on my left shoulder. A slight squeeze. A deep sigh. No words. Again, I realized that the professor must have been a good priest.

The acrid/sweet scent of cigarette smoke flavored the air. Normally I hate the odor, but this time it said Brenda was here. I heard her take a ragged breath.

Only one was missing: Daniel. But if Brenda was here, Daniel had to be here, too.

I opened my eyes and saw his small form in front of me, just out of arm's reach. I knew so little about Daniel. He saw things no one else did, he almost never spoke, but he had a courage no child should have to have. We stared at each other for a moment. I forced a smile. He burst into tears and ran into my arms.

He cried. I broke into sobs. Sobs loud enough to embarrass me. I was brought up to believe that men didn't cry in public, especially big guys like me. I wish that were true. It's not. I melted into the chair, comforted by the touch of four other misfits . . . friends as dear to me as family.

"They've been at it all night." Brenda moved to the seat the professor had vacated a couple of hours before. He and Andi had moved to the corner of the room, each fixated on their iPads. Brenda jerked her head in their direction. "They're obsessed with figuring out the kid's scroll."

"I'm glad they're working on it," I said. "I got no idea what it is."

"Me neither. I'm pretty useless in the intellect department."

"Don't say that, Miss Brenda. You're smart. Better, you're wise. We would be a much weaker team without you."

She studied me. "Is that what we are, Cowboy? A team? Really?"

"Yes."

"I dunno. We barely tolerate each other."

It was good to be talking again. "Teams fight, Miss Brenda. Don't let that throw you. My dad thinks football represents life. I think it's just a game, but he sees more. In some ways I think he's right." I shifted my bulk in the seat. "Look, I've been playing football since my peewee days, and it has taught me a few things."

"Like what?"

"I'm not a great player, but I get to play because of my size. I'm not the smartest guy on the field, but I'm not dumb. We need the really smart, the really fast, the really strong, the really determined. There has to be a mix. That means players get on each other's nerves. They fight during practice; they fight in the locker room. They call each other names and blame one another for just about everything. Come game time, they are a unit. The other team is the enemy, not one another. So they pull together. Or as every coach I've had has said, 'Pull together or pull apart.' That's us. We bicker, but I know that when I need you—like right now—you'll be there for me. And I will always be there for you guys."

"I dunno, Cowboy."

"I do. Daniel needs you. Daniel and me are buds . . ." I turned to him. "Ain't that right, Daniel?" As usual, he didn't speak, but held up a clenched hand. I gave him a fist bump. "Daniel needs more than a buddy, he needs you. I don't know what part Daniel plays in all this, but I know he's part of the team. I know you're part of the team. You are . . ."

"I'm what?"

"I was going to say that you are the perfect mother for Daniel."

She pulled back as if I had slapped her. She worked her mouth like she was going to say something but couldn't get the words to flow. She looked to me like someone with a secret.

She collected herself. "The way you said that makes me think you were going to say something else."

I hesitated.

"Go ahead, Cowboy. I'm tough. I can take it."

She had found a way to make me chuckle. "You're tough all right. Sometimes you're downright scary. I mean that as a compliment. What I was going to say is that there are days when I think you're a mother to all of us."

"Shuddup! No way. I ain't that old coot's mother."

"He's not an old coot, Miss Brenda. The professor is just sixty."

"Ancient. A fossil."

"And you know how to handle him. It takes you and Andi both to keep him on the path."

Daniel shot to his feet and looked to the far wall. I'm glad Brenda, me, Andi, and the professor were the only ones in the room. I didn't have to worry about what others would think.

"Daniel, what is it, honey?" Brenda slipped from her seat

and knelt next to the boy. He continued to stare at the wall. "Is your friend-who's-not-Harvey back?"

He nodded. The professor and Andi stared at him.

Judging by the tilt of Daniel's head, his friend had to be seven feet tall. We're pretty sure Daniel sees angels, and who knows how tall they are.

"Is something wrong?" Brenda asked. Daniel smiled, then the corners of his mouth turned down and his eyes widened. He turned sharply, stepped to me, took my hand, and made me rise. I let him lead me to the waiting room door. He stopped.

Ten seconds later, a doctor appeared. "I'm looking for family of the young girl brought in this morning."

The others were on their feet a moment later. "She doesn't have family, Doctor. I'm Bjorn Christensen, her friend."

"That complicates things. There are laws that keep me from revealing patient information—"

Brenda stepped up. "Tank—I mean, Bjorn—is the sheriff's nephew. He's working with law enforcement on the little girl's situation." She sure knew how to take over a conversation.

The doctor studied Brenda the way a prisoner studied his executioner. "Still—"

"You want us to get Sheriff Christensen on the phone?" Brenda hit the last name hard.

"No. It's been a long morning."

He looked at the others, then directed his attention to me. "She came through the surgery, but she still has a long way to go. She lost a lot of blood and we had to keep hanging units. We also did a lot of stitching, but she's gonna make it."

"Praise God," I said.

Brenda was still in control. "So the stab wounds were deep?"

"Those weren't knife wounds. Those are bite marks."

It was time for me to sit down again.

The professor found his seat. "I'm starting to hate this job."

CHAPTER

12

A Spark of an Idea

3:30 P.M.

Waiting is the toughest thing I've ever done. I have developed a high tolerance for pain. Hours in the gym and on the practice field have a way of toughening a man up. But waiting to see Littlefoot ate away at me. Of course, seeing her after the surgery, gazing at the bite marks might be worse, but I needed to be with her, to watch her little chest rising and falling, telling me she was breathing—telling me she was still alive. I needed that.

At least Andi and the professor had the scroll to occupy their minds. They stayed in their huddle, looking at their iPads and whispering. They had taken digital photos of it and were examining every inch and every letter, or picture, or whatever it was on the document. My gaze lingered on Andi and I remembered how good it felt when she rested her head on my shoulder. I know it wasn't a romantic gesture. She was trying to comfort me. Still, it was a light in the darkness that swallowed me.

"Think they'll figure anything out?" Brenda walked back into the waiting room. After the doctor left, she had taken Daniel to find a bathroom and then for a walk through the halls. At first I figured she was trying to get his mind on other things. Although he seldom spoke, he seemed quieter now, if such a thing was possible. She may have been trying to get *her* mind on other things.

I shrugged. "If anyone can, they can. They're the smartest people I know."

"Thanks." Brenda tried to look hurt.

"You know what I mean."

"You know how to butter up a girl, don't you, Cowboy." She patted her dreadlocks as if trying to look prettier.

"I only meant—"

"I know what you meant, Cowboy. I'm just trying to pull you outta your funk. Not that you don't have a right to be in a funk."

I didn't know what to say to that.

She stared at Andi and the professor for a moment. "Hey, Computer Girl, I got a question for ya."

Andi looked up. "Computer Girl? Really? Computer Girl? Maybe I need a cape and some tights."

"You'd look good," Brenda said.

"Really?" Andi raised one eyebrow.

Brenda snorted. "No. I don't have the best schoolin' in the world, but something occurred to me on my little walk."

"Like what?" Andi exchanged glances with the professor.

"What are the odds of us getting two messages in a row?"

"Two?" the professor asked. "There's another scroll?"

Brenda sighed dramatically. "Why is it that brilliant people are so forgetful?"

"Wait." Andi wasn't as forgetful as Brenda implied. "You

mean that note you got when we were in Florida a few months ago?"

"Yep. The one the professor said to forget. The one he called a joke."

Andi furrowed her brow. "I looked at it and the page was blank."

"You peeked at it, girl. Tank saw the message."

I had seen it. In fact, I had read it out loud. We were getting ready to go to the airport. We had done all we could in Florida. A kid on a bike rode up and handed an envelope to Brenda. "That's right. I remember it."

"I don't," the professor said.

"That's because you declared it unimportant. A joke. You told us to forget it." Brenda pulled a familiar envelope from her coat pocket. It looked worn, probably because she'd stuffed it into various pockets over the past couple of months. "Wanna hear it again?"

"Stop being dramatic, Brenda. Just read the thing."

She cleared her throat as if she was about to launch into a speech. "'Likewise you, human being—I have appointed you as watchman. Yechizk'el.'"

The professor's eyes darted back and forth like a Ping-Pong ball.

"Yechizk'el sounds familiar." I could almost see Andi's brain working.

"With your Jewish background, it should. Yechizk'el is the Hebrew way of pronouncing Ezekiel," the professor said.

"Like in the Bible?" I straightened in my chair. "Like the Old Testament prophet?"

The professor nodded. "Exactly, Tank. Exactly."

"So maybe we shouldn't have ignored it," Brenda said.

"Not necessarily, my young artist friend. As is, it doesn't mean much." The professor rose and moved to the seat next to Brenda. "May I?"

Brenda looked stunned. "Well, lookie who just found his manners." She handed it over.

Andi moved to sit next to the professor. "Odd handwriting. Squarish printing."

"Similar to the scroll, but using letters, not pictography." The professor rubbed his forehead so hard I thought he'd push his fingers through his skin. He shot to his feet. "Think, James, think."

I don't think he was used to working this hard to make a connection.

"The phrasing is odd. It can't be from the original texts. *Human being*. That's not a term the Bible writer would use."

He paced the floor. I pulled my smartphone from my jeans, activated my Bible app, and did a search for *human being*.

"Of course some newer translations might make use of the term."

"They did, Professor." I held up my smartphone. "There are several translations that use it." I looked at the phone again. "He does use the word *human* several times."

The professor snapped his finger. "Son of man. If memory serves, Ezekiel used the phrase 'Son of Man.'"

"God uses it, Professor. . . . I know, you don't believe in God." I did another search. Sure enough, "Son of Man" appeared several times. "Ezekiel 3:17: 'Son of man, I have appointed you a watchman to the house of Israel.' That's the first part of the verse."

"What translation?" The professor was staring at me.

"New American Standard. I have others."

"No, that's fine. It's a decent translation. A little too conservative in their renderings for my tastes, but respectable."

Brenda huffed. "I'm sure they'll be glad to hear you approve."

I expected Andi to defend the professor, but she didn't. Truth is, I've heard Brenda say worse to him.

"May I?" The professor held out his hand. I let him have my phone. He began to read:

"'Son of man, I have appointed you a watchman to the house of Israel; whenever you hear a word from My mouth, warn them from Me. When I say to the wicked, "You will surely die," and you do not warn him or speak out to warn the wicked from his wicked way that he may live, that wicked man shall die in his iniquity, but his blood I will require at your hand. Yet if you have warned the wicked and he does not turn from his wickedness or from his wicked way, he shall die in his iniquity but you have delivered yourself. Again, when a righteous man turns away from his righteousness and commits iniquity, and I place an obstacle before him—'"

The professor stopped suddenly and stared at the screen for a moment. He went pale. Before I could ask what was wrong, he returned the phone to me and walked from the room without a word.

Andi looked at us. "What just happened?"

"I don't know." Brenda didn't offer a quip. She looked concerned.

"Tank?" Andi stared at me.

I lifted the phone and found the text that made him stop:

"'Again, when a righteous man turns away from his righteousness and commits iniquity, and I place an obstacle before him he will die; since you have not warned him, he shall die in his sin, and his righteous deeds which he has done shall not be remembered. . . .'"

Brenda shuddered. "Yep, that would do it."

Andi stared at the door. "He sees himself as the righteous man who turned away."

"I think so," I said.

"He thinks God is going to kill him?" Brenda spoke softly so Daniel wouldn't hear, but my guess is he knew more than we did.

"Worse," Andi whispered. "The verse says the righteous man who commits iniquity will die and all his accomplishments will be forgotten. For an academic, that's worse than death."

Daniel stood abruptly. Looked at someone who wasn't there, at least as far as we could tell, then moved to the door and waited. A nurse appeared. She smiled, but her expression didn't seem genuine. "She's out of recovery and in a room now. You may visit, but please keep it short. She needs her rest. Room 227."

It took all my willpower not to run.

CHAPTER 13

Thirteen O'clock

5:30 P.M.

The sky was beginning to darken, but at these high latitudes, the sun set later than it did in Southern California. Light pressed through thin drapes, illuminating tiny dust motes floating in the air. There was one bed, one IV unit, one chair, one television, and one lost little girl. I hadn't seen her when she reappeared in the middle of town early this morning. As before, as with each new appearance, she seemed younger, smaller, more needy. Looking at her, what was left of my heart shattered to pieces.

Littlefoot lay still as a corpse. Her body was covered in a white sheet that looked too much like a shroud. What was wrong with hospitals? A pink sheet, or a blue one, or just about any other color would be better than the lily-white material that implied death. Maybe that doesn't make sense. My brain was on fire when I thought it.

I took two steps into the room. I heard Andi gasp behind me. Brenda whispered, "Oh God." It was the closest I had ever heard her come to praying.

Littlefoot—she would always be Littlefoot to me—didn't move when we entered. We tried to be as quiet as we could. Her face was lovely and serene. The sight of her all bandaged up brought images of her little frame in the jaws of a monster. I could imagine it thrashing her around as if she were a rag doll. Tears crept down my cheeks and I didn't care. Brenda held my right arm; Andi my left. I needed their strength. I needed their touch to remind me that there was still good in the world.

My mind was unraveling.

Daniel pushed by and walked to the side of the bed. I started to tell him to stay back, but it didn't seem right. Had it been any other kid I would have said something, but Daniel was, well, Daniel. He looked at her arms, something no kid should see. He looked at her face as if studying it for signs of life. Again he moved his gaze to her left arm and traced it with his eyes, until he settled on a finger that appeared unharmed.

He touched it. The gesture was so light it wouldn't have moved a feather. I love that kid.

Littlefoot opened her eyes, eyes the color of unsweetened chocolate, and looked at Daniel. He smiled. She smiled. I had a feeling an entire conversation was carried on in those seconds.

Then she stuck her tongue out. In and out. It was the peanut-butter-in-the-dog's-mouth-thing again. Seeing that made me feel like things might be all right.

Daniel turned to Brenda. He didn't speak, but Brenda got the message. "I'm on it, honey." To me she said, "I'll see if the cafeteria has milkshakes."

I managed to nod.

"Tank?"

I didn't need to turn to know Uncle Bart had shown up.

"The nurses told me you guys were up here." He stepped to the spot Brenda had occupied. "How's she doing?"

"I just got here."

"She looks younger—again."

I nodded and walked to the right side of the bed. I moved under compulsion. Nothing in the universe could have kept me away. She turned her face to me and I stroked her cheek. Precious. Beautiful. Everything good in the world contained in one little girl's body.

Like Daniel, I studied her arms and hand. Her arms were swollen like sausages. The sight of them pulled my strength through a paper shredder. Her right hand was completely encased in gauze, but her thumb was unwrapped. Using two fingers, I held her thumb and stroked her hair with my other hand.

A few deep breaths later I gazed into her eyes . . . that were now blue.

I closed my eyes.

The sounds were the first thing to go, then the room, the sense that others were present. All of that was replaced by darkness. It sounds strange to some, but God is often found in the darkness—in the holy dark.

It was warm. It felt safe. I had been here before, good had come out of—

The growl startled me. The scream brought me back. Littlefoot was sitting up in bed, her eyes white as chalk and looking toward the door. I snapped my head around. Andi was seated on the floor doing her best to back away from the doorway. Brenda was slumped next to one of the walls, a milkshake toppled and gushing its contents on the floor. Uncle Bart was struggling to get to his feet. He fumbled for his gun.

It was there. The black thing. The blurry thing I had seen in my dream. The thing with the white fangs—fangs that pierced the skin and muscles of Littlefoot. It looked at me with eyes that blazed like molten steel, then fixed its stare on Littlefoot. It took a slow step, then another. The remembered pain of my dreams was now alive.

Then it sprang.

So did I.

I don't know who made the most noise, the Beast or me. We both screamed as we met near the foot of the bed. Its front paws passed over the foot of the mattress before I reached it with my right hand. I caught it at the neck and clamped my big mitt shut. It turned on me, just like I wanted it to do. One claw ripped my right arm, the other caught my left shoulder. I didn't much care.

I pulled it close.

I embraced it, pulling it tight to my chest. If need be, we were going to die together, me and this attacker of little girls. Maybe I was born for this one moment; maybe not, but I did know that only God himself could break my grip.

We hit the floor, me on my back, the IT on top of me. It writhed. It twisted. It lurched. It snapped its jaws. Its breath reeked of rotted meat, a breath it inflicted on Littlefoot. That thought gave me new strength, new power, new purpose.

"Tank." Uncle Bart came into my vision but I couldn't pay him any attention. He had his gun drawn. "Tank, let go. I can't get off a shot with you holding it."

I don't know if shooting would have done any good. Besides, to let go was to let it rip out my throat. Instead, I tried to tighten my grip, but it pulled its head away.

The bite was crushing. I felt its teeth make contact with the bones of my arm. Fine. Instead of trying to pull my arm out, I pushed it farther into the Beast's mouth. If it was going to eat me, then it was going to choke on me.

Uncle Bart moved closer.

"No. Stay back. Stay back."

I caught sight of Littlefoot. The look of fear on her face hurt more than the thing chewing my arm—

The hospital room vanished. The ceiling became a beautiful green sky. The ground was firm, but somehow different. The light was wrong, but I didn't know how. And I didn't have time to think about it. One thing I did notice was the fuzzy, indistinct, hard to see IT had become clearer. I liked it better the other way.

A flash of light. A sense of falling and then I was flying through the air and back in Littlefoot's room. We hit the wall with the window. I heard the glass rattle—

The hospital disappeared again.

Then I was back.

I wrapped my legs around the creature and continued to hold on. One of us would run out of energy sometime. I just had to make sure it wasn't me.

"Ta—"

Back in the green sky world, but this time I wasn't alone. Two people. Two men—I guess they were men. They were taller than me and wider at the shoulders, and they looked very unhappy. I could only hope they were on my side.

The IT clamped down. This time I was certain the thing would bite my arm off. I'd be dead soon after. I fought on. What choice did I have?

One of the men spoke and the IT released its jaws and snapped its head around. Its eyes widened. I felt it tremble. With impossible speed, one of the men ripped the Beast from my arms with one hand. He lifted it high. Said something I didn't understand and then disappeared.

I glanced around but can't describe what I saw. Things didn't make sense to me. The best I could tell, I was flat on my back on some open plain. There was grass beneath me. The horizon seemed to curve up instead of down.

The second man moved closer. He looked sad.

He smiled. It was a weird smile, like someone who wasn't quite sure how to do it. "Hi, Tank."

"You're . . . you're Daniel's friend, aren't you?" He nodded. I rolled to my other side, holding my bleeding arm. The thing had pierced an artery. If I let go, I would be dead in short order.

I looked over at my little friend. "Daniel?"

"Yep."

"What are you doing here?"

"I've been here before." He seemed to be a little older.

"Is this heaven?" I had had a glimpse of heaven in the House some months back, but it didn't look like this.

He shook his head. "Nope. It's a different place."

"Littlefoot?"

"She's good. This is her world." He crouched near me. "Time to go home."

I was on the floor. On my back. Clutching my wounded arm. Blood gushed.

"Dear God, Tank." Uncle Bart was at my side applying pressure to the wound. "We need a doctor. Now. NOW. We need a doctor. Now!"

I looked at Littlefoot. She looked well. Whole. Healed. Whaddya know? It worked this time.

Outside the window, the sun continued to provide light for the world.

Sunset pulled a thick blanket of black over me.

EPILOGUE

10:00 P.M.

"Man, my arm hurts."

I was in a hospital bed, an IV needle in my arm. It hurt. My other arm, where they did surgery, hurt; my back hurt, my head hurt. In comparison, my busted toe felt pretty good.

My friends were around me. So was the doctor who did surgery on Littlefoot.

"You've had a long day, Doc."

He laughed. "*I've* had a long day? You know, I used to work in a big city hospital. Saw it all there. At least I thought I did. I'm confused by all this. I don't even know what questions to ask."

"We don't either, Doc." Andi stood close to the right side of the bed. She looked like she had been down a long, hard road, but she looked good to me. Brenda was biting her nails. Even tough chicks get shook from time to time. The professor looked like a scolded dog and stood near the wall. He hadn't been in the room, but my guess is they told him all about it.

To make things better, I had another visitor: Littlefoot. She looked about six years old, and her skin was unmarked. Seeing that made me the wealthiest man in the world. She held a milkshake in one hand. Daniel had one, too. Each time they took a sip, they did the tongue thing, then giggled.

"Give him the rundown, Doc." Uncle Bart managed to look worried and joyful at the same time.

"Okay. As you know, we did surgery on your right forearm. We had to repair a damaged artery and pick out bone fragments. You had several puncture wounds to your legs and torso, we assume from the creature's claws. You also separated a couple of ribs. You have a ton of bruises."

"'Ton of bruises'—is that a medical term?" Andi asked.

"Don't mind her, Doc. She's a little too attached to details." For Brenda, it was a kind comment.

The doctor excused himself and said he was going home. He was done with the day. So was I.

We spent the next few minutes relating what we had seen. I told what I saw and even mentioned Daniel's appearance on the other side. "He looked older and he said it wasn't heaven. It didn't look at all like the heaven I saw in the House."

"I doubt it was heaven," the professor said.

"Oh, don't start, Professor," Brenda said. "We all know you don't believe in anything but your gigantic intellect."

That seemed to wound him. He looked more vulnerable than usual. "Let me explain. We think Daniel sees angelic beings. Now it appears that Tank does, too. According to Tank, one admitted to being Daniel's friend. And, of course, I had an encounter with something at the House. Maybe it was illusionary, I don't know. Anyway, I don't think Littlefoot is an angel. Not in the sense that we use the term today. Technically, the word *angel* means *messenger*, so anyone carrying a message is an angel. In that way, Littlefoot *is* an angel, but not an angelic being. Am I making sense?"

"I'm with you, Professor," I said. "For a change."

"This is hard to explain in a few words." The professor inhaled as if he hadn't taken a breath for an hour or so. "The world of science has turned things upside down of late. Quantum theory describes quantum entanglement, indicating that things in the subatomic world are somehow connected, at least in certain conditions. That deals with the very small things. On the cosmic level, many physicists believe that we live in a multiverse instead of a universe."

"Meaning what?" Uncle Bart asked.

"The idea is that all we see is our universe, but ours is just one of many others. They're similar but not identical to ours, and a new one is created each time we make a decision. And with so many decisions being made, these other universes can vary wildly. I know, I know. It's difficult to fathom, but there are many excellent scientists who have hung their hats on the idea.

"Each universe is independent of the others, but there might be ways to cross over. Then there's the whole multidimensional thing that is totally different. Lots of folks believe there are eleven or twelve dimensions. But that's different because dimension deals mostly with spatial things. Most Christian thinkers, especially among conservative Protestants, believe that angels are beings from another dimension and can move between dimensions as is shown in the Bible. The truth is, there's a lot we don't know."

I looked at him. "My head is beginning to hurt."

He moved closer to the bed. "Don't worry, Tank. I don't expect you to understand. My guess, and that's all it is at this point, is that Littlefoot is from another universe close to ours and somehow related to it. Time flows differently for her. That's why she grows younger when she comes to us and why Daniel appeared older wherever you were. I assume you were in Littlefoot's land."

"You're breaking my brain," Brenda said.

I expected a cutting reply, but the professor let it pass. "I want to show you something." He extracted his smartphone and took a photo of me, then showed me the picture. I saw a few bruises, but the most shocking thing was the hair on my face. I rubbed my chin with my good hand.

"How long does it take for your beard to grow that long?" The professor kept his eyes on me as I handed his phone back.

"A week and a half, maybe."

"I missed the action, but they tell me the fight only lasted a few seconds."

"It felt a lot longer than that."

"When Littlefoot is here, she grows younger. When you were there, you grew older."

"How can that be?" Uncle Bart wasn't used to hearing such things.

"I don't know, Sheriff. No one does. We are experiencing things that no one else has, and we don't have enough information yet to give solid answers. Yet."

"Yet?" Brenda lowered her head. "You sayin' there will be more of this?" She added a term I'm uncomfortable repeating.

"Yes. Maybe the weirder stuff is yet to come."

Andi touched my hand. Just a finger or two. "You should tell them the rest," she said to the professor.

"It's about the scroll."

"You figured it out?" I hoped so. I don't like puzzles.

"Not completely. It might be impossible to understand fully, especially if it's a language from Littlefoot's universe. However, I think Brenda was right when she began to wonder if the message that was handed to her at Andi's was related. Some smart thinking there."

Brenda snorted. "You make me blush."

The professor ignored her. "Andi and I spent the time you were in surgery arguing over this and reviewing the document. The first note was in English, but it looked as if a non-English-speaking writer penned it. You already know—well, the sheriff doesn't know since he wasn't there—but the first note was a variation of a passage in Ezekiel. Ezekiel experienced some very odd things: multi-faced beings, winged angels, God's throne on a set of wheels within wheels. We still don't understand all that he saw. If he really saw them." He raised a hand. "I know, I know, we've seen equally strange things."

"What's the point, Professor?" Brenda asked.

"I suspect that the verse given you was changed to fit our situation. Ezekiel was being set apart to be a watchman over Israel, and to call his people back to faith. Maybe we're being called to do the same thing. Not to Israel, but to the world."

"This is a calling, Professor?" I asked.

He looked like he was choking on a bone. "I think so. Tank, you've called us a team several times. I've always looked at our past adventures as a few bizarre happenings with no purpose, no message, no meaning. I'm not so sure now. We may be stuck with each other."

"So what's the mission?" I asked.

He shrugged. "I really don't know. Andi has noticed a few things in common."

"I need to give it deep thought, but we do know that in each case we've encountered opposition and things beyond this world, and it has taken our combined skills to solve the problem, even to save lives. I think we've just started our journey." Andi sounded a little like the professor.

"Will you be able to read the whole scroll?" Uncle Bart asked the professor.

"I can't. I've taken it as far as I can. I've sent digital photos to Cardinal Hartmann in the Vatican. If I may, I would like to send him the original document. I know he's going to ask for it. He's a genius with languages, and I'm hoping his contacts in the Vatican might help. Brenda's message is from Ezekiel chapter three. It's not a modification of a verse as I first suspected. I found the exact translation in a Messianic Bible. At least we can understand that message. I can't be certain, but the two documents seem to be related."

"Not knowing is as much a part of being human as knowing, Professor," I said.

"Perhaps, Tank. Perhaps."

Littlefoot set her milkshake down, walked to the bed, touched my hand, and smiled. Then she began to blur. At first I thought the drugs were affecting my vision, then I realized the creature looked that way when it came to our world.

"No. No, stay, Littlefoot. I don't want to lose you." I tried to get up. The professor pushed me back in the bed.

"Let her go, son. She can't stay here. She will just get younger and younger, then what? She needs to be in her home just like you need to be in yours."

"But—"

"She has to go, Tank."

Littlefoot waved at me, giggled at Daniel, then waved at the others.

She was gone, and with her, my joy.

Uncle Bart took me to his home the next day. He was holding a January barbecue for the others who were leaving later that evening. The snow around Uncle Bart's house was all but gone, but the air was still cold, so most of us stayed in the house. Mr. Weldon, the diabetic rancher, had been invited. He stood outside by the barbecue while Uncle Bart kept a practiced eye on the grill. I watched through a window. I was a little too sore to be outside shivering. Weldon looked strong, spry, and healthy. He looked at me and raised a cup of whatever he was drinking in an unspoken toast.

I guess sometimes I do some good.

Keep reading for a sneak peek of episode 5,

THE REVEALING.

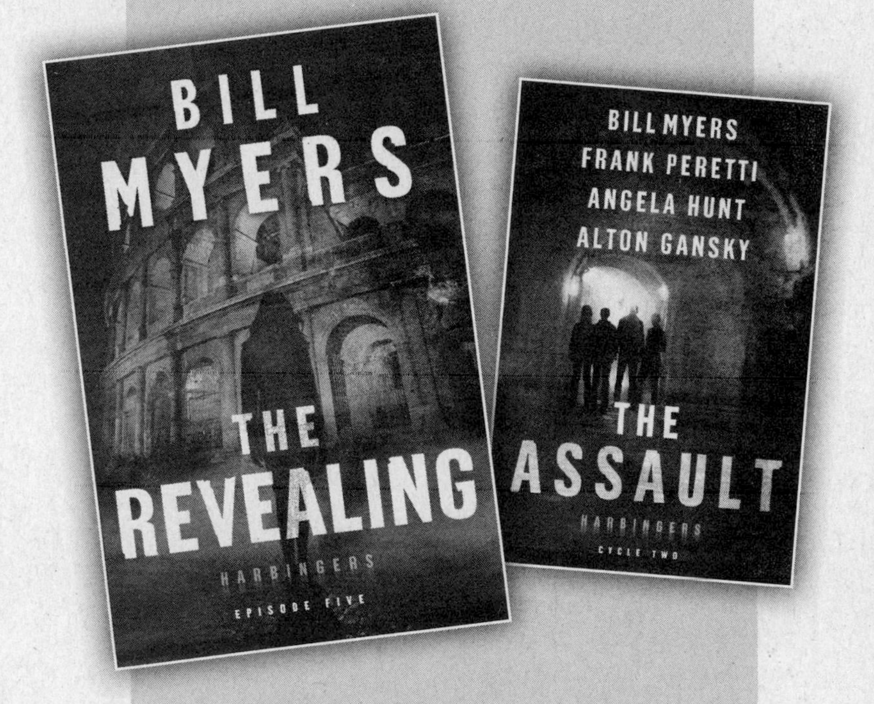

***From* HARBINGERS 5**

What're you sketchin' now?" Cowboy asked.

I flipped my notebook shut like a kid caught with porn.

The big guy smirked. "You know, Miss Brenda, you don't have to keep hidin' your gift under a bushel."

I gave him a look. He gave me one of his good-ol'-boy shrugs. Daniel's sittin' on my other side and stifles a giggle.

I shoot him a look. "You think that's funny?"

He grins and imitates Cowboy's shrug.

I scowl. But the truth is I like that grin. It don't happen much, but whenever it does, it warms somethin' up inside me.

The sketch is a blue velvet armchair. It's got peeling gold paint on its arms. I've been seeing it ever since we got on the plane to Rome. Never left my head. Not during the eight-hour flight with its crap food and rerun movies, not during Mr. Toad's wild taxi ride from Da Vinci airport to the Vatican, and not as we sat on this butt-numbing wood bench listening to the professor lay into some pimply-faced, man-boy receptionist.

"Well, look again." The old man waved at the computer screen. "Cardinal Hartmann. You do know what a Cardinal is, do you not? *Cardinal* Hartmann invited us to this location at this this particular date and this particular time to—"

"*Mi scusi*, Signor, but you cannot have an appointment with—"

"Blast it all, don't tell me what I can and cannot have."

"But, such a thing, it is not—"

"I'm sorry, are you part of some special-needs program?"

"Professor . . ." As usual, Andi, his ever-cheerful assistant, stepped in to try and prove her boss was a human being. As usual, the odds were not in her favor.

Meanwhile, Daniel scooted off the bench to get another drink of water. At least that's what I figured. But the way he cocked his head upward like he was listening, told me one of his "friends" was around.

Miss Congeniality continued smoothing things over. "What the professor means is, we've just come from the airport. In fact, we haven't even gone to our hotel because Cardinal Hartmann sent a very urgent and very personal request for us to visit him today."

Cowboy and I traded looks. It was true. It hadn't even been a month since the professor sent the Cardinal that scroll with the fancy writing on it. The one that some kid, supposedly from another universe, gave us. I know, I know, long story and I'm not in the mood. The point is, this Cardinal guy, who used to be the professor's mentor back when the professor believed in God, begged us to come. He sweetened the deal by springing for our plane tickets. And since I couldn't cash them in, and the professor had pulled some strings to get us some quick passports . . . well, here we were with our ol' pals—stuck in some back-room reception area that smelled like old floor wax and old men.

I glanced over at Daniel. He'd passed the water fountain and stood at a wooden door built into the wall. Hardly visible. He looked back at me like he wanted something.

What? I mouthed.

He just stood there.

What?

Meanwhile, the professor cranked up his personality to super-jerk. "Okay, you do that."

The receptionist got up and headed out of the room.

"Only make sure you bring back someone with a rudimentary understanding of communication skills."

Daniel cleared his throat, real loud to get everyone's attention. We turned to him and he reached for the door. He pushed it open and motioned for us to join him.

"What is it now?" the professor said. "Do you wish for us to follow? Do you believe there is something inside there?"

Daniel sighed like it was obvious. And for him it probably was. 'Cause like it or not, the kid heard things we never heard. Saw things we never saw. And whether the professor believed in any type of "higher power" or not made no difference. Our last couple of road trips made it clear Daniel was connected to something.

So, without another word, Dr. Stuffy-Butt headed over to join the boy. Something was up and he knew it.

So did Cowboy. "What's goin' on, little fella?" the big jock asked as he rose to his feet.

Daniel pointed to the open doorway. It was dark, but you could make out some real narrow steps. Me and Andi glanced at each other, then followed. None of us knew what was going on in that little head of his, but, whatever it was, it wouldn't hurt to pay attention.

Selected Books by Bill Myers

Novels

Child's Play

The Judas Gospel

The God Hater

The Voice

Angel of Wrath

The Wager

Soul Tracker

The Presence

The Seeing

The Face of God

When the Last Leaf Falls

Eli

Blood of Heaven

Threshold

Fire of Heaven

Non-Fiction

The Jesus Experience—Journey Deeper into the Heart of God

Supernatural Love

Supernatural War

Children Books

Baseball for Breakfast (picture book)

The Bug Parables (picture book series)

Bloodstone Chronicles (fantasy series)

McGee and Me (book/video series)

The Incredible Worlds of Wally McDoogle (comedy series)

Bloodhounds, Inc. (mystery series)

The Elijah Project (supernatural suspense series)

Secret Agent Dingledorf and His Trusty Dog Splat (comedy series)

TJ and the Time Stumblers (comedy series)

Truth Seekers (action adventure series)

Teen Books

Forbidden Doors (supernatural suspense)

Dark Power Collection

Invisible Terror Collection

Deadly Loyalty Collection

Ancient Forces Collection

For a complete list of Bill's books, sample chapters, and newsletter sign-up, go to www.billmyers.com or check out his Facebook page: www.facebook.com/billmyersauthor

Selected Books by Frank Peretti

Illusion: A Novel

This Present Darkness

Piercing the Darkness

The Oath

Prophet

Tilly

The Visitation

Monster

www.frankperetti.com
www.facebook.com/officialfrankperetti

Selected Books by Angela Hunt

Roanoke
Jamestown
Hartford
Rehoboth
Charles Towne
Magdalene
The Novelist
Uncharted
The Awakening
The Debt
The Elevator
The Face
Let Darkness Come
Unspoken
The Justice
The Note
The Immortal
The Truth Teller
The Silver Sword
The Golden Cross
The Velvet Shadow
The Emerald Isle
Dreamers
Brothers
Journey
Doesn't She Look Natural?
She Always Wore Red
She's In a Better Place
Five Miles South of Peculiar
The Fine Art of Insincerity
The Offering
Esther: Royal Beauty
Bathsheba: Reluctant Beauty
Delilah: Treacherous Beauty

www.angelahuntbooks.com
www.facebook.com/angela.e.hunt

Selected Books by Alton Gansky

By My Hands
Through My Eyes
Terminal Justice
Tarnished Image
Marked for Mercy
A Small Dose of Murder
A Ship Possessed
Vanished
Distant Memory
The Prodigy
Dark Moon
A Treasure Deep
Out of Time
Beneath the Ice
The Incumbent
Before Another Dies
Submerged
Director's Cut
Crime Scene Jerusalem
Zero-G
Finder's Fee
Angel
Enoch
Wounds

www.altongansky.com